History of

History of Prince Edward Island

by Duncan Campbell

Copyright © 2/9/2016
Jefferson Publication

ISBN-13: 978-1523971022

Printed in the United States of America

Table of Contents

PREFACE.

The principal aim of the Author has been to produce a History of Prince Edward Island, which might claim some degree of merit as to conciseness, accuracy, and impartiality, from the period it became a British possession until its recent union with the other confederated provinces of British North America. With the view to secure these ends, it was necessary that not only all available books and pamphlets relating to the island should be attentively perused, and the correctness of their statements tested; but that a vast mass of original papers, hitherto unpublished, should be carefully examined. Application having been made to His Excellency Lord Dufferin, through Sir Robert Hodgson, the Lieutenant-governor of the island, permission was granted to examine all the numerical despatches. This task imposed an amount of labor which had not been anticipated, and which seemed incompatible with the production of so small a volume. The Author is aware that there lies in the French archives at Paris a large deposit of interesting matter bearing on the history of the Maritime Provinces, and it is to be hoped that it will soon be rendered accessible to the English reader.

It was necessary that a considerable portion of the work should deal with the Land Question. To its consideration the Author came in comparative ignorance of the entire subject, and therefore unprejudiced by ideas and associations of which it might be impossible for a native of the island entirely to divest himself. The soundness of the conclusions arrived at may be questioned; but it can be truly said that they have not been reached without deliberate consideration, and an anxious desire to arrive at the truth.

The Author desires to express his special obligations for valuable matter to His Honor Sir Robert Hodgson, the Honorable Judge Pope, Professor Caven, Mr. Henry Lawson, the Honorable Judge Hensley, the Honorable Mr. Haviland, Mr. John Ings, Hon. Francis Longworth, Mr. J. B. Cooper, Mr. Arthur DeW. Haszard, Mr. Donald Currie, the Reverend Mr. McNeill, Mr. T. B. Aitkins, of Halifax, Mr. John Ball, Mr. F. W. Hughes, the Reverend Dr. Jenkins, Mr. Charles DesBrisay, Mr. J. W. Morrison, and others too numerous to mention.

The Honorable Judge Pope possesses rare and most important documents connected with the island, without which it would have been impossible to produce a satisfactory narrative, and which he at once courteously placed at the temporary disposal of the Author, rendering further service by the remarkable extent and accuracy of his information.

The Author has also to thank the People of Prince Edward Island, especially, for the confidence reposed in him, as proved by the fact of his having received, in the course of a few weeks, orders for his then unpublished work to the number of more than two thousand seven hundred copies,—confidence which he hopes an unprejudiced perusal of the book may, to some extent, justify.

Charlottetown, October, 1875.

CHAPTER I.

Geographical position of the Island—Early possession—Population in 1758—Cession by Treaty of Fontainebleau—Survey of Captain Holland—Holland's description of the Island—Position of Town sites—Climate—The Earl of Egmont's scheme of settlement—Proposed division of the Island—Memorials of Egmont—Decision of the British Government respecting Egmont's Scheme.

Prince Edward Island is situated in the Gulf of Saint Lawrence. It lies between 46° and 47° 7' north latitude, and 62° and 64° 27' longitude west, from Greenwich. As viewed from the north-east, it presents the form of a crescent. Its length, in a course through the centre of the Island, is about one hundred and forty miles, and its breadth, in the widest part, which is from Beacon Point to East Point, towards its eastern extremity, thirty-four miles. It is separated from Nova Scotia by the Strait of Northumberland, which is only nine miles broad between Cape Traverse and Cape Tormentine. From the Island of Cape Breton it is distant twenty-seven miles, and from the nearest point of Newfoundland one hundred and twenty-five miles.

The Island was amongst the first discoveries of the celebrated navigator, Cabot, who named it Saint John, as indicative of the day of its discovery. Britain failing to lay claim to it, the French afterwards assumed it as part of the discoveries made by Verazani in 1523. In 1663 it was granted, with other Islands, by the Company of New France, to the Sieur Doublet, a captain in the French navy, with whom were associated two adventurers who established a few fishing stations, but who did not reside permanently on the island.

In the year 1713 Anne, the Queen of Great Britain, and Louis XIV, the King of France, concluded the celebrated treaty of Utrecht, by which Acadia and Newfoundland were ceded to Great Britain. The fourteenth article of that treaty provided that the French inhabitants of the ceded territory should be at liberty to remove within a year to any other place. Many of the Acadians, availing themselves of this liberty, removed to the Island of Saint John, which was then under French rule. Subsequently a French officer, who received his instructions from the Governor of Cape Breton, resided with a garrison of sixty men at Port la Joie (Charlottetown).

A Frenchman who had visited the island in 1752 published an account of it shortly afterwards. His report as to the fertility of the soil, the quantity of game, and the productiveness of the fishery was extremely favorable, and he expressed astonishment that with these advantages the island should not have been more densely populated—its inhabitants numbering only 1354.

The great fortress of Louisburg fell in 1745, but was restored to the French in 1748. War was again declared by Britain against France in 1756, and in 1758 Louisburg again fell under the leadership of the gallant Wolfe. After the reduction of the fortress several war ships were detached to seize on the Island of Saint John; an object which was effected without difficulty. Mr. McGregor, in his account of the island, says that the population was stated to be at this time ten thousand, but an old Acadian living when he wrote informed him that it could not have exceeded six thousand. A little over four thousand seems to have been the number of inhabitants at this period. [A] The expulsion of the Acadians from Nova Scotia took place in 1755, and many of them having escaped to the island in that year, its population must have been nearly doubled by the influx of fugitives.

The fall of Quebec followed that of Louisburg, and by the treaty of Fontainebleau, in 1763, Cape Breton, the Island of Saint John, and Canada were formally ceded to Great

Britain, Cape Breton and the Island of Saint John being placed under the Government of Nova Scotia.

In the year 1764 the British Government resolved to have a survey of North America executed, and with that view the continent was divided into two districts,—a northern and southern,—and a Surveyor General appointed for each, to act under instructions from the Lords' Commissioners for Trade and Plantations. Captain Samuel Holland was appointed to superintend the survey of the northern district, which comprehended all the territory in North America "lying to the north of the Potowmack River, and of a line drawn due west from the head of the main branch of that river as far as His Majesty's dominions extend." Captain Holland received his commission in March, and was instructed to proceed immediately to Quebec, in order to make arrangements for the survey. He was instructed to begin with the Island of Saint John. The government vessel in which Captain Holland had left sighted the Island of Cape Breton on the eleventh of July, 1764. A thick fog having come on, the vessel had approached too near to the land, when the crew heard a musket shot, and the alarming cry of breakers ahead, which had proceeded from a fishing boat. The ship barely escaped the rocks. Contrary winds were subsequently encountered, and Captain Holland resolved to proceed in a rowing boat to Quebec. He accordingly left the ship on the nineteenth of July, and arrived in Quebec on the second of August. In Quebec Captain Holland met Captain Dean, of the *Mermaid*, who had visited the Island of Saint John during the summer, and who advised him to take "all sorts of material and provisions with him, as there was nothing left on the island but a detachment posted at Fort Amherst, who were indifferently provided, and could not furnish himself and his staff with lodgings." Captain Holland arrived on the island in October, 1764. He describes Fort Amherst "as a poor stockaded redoubt, with barracks scarcely sufficient to lodge the garrison,—the houses near it having been pulled down to supply material to build it." "I am obliged," he adds, "to build winter quarters for myself. I have chosen a spot in the woods, near the sea shore, properly situated for making astronomical observations, where I have put up an old frame of a barn, which I have covered with what material I brought with me, and some boards that we collected from the ruins of some old houses. I fear that it will not be *too* comfortable." The vessel in which Captain Holland was conveyed to North America was called the *Canceaux*, and had been fitted out by the government with the view of aiding him in his professional operations; but on applying to Lieutenant Mowatt, her commander, for boats and men, he was coolly told that such aid could not—according to instructions—be granted. Having complained to Lord Colville, then in command of the naval force in North America, instructions were at once issued to Lieutenant Mowatt to give the required assistance; and Governor Wilmot instructed Captain Hill, the commanding officer on the island, to render all the assistance in his power in forwarding the important service in which Captain Holland was engaged.

In a letter addressed to the Earl of Hillsborough, Captain Holland reports most favourably respecting the capabilities of the island. He adds, "There are about thirty Acadian families on the island, who are regarded as prisoners, and kept on the same footing as those at Halifax. They are extremely poor, and maintain themselves by their industry in gardening, fishing, fowling, &c. The few remaining houses in the different parts of the island are very bad, and the quantity of cattle is but very inconsiderable." At Saint Peter's, Captain Holland met an old acquaintance, Lieutenant Burns, of the 45th Regiment, who had removed with his family to the island, and had built a house and barn, and of whom he writes to the Board of Trade very favorably.

The energy with which Captain Holland prosecuted the survey is sufficiently proved by the fact that in October, 1765, he sent home by Mr. Robinson, one of his deputies, plans of the island, as well as of the Magdalen Islands; also, a description of the Island, from which we shall quote copiously as conveying the impressions of an acute and reliable observer.

"The soil," says Captain Holland, "on the south side of the island is a reddish clay, though in many places it is sandy, particularly on the north coast. From the East Point to Saint Peter's it is a greyish sand. The woods upon this coast, from the East Point as far southward as Hillsborough River, and to Bedford Bay on the west, were entirely destroyed by fire about twenty-six years ago. It was so extremely violent that all the fishing vessels at Saint Peter's and Morell River, in Saint Peter's Bay, were burned. In many parts round the island is a rough, steep coast, from forty to fifty feet high, in some places a hundred, composed of strata of soft red stone, which, when exposed to the air for some time, becomes harder, and is not unfit for building. Wherever this sort of coast is, it diminishes considerably every year upon the breaking up of the frost, which moulders away a great part of it. It may probably be owing to this cause that the sea betwixt the island and the Continent is frequently of a red hue, and for that reason by many people called the red sea. The rivers are properly sea creeks, the tide flowing up to the heads, where, generally, streams of fresh water empty themselves. In most parts of the island the Sarsaparilla Root is in great abundance, and very good. The Mountain Shrub and Maiden Hair are also pretty common, of whose leaves and berries the Acadian settlers frequently make a kind of tea. The ground is in general covered with strawberries and cranberries, in their different seasons, which are very good. In those places which have been settled, and are still tolerably cleared, is very good grass, but a great part of the land formerly cleared is so much overgrown with brush and small wood that it would be extremely difficult to make it fit for the plough. It may be proper to observe that very few houses mentioned in the explanation of the Townships are good for anything, and by no means tenantable, except one or two at Saint Peter's, kept in repair by the officers, and one kept by myself at Observation Cove."

After describing the kinds of Timber to be found on the island, Captain Holland proceeds to say: "Port la Joie (Charlottetown), Cardigan and Richmond Bays are without dispute the only places where ships of burthen can safely enter, and consequently most proper to erect the principal towns and settlements upon. In point of fishing, Richmond Bay has much the advantage of situation, the fish being in great plenty most part of the year, and close to the harbour.

"The capital, to be called Charlottetown, is proposed to be built on a point of the harbour of Port la Joie, betwixt York and Hillsborough Rivers, as being one of the best and central parts of the island, and having the advantage of an immediate and easy communication with the interior parts by means of the three fine rivers of Hillsborough, York, and Elliot. The ground designed for the town and fortifications is well situated upon a regular ascent from the waterside. A fine rivulet will run through the town. A battery or two some distance advanced will entirely command the harbour, so that an enemy attempting to attack the town cannot do so without great difficulty. Having passed the battery at the entrance to the harbour, he must attempt a passage up Hillsborough and York Rivers, the channels of both which are intricate; and the entrance of the respective channels will be so near the town that a passage must be attended with the greatest hazard. Should an enemy land troops on either side the bay of Hillsborough, they must still have the river of the same name on the east, or Elliot or York rivers on the west to pass before they can effect anything of consequence.

"As this side of the Island cannot have a fishery, it may probably be thought expedient to indulge it with some particular privileges; and as all the judicial and civil, as well as a good part of the commercial business will be transacted here, it will make it at least equally flourishing with the other county towns.

"Georgetown is recommended to be built on the point of land called Cardigan Point, there being a good harbour for ships of any burthen on each side of Cardigan river on the north, or on Montague river on the south side; but the latter—though a much narrower channel in coming in—is preferable, as the bay for anchoring will be close by the town immediately on entering the river, and going round the Goose Neck—a long point of dry sand running half over the river and forming one side of Albion Bay—the place of anchorage. On the Goose Neck may be a pier, where goods may be shipped with great facility and convenience. The place proposed is so situated as to be easily made secure, as well as the entrance into the two respective harbours. There is a communication inland by means of Cardigan, Brudenell, and Montague rivers, from the top of which last to the source of Orwell river, is not quite ten miles; and Orwell river, emptying itself into the great bay of Hillsborough, makes a safe and short communication, both in winter and summer, betwixt two of the county towns.

"Princetown is proposed to be built on a most convenient spot of ground as well for fishery as fortification. The site is on a peninsula, having Darnley Basin on the northeast, which is a convenient harbour for small vessels, and where they may lie all winter. The town will have convenient ground for drying fish, and ships of burthen can anchor near it in the bay. It can be fortified at little expense; some batteries and small works erected along the shore would entirely secure it."

It is interesting to note what Captain Holland, writing upwards of a century ago, says respecting the climate:—"The time of the setting in of the frost in winter, and its breaking up in the spring, is very uncertain. In general it is observed that about October there usually begins to be frost morning and evening, which gradually increases in severity till about the middle of December, when it becomes extremely sharp. At this time north-west wind, with small sleet, seldom fails. In a little time the rivers on the island are frozen up, and even the sea some distance from land. The ice soon becomes safe to travel on, as it is at least twenty-two to thirty inches thick. The snow upon the ground, and in the woods, is often a surprising depth, and it is impossible to travel except on snow-shoes. The Acadians now have recourse to little cabins or huts in the woods, where they are screened from the violence of the weather, and at the same time have the convenience of wood for fuel. Here they live on the fish they have cured in the summer, and game which they frequently kill, as hares and partridges, lynxes or wild cats, otters, martins, or musk rats,—none of which they refuse to eat, as necessity presses them. In the spring the rivers seldom break up till April, and the snow is not entirely off the ground until the middle of May. It ought to be observed that as Saint John is fortunately not troubled with fogs, as are the neighboring Islands of Cape Breton and Newfoundland, neither has it so settled and constant a climate as Canada. Here are frequent changes of weather, as rain, snow, hail, and hard frost."

On the completion of the survey of the Island of Saint John, Captain Holland proceeded to prosecute that of Cape Breton. Here he had the misfortune to lose his most efficient deputy, Lieutenant Haldiman, who was drowned, by falling through the ice on the 16th of December, 1765. He was a Lieutenant, on half pay, when Captain Holland engaged him, having served since the age of fifteen in America. He was an excellent mathematician, and quite an adept in making accurate astronomical observations. This excellent young man perished in the twenty-fourth year of his age. Whilst Captain Holland was busy on the Island of Saint John, Haldiman was detached to superintend the survey of the Magdalen Islands. In the report sent by Holland to the Board of Trade, from which we have given extracts, was embodied Haldiman's account of the Magdalen Islands, which is extremely interesting. We regret our space will not permit its insertion.

In December, 1763, the Earl of Egmont, then first Lord of the Admiralty, presented an elaborate memorial to the King, praying for a grant of the whole Island of Saint John, to hold the same in fee of the Crown forever, according to a tenure described in the said memorial. On the supposition that the island contained two millions of acres,—for it had not then been surveyed,—he proposed that the whole should be divided into fifty parts of equal extent, to be designated *Hundreds*, as in England, or *Baronies*, as in Ireland; forty of these to be granted to as many men who should be styled Lords of Hundreds, and each of whom should pay to the Earl, as Lord Paramount, twenty pounds sterling yearly. On the property of the Earl—to whom, with his family of nine children, ten hundreds were to be allotted—a strong castle was to be erected, mounted with ten pieces of cannon, each carrying a ball of four pounds, with a circuit round the castle of three miles every way. The forty *Hundreds* or *Baronies* were to be divided into twenty manors of two thousand acres each, which manors were to be entitled to a Court Baron, according to the Common Law of England. The Lord of each *Hundred* was to set apart five hundred acres for the site of a township, which township was to be divided into one hundred lots, of five acres each, and the happy proprietors of five acres were each to pay a yearly *free-farm* rent of four shillings sterling to the Lord of the Hundred. Each Hundred was to have a fair four times a year, and a market twice in every week. There were also to be Courts Leet and Courts Baron, under the direction of the Lord Paramount. A foot-note referring to these Courts, attached by the framers of the memorial, indicates the ideas which were entertained at this time in the old country respecting protection to life and property in the North American Colonies. "These courts—established by Alfred and others of our Saxon Princes, to maintain order, and bring justice to every man's door—are obviously essential for a small people, forming or formed into a small society in the vast, impervious, and dangerous forests of America, intersected with seas, bays, lakes, rivers, marshes, and mountains; without roads, without inns or accommodations, locked up for half the year by snow and intense frost, and where the settler can scarce straggle from his habitation five hundred yards, even in times of peace, without risk of being intercepted, scalped, and murdered."

To epitomise the proposal: there was to be a Lord Paramount of the whole island, forty Capital Lords of forty Hundreds, four hundred Lords of Manors, and eight hundred Freeholders. For assurance of the said tenures, eight hundred thousand acres were to be set apart for establishments for trade and commerce in the most suitable parts of the island, including one county town, forty market towns, and four hundred villages; each Hundred or Barony was to consist of somewhat less than eight square miles, and the Lord of each was bound to erect and maintain forever a castle or blockhouse as the capital seat of his property, and as a place of retreat and rendezvous for the settlers; and thus, on any alarm of sudden danger, every inhabitant might have a place of security within four miles of his habitation. A cannon fired at one of the castles would be heard at the next, and thus the firing would proceed in regular order from castle to castle, and be the means, adds the noble memorialist, "of putting every inhabitant of the whole island under arms and in motion in the space of one quarter of an hour."

As we have already stated, Lord Egmont's memorial was presented in December, 1763, and in January, 1764, it was backed by three different communications, addressed to the Lords of Trade and Plantations, and signed by thirty influential gentlemen, who were supposed—on account of military or other services—to have claims on the government.

On the 13th February, 1764, a report was made on the memorial by the Board of Trade, to which it had been referred by the King. The Board reported that the scheme was calculated to answer the purposes of defence and military discipline rather than to encourage those of commerce and agriculture, and seemed totally and fundamentally adverse in its principles to that system of settlement and tenure of property which had of late years been adopted in the colonies, with so much advantage to the interests of the kingdom; and they therefore could not see sufficient reason to justify them in advising His Majesty to comply with Lord Egmont's proposal.

In forming plans for the settlement of the American Colonies, the object the Commissioners had principally in view was to advance and extend the commerce and navigation of the kingdom, to preserve a due dependence in the colonies on the mother country, and to secure to them the full enjoyment of every civil and religious right, so that the colonists might have just reason to value themselves on being British subjects. In order to attain these objects, the Board had recommended such a mode of granting lands as might encourage industry, which is the life and spirit of commerce; and in the form of government, they recommended a constitution for the colonies as nearly similar to that of Britain as the nature of the case would permit. In adopting this policy they had followed what appeared to have been almost the invariable practice of Government ever since the surrender and revocation of those charters which were formerly granted for the settlement of America; and the effects could be best judged of by the present flourishing state of the colonies, and the progress they had made in cultivation and commerce, compared with their condition under those charters, which, though granted to persons of rank and consequence, and accompanied by plans of government,—the result of the study and reading of wise and learned men,—yet, being founded in speculation more than in experience did, in the event, not only disappoint the sanguine expectations of the proprietors, but check and obstruct the settlement of the country.

The report pointed to the grant made to the Lords Proprietors of Carolina, as a striking example of the inexpediency of such a plan of settlement, little progress having been made in the execution of it till the property, being reinvested in the crown, a new foundation was laid, which resulted in prosperity and advancement. The report, of which we have attempted to give a sketch, ended with the following words:—"We have not thought proper to take the opinion of Your Majesty's servants in the law upon the question whether Your Majesty can legally make the grant desired by the Earl of Egmont, because we cannot think it expedient, either in a political or commercial light, for Your Majesty to comply with his Lordship's proposals; and as Your Majesty has been pleased to annex the Island of Saint John to your Province of Nova Scotia, we humbly recommend the settling it upon the plan and under the regulations, approved of by Your Majesty for the settlement of that province in general."

On receiving this reply to his memorial, the Earl addressed a second one to the King, substantially the same as the former, to which no reply seems to have been made. He accordingly had a third one drawn out and presented, attaching the names of his co-adventurers, who had agreed to assist his Lordship in the settlement of the island. The list included four admirals, a large number of officers, and eight members of parliament. This memorial, like the first, was referred to the Board of Trade, who prepared a lengthened report in answer to it. The opening passage was of such a nature as to make the memorialists imagine that all desired was to be granted. "We are of opinion," said the Board, "it may be highly conducive to the speedy cultivation of your Majesty's American Dominions that the nobility and other persons of rank and distinction in this country should take the lead, and show the example in the undertaking and carrying into execution the settlement thereof, and that all due encouragement should be given to officers of Your Majesty's fleet and army, to whose distinguished bravery and conduct this kingdom is so much indebted for the acquisitions made in the last war." But this soothing paragraph was followed by others which blasted the hopes of the ardent adventurers, by insisting on the distribution of land on the island being made in conformity to those principles of settlement, cultivation, and government which had been previously adopted, and were founded on experience.

The King referred this report, and all the other papers, to a committee of council, to whom Lord Egmont sent observations on the report, drawn up with great ability, in which his former arguments were repeated, and others adduced to strengthen them. These observations are pervaded by a bitterness of expression which, in the circumstances, is pardonable. The committee of council coincided in the views of the Board of Trade, and on the 9th of May, 1764, came the climax to Lord Egmont's proposal, in the form of a minute of council, embodying a report adverse to the proposition of the Earl, and ordering that no grants be made of land in the Island of Saint John upon any other principles than those comprised in the reports of the Lords Commissioners of trade and plantations.

About the time of the arrival in London of Captain Holland's plans of the island, the friends of Lord Egmont again mustered in great strength, including officers of high rank in the naval and military service, bankers, and merchants, and drew up a final memorial in behalf of his Lordship's scheme, which closed with these words:—"That if at the end of ten years any ill consequence should be found to have arisen therefrom, upon an address to the two houses of parliament, His Majesty in council might change the jurisdiction in such manner as experience of the use or abuse might then dictate or demand." That Lord Egmont was sanguine as to the success of this last appeal in his behalf, appears evident from a manuscript letter now before us, addressed by him on the 8th October, 1765, to Captain Holland, in which he says:—"I think it proper to let you know that a petition will be again presented to His Majesty in a few days for a grant of the Island of Saint John, upon the very same plan as that proposed before, which I have now reason to expect will meet with better success than the former. The same persons very nearly will be concerned, those only excluded who were drawn away by proposals and grants elsewhere by the Board of Trade, in order if possible to defeat my scheme. For yourself, you may be assured of your Hundred, as formerly intended, if I have anything to do in the direction of the affair,—which probably I shall have in the same mode and manner. Whether the grant may be made before the arrival of the survey or not I cannot certainly say, but we wait patiently for it, and hope it will be done accurately as to Hundreds, Manors, Freehold Villages, Towns, and Capitals, that a moment's time may not be lost afterwards in proceeding to draw the lots, and then in proceeding to erect the Blockhouses of the Hundreds on a determined spot, which is the very first work to be put in execution, and agreed to be completed by all the chief adventurers within one twelvemonth after the grant shall be obtained." This communication leads to the conviction, that if the island had been then granted no time would have been lost in erecting the strongholds referred to. It is evident that the erections were intended to consist mainly of wood. The adventurers were, for the most part, wealthy and influential, and under their auspices thousands would have emigrated to the island. It were vain to speculate as to the effect which would be produced if Egmont's scheme had been put in execution. In looking over the list of those to whom Hundreds were to be allotted, we find that of the forty persons specified, thirty-two were military or naval officers,—men whose profession did not, as a rule, fit them for the direction of the settlement of a new colony. It is probable, however, that the expense to which, at the outset, the forty Lords of Hundreds were to be put would prompt them to take a more lively interest in their property than was exhibited by the subsequent grantees. It is, however, possible that not a few of the proposed lords intended to dispose of their property to the highest bidder soon after the lots were drawn, and thus to avoid the expense of the blockhouse erections, such a transference of interest being allowable under the proposed original grant. That Egmont intended to carry out his scheme in its integrity, there is no room to doubt. He must have employed the highest legal ability to frame his memorials, which are distinguished by a mastery of the ancient feudal tenures of the kingdom, which elicited expressions of admiration from the government. The pertinacity with which he urged his scheme showed that he was not a man easily diverted from any settled purpose, and few governments could have resisted the powerful influence he brought to bear for the attainment of his object. There can be little doubt that whatever might be the consequences of possession to the Lord Paramount himself and his family of nine children, the destiny of the island would have been far better in his keeping than in that of the men to whom it was afterwards unfortunately committed. In order to conciliate Lord Egmont, and make reparation to him for the trouble and expense to which he had been put in urging his scheme, the Board of Trade, by a minute dated the 5th of June, 1767, offered him any entire parish,—comprehending about one hundred thousand acres,—which he might select, but his lordship addressed a letter to the Board on the eleventh of the same month declining to take the grant. [B]

CHAPTER II.

Determination of the Home Government to dispose of the whole Island—The manner in which it was effected—Conditions on which grants were made—Appointment of Walter Patterson as Governor—Novel duties imposed on him—Callbeck made prisoner by Americans—Arrival of Hessian Troops—Sale of Land in 1781—Agitation in consequence—Complaints against the Governor, and his tactics in defence—Governor superceded, and Colonel Fanning appointed—Disputes between them—Charges of immorality against Patterson—His departure from the Island.

Although the government had resolutely opposed the scheme of settlement proposed by Lord Egmont, yet it was disposed to divide the island among persons who had claims on the ground of military or other public services; and it was accordingly determined, in order to prevent disputes, to make the various allotments by ballot. [C] The Board of Trade and Plantations accordingly prepared certain conditions, under which the various grants were to be made. On twenty-six specified lots or townships a quitrent of six shillings on every hundred acres was reserved, on twenty-nine lots four shillings, and on eleven lots two shillings, payable annually on one half of the grant at the expiration of five years, and on the whole at the expiration of ten years after the date of the grants. A reservation of such parts of each lot as might afterwards be found necessary for fortifications or public purposes, and of a hundred acres for a church and glebe, and of fifty acres for a schoolmaster, was made, five hundred feet from high-water mark being reserved for the purpose of a free fishery. Deposits of gold, silver, and coal were reserved for the Crown. It was stipulated that the grantee of each township should settle the same within ten years from the date of the grant, in the proportion of one person for every two hundred acres; that such settlers should be European foreign protestants, or such persons as had resided in British North America for two years previous to the date of the grant; and, finally, that if one-third of the land was not so settled within four years from the date of the grant, the whole should be forfeited. Thus the whole island was, in 1767, disposed of in one day, with the exception of lot sixty-six, reserved for the King, and lots forty and fifty-nine,—which had been promised to Messrs. Spence, Muir, and Cathcart, and Messrs. Mill, Cathcart, and Higgens, by the government, in 1764, in consideration of their having established fisheries, and made improvements on the island, [D]—and three small reservations, intended for three county towns. A mandamus addressed to the Governor of Nova Scotia, the island being now annexed to that province, was handed to each of the proprietors, instructing the governor to issue the respective grants, on the conditions specified. In the following year, 1768, a large majority of the proprietors presented a petition to the King, praying that the island should be erected into a separate government; that the quitrents which would become payable, according to stipulation, in 1772, should become payable from the first of May, 1769, and that the payment of the remaining half should be deferred for the period of twenty years. This proposition was accepted by the government, and accordingly Captain Walter Patterson, one of the island proprietors, was appointed governor. He, accompanied by other officers, arrived on the island in 1770, at which period, notwithstanding the conditions of settlement attached to the land grants, there were only one hundred and fifty families and five proprietors residing on it. It was calculated by the government that the quitrents would amount in the aggregate to fourteen hundred and seventy pounds sterling. The governor was instructed to pay out of that fund the following annual salaries, in sterling currency: to himself, as governor, five hundred pounds, to the secretary and registrar, one hundred and fifty pounds, to the chief justice, two hundred pounds, to the attorney general, one hundred pounds, to the clerk of the crown and coroner, eighty pounds, to the provost marshal, fifty pounds, and to a minister of the Church of England, one hundred pounds. This arrangement was to remain in force not more than ten years, and in the event of the quitrents falling short, from any cause, of the required sum, the salaries were to be diminished in proportion.

The governor was required to perform other duties, which were grossly unjust, and in some cases beyond human capability. He was, for example, enjoined by the twenty-sixth and twenty-seventh articles of his instructions to permit "liberty of conscience to all persons (except Roman catholics), so they be contented with a quiet and peaceable enjoyment of the same, not giving offence and scandal to the government," and he was also "to take especial care that God Almighty should be devoutly and duly served throughout his government." No schoolmaster, coming from England, was permitted to teach without a license from the Bishop of London; and it was assumed in his instructions that all Christians, save those connected with the Church of England, were heterodox. Some denominations were, indeed, *tolerated*; but in conformity to the bigoted British policy of the times, Roman catholics were not permitted to settle on the island. This sectarian policy has borne bitter fruit in Ireland, in the alienation of a great mass of the Irish people. So deeply has alienation struck its roots, and so widely spread are its branches, that, notwithstanding catholic emancipation, its effects are still painfully visible, not only in Ireland, but also in the masses of the Irish people located in the United States, as strikingly evinced in the election of the late John Mitchell, for Tipperary, and in the honors which have been paid to his memory in the States. More than one generation will pass away ere the evil effects of unjust anti-catholic legislation are totally obliterated from the continent of America.

The little progress made in the settlement of the island, from the time it was granted until the year 1779, is indicated by the fact that no step had been taken to introduce settlers into all the lots, ranging from one to sixteen, besides other thirty-three which were in the same condition. Thus, although more than ten years had elapsed since the ballot took place, in scarcely a score of lots was there any attempt made to conform to the conditions attached to the sixty-seven townships.

Notwithstanding the very small population of the island, it was resolved to grant it a complete constitution. This step the governor was commanded in his instructions to take as early as possible. "The forming a lower house of representatives for our said Island of Saint John," said His Majesty, "is a consideration that cannot be too early taken up, for until this object is attainable, the most important interests of the inhabitants will necessarily remain without that advantage and protection which can only arise out of the vigor and activity of a complete constitution." In the year 1773, the first assembly was convened. The first act passed was one confirming the past proceedings of the governor and council, and rendering valid all manner of process and proceedings in the several courts of judicature within the island, from the first day of May, 1769, to the present session of assembly.

The proposal to pay the government officials in the island from the amount realized from the quitrents completely failed, as but few of the proprietors acted as if they had been under obligation to comply with the conditions on which they obtained their grants. The sum realized from the amount of quitrents paid was totally inadequate to pay the official salaries. Hence it was necessary that some other arrangement should be adopted. The governor was reduced to such straits for want of money, that he was under the necessity of appropriating three thousand pounds, granted by parliament for the erection of public buildings in the island, for the maintenance of himself and the other government officers. The governor went to England in 1775, when it was agreed that the proprietors, in order to meet the difficulties of the case, should present a memorial to the Secretary of State for the colonies, praying that the civil establishment of the island should be provided for by an annual parliamentary grant, as in the case of the other colonies. By a minute of the seventh August, 1776, it was ordered by the government that the arrears of the quitrents due should be enforced by legal proceedings, and that the sum thus obtained should be devoted to the refunding of the amount expended, in a manner incompatible with the object for which it was voted. The power for the recovery of the quitrents, with which the governor was thus invested, was not speedily exercised, as he was anxious not to offend the proprietors, through whose influence the payment of the civil establishment of the island was placed on a more satisfactory footing.

During the governor's absence in England the Hon. Mr. Callbeck, being the senior member of the council, was sworn in as administrator. In November of that year, a ship from London, having on board a number of settlers, and loaded with a valuable cargo, was unfortunately wrecked on the north side of the island. All on board were saved, but the cargo was either lost, or destroyed to such an extent as to be of little value,—an accident which involved no small hardship to the inhabitants.

In this year too a memorable incident occurred. Whilst the good people of Charlottetown were living in apparent security from hostile aggression, two American armed vessels which had been sent to cruise in the Gulf of Saint Lawrence, in order to intercept English ordnance store-ships, supposed to be on the way to Quebec, entered the harbor, and a landing was effected without any opposition, when the administrator, Mr. Callbeck, Mr. Wright, the surveyor general, and other officers of the government were made prisoners, and put with such valuable booty as the Americans could lay hands on, on board ship, and conveyed to New England. On arriving at the head-quarters of the American army, then at Cambridge, General Washington disapproved of the hostile act, dismissing the principal officers from their commands, telling them that "they had done those things which they ought not to have done, and left undone those things which it was their duty to have done." At the same time he discharged the prisoners with expressions of regret, and returned all the property.

In the following year the *Diligent*, an armed brig, was detached by the admiral, commanding in America, to protect the island, which vessel was replaced by the *Hunter*, sloop of war, towards the end of the year, and which remained till November, 1777. The arrival of the latter vessel was extremely opportune, as a hostile expedition to the island was being organized by rebels from Machias, in Massachusetts, who had arrived at Fort Cumberland, in Nova Scotia. These men paid a visit to Pictou, where they seized on an armed merchant ship, then loading for Scotland. Fearing resistance, which they were not in a condition to overcome successfully, these rebels entered, with their prize, into the Bay of Verte, for the purpose of receiving reinforcements. But not being successful in this effort, on account of a defeat at Fort Cumberland, the vessel was given up to one of the officers, the rebels escaping on shore. The vessel then came to Charlottetown, where she remained during the winter.

In 1777 the administrator received instructions from the secretary of state for the colonies to raise an independent force for the defence of the island; but from the small number of the male population, which had been previously considerably reduced by recruiting officers, this force was never completed. In the following year, however, four provincial companies were sent from New York, under the command of Major Hierliky, for whom barracks were erected, under the direction of an engineer from Nova Scotia, and the island was thus placed in a defensive position, which greatly reduced the chances of a successful attack during the American war. With the exception of a few sheep, occasionally taken by the men of privateers, and some valuable property seized at the harbor of Saint George (now Georgetown), the inhabitants of the island experienced no further annoyance from the Americans during the continuance of the contest. The monotony of Charlottetown was betimes enlivened during the summer by the presence of the British war vessels employed in accompanying convoys to Quebec, and the occasional conduct into the harbor of American privateers which had been captured at sea by the British cruisers, and whose men were marched as prisoners through the woods to Halifax.

An interesting trial took place in Charlottetown in 1779, in the case of *Thomas Mellish, v.* the Convoy ship *Dutchess of London*, which Mr. Mellish seized for smuggling. The trial lasted for several months. Mr. Mellish was an officer in the First Troop of Horse Guards, and served also in the colonial military service. He was a member of the house of assembly, and held the office of collector of customs and other public positions for many years. His son, Thomas Mellish, died at an advanced age in 1859. Referring to his death, the *Islander* describes him as a most loyal British subject, and a devoted adherent of the Church of England.

Towards the end of October, 1779, the town of Charlottetown received a temporary accession to its inhabitants, by the arrival of the Hessian regiment of Knyphansen, under convoy of the war ship *Camilla*. Severe gales were encountered in the River Saint Lawrence, which compelled the ship to take refuge in the island. The troops were landed, and there being no barrack accommodation for them, some succeeded in hutting themselves most comfortably. Some of the men were suffering from fever, but speedily recovered, on account of the admirable character of the climate. The town supply of provisions was utterly inadequate to meet the demand occasioned by so large an addition to the population, but the farmers soon made up the deficiency, and the Hessians remained till the month of June, when they left for their destination. Not a few of the men were so favorably impressed with the island, that they returned to it from Germany, many years afterwards, and became industrious settlers.

Governor Patterson returned to the island in 1780, relieving the Honorable T. DesBrisay, who had succeeded Mr. Callbeck as administrator; and shortly after his arrival he appointed Mr. Nisbet, his brother-in-law, then clerk of the council, to the office of the receiver of quitrents. It was now determined by the governor to enforce a law passed by the assembly in 1773, "for the effectual recovery of certain of His Majesty's quitrents in the Island of Saint John," and in conformity to the treasury minute of the seventh of August, 1776, to which reference has already been made. Accordingly, early in 1781, proceedings were commenced in the supreme court against the townships in arrear of quitrents, as enumerated in the act of 1773, and the sale of a number of townships was thus effected. These reasonable proceedings were complained of to the British government, and powerful influence was brought to bear for the purpose of counteracting them. As the act of 1773, which had been confirmed by His Majesty, only applied to a part of the lands granted, it was deemed necessary to pass another act in 1781, which was intended to take a wider scope, and to render the sale of all lands in the island, where quitrents remained unpaid, legal. This act had, however, a clause suspending its operation till the King's pleasure should be known. It appears by a manuscript copy of a report, dated tenth of July, 1783, by the lords of the committee of council for plantations, now before us, that this act was referred to Andrew Jackson, one of the King's council, who reported that, in point of law, no objection could be made to it; and the same report also furnishes interesting information as to the considerations by which the government was influenced in its treatment of the action of the House of Assembly in regard to land. An application was made in behalf of officers abroad in the King's service, who were proprietors of land, praying that the arrears of quitrent due on their lands should be remitted, and that no proceedings should be taken to dispose of those lands for future arrears until the conclusion of the war, when they might be enabled to settle and improve the same. Thomas Townshend, the colonial secretary, accordingly recommended that no action during the war should be taken against the property of absent officers. A petition was about the same time presented by other proprietors of land in the island, reciting the difficulties peculiarly incident to the island, showing that their expectations, mainly in consequence of the American war, had proved abortive, and complaining that many of the allotments in the island had been sold under the assembly act of 1774, and of the treasury order of 1776, *to officers resident in the island,* for little more than the arrears and charges of confiscation. They further prayed for a remission of the quitrents in arrear, and that in future they might have the option of paying the quitrents either in London or the island. The council proceeded, on the first of May, to take these matters into consideration, when it was agreed "that all such as, on or before the first of May, 1784, should have paid up all the arrears of quitrent due upon their respective lots to the first of May, 1783, should, from the said first of May, 1783, until the first of May, 1789, be exempted from the payment of more than the quitrent now payable upon each of their lots, and that, for and during the further term of ten years,—to commence from the said first of May, 1789,—the same quitrent only as is now payable on each of their lots should continue to be paid in lieu of the advanced quitrent, which, by the terms of the grants, would have become due and payable from the said first of May, 1789." In accordance with this decision, a bill was prepared, which not only granted the redress specified in the above quotation, but also disallowed the act of 1781, and repealed the act of 1774, and rendered all the sales effected under it void, on the payment by the original proprietors of the purchase-money, interest, and charges incurred by the present holders, compensation being also required for any improvements made on the lands since the date of sale. This bill was drawn out in London, and sent to Governor Patterson in 1784, in order that it might be submitted to and adopted by the house of assembly. But the governor, having been himself a purchaser to a large extent of the confiscated property, assumed the responsibility of postponing official action in the matter, on the ground that the government was mistaken as to facts connected with the sale of the land, and, on consulting with the council, it was resolved to send to the home government a correct representation of the circumstances under which confiscation took place, in justification of delay in submitting the bill to the assembly for approval.

A Mr. John Stuart, [E] an intimate friend of Governor Patterson, and who had resided in London for fourteen years, was in 1781 appointed by the house of assembly as their London agent. We have been favored with the perusal of a number of private and confidential letters which passed between the governor and this gentleman. These throw considerable light on the island history of this period. The sales of land recently made excited intense indignation against the governor on the part of those whose property had been confiscated, who were backed in their applications for redress by the general body of proprietors. The act sent to the governor, and which he failed to present to the house of assembly, was the result of these applications. In the preamble of that portion of the act which provided for relief to the complainants, it was stated that the governor and council, on the first day of December, 1780, unanimously resolved, in order to give absent proprietors whose lands were liable to be sold an opportunity of relieving their property, that no sales should take place until the first Monday of November following, and that in the meantime the colonial agent in London should be instructed to inform the proprietors of the proposed sale; and "whereas," runs the act, "notwithstanding such determination and resolution, no such notice was given by the colonial agent to the proprietors, it seems reasonable that they should obtain effectual relief in the premises." It is only fair that the governor should be allowed to reply in his own words, as contained in a letter now before us, which he addressed to his friend Stuart on the twelfth of May, 1783. In order that a portion of that letter may be understood, it is necessary to say that Captain McDonald, one of the proprietors resident in London, had written a pamphlet reflecting on the conduct of the governor in disposing of the land, which contributed in no small degree, as Mr. Stuart affirms, in causing the act of relief to be prepared. After referring to business matters, which have no bearing on our story, the governor says: "What appears most pressing at present is to say something in answer to my friend Captain McDonald's proceedings. But first I must express my astonishment at your not having received any letters from me since December, 1781. I wrote and sent two by the express, which went to the continent in February, 1782,—not to you, indeed, because I thought you had sailed for India; but Mr. Townshend received them, I am certain, for I have answers to them from you. I wrote a long one to you in October, 1782, on a variety of subjects. If this letter has not reached you, I am very unfortunate, as I have no copy of it. I wrote you three others in the course of the winter, copies of which shall accompany this, though they will be now, I fear, of little use, except to show that I have not been idle, or negligent in my attention to the interests of this government. If I succeed, I may be rewarded by my own feelings, but as to any grateful returns, I expect them not. In bodies of men there is no such virtue as gratitude, nor indeed but very rarely in individuals. I feel this, and in few instances more sensibly than in the behaviour of Captain McDonald. Believe me, my friend, I have rendered him and his family many disinterested and essential services; nor do I know that I can let an opportunity slip of doing so, when in my power. But *now*, when he thinks his interest is in the least affected, he becomes my enemy, and that, too, in a matter where I am only a spectator, or rather, when I ought to have been only such; for the fact is, I did step out of my line in the business of forfeiting the lots, but then it was only to continue my wonted practice to benefit the proprietors. For this purpose I advised sending the advertisements to England, which the law did not require. I, by the advice of council, postponed the sales from time to time, in hopes the proprietors would take some steps in consequence of the advertisements, and, with this view, prevented their taking place till the latter end of November, when every hope was over. This the law did not require, and the advertisements not reaching England in time was not my fault, as the resolution of council directing their being sent is dated twenty-sixth November, 1780, and the sales did not take place for a year afterwards. I did more: I prevented all the lots from being sold belonging to proprietors who I knew were inclined to improve their lands, and this I did by taking the debt upon myself, which was not required by the law, nor perhaps in justice to my own family; nor do I believe there is an instance of such conduct in any other man. Among the number so saved is the lot belonging to this same Captain McDonald, though I had no hopes of his paying his quitrents, or of his doing any one thing relative to the settling of it; for he has repeatedly told me himself that he would not, as he thought he had engaged to pay too much money for it to the chief baron from whom he bought it. What I did was out of tenderness to his sisters, who live upon the lot, and to give him time to think better. I saved Lord

Townshend's, the chief baron's, etc., and, in short, what I thought worth the saving,—and all at my own risk. I have done still more, for I have prevented any further sales since the first. This I also did for the benefit of the proprietors, knowing the lands would not bring their value; and I did it at the risk of my commission, for I did it in the face of a positive order from the treasury. So far, I hope I am not to blame.

"As to the regularity and legality of the proceedings in other respects, I am not accountable. The lands were seized in terms of a law passed near ten years since, and the proceedings conducted by the law officers,—I have no doubt properly.

"There is some idea, I find, of rescinding the purchases, and that government will order it. Whoever has formed such an idea must have strange notions of government. Government may order me; and, if I have a mind to be laughed at, I may issue my orders to the purchasers; but can anyone believe they will be obeyed? Surely not; nor would I be an inhabitant of any country where such a power existed. My money may with as much justice be ordered out of my pocket, or the bread out of my mouth. A governor has just as much power to do the one as the other. I should like to know what opinion you would have of a country where the validity of public contracts depended on the will of the governor.

"The purchases were made in the very worst period of the war, when the property was very precarious indeed, and when no man in England would have given hardly a guinea for the whole island. It is now peace, and fortunately we still remain a part of the British Empire. The lands are consequently esteemed more valuable, and the proprietors have become clamorous for their loss. Had the reverse taken place,—had the island been ceded to France,—let me ask, what would have been the consequence? Why, the purchasers would have lost their money, and the proprietors would have been quiet, hugging themselves on their own better judgment. There can be no restoring of the lots which were sold. There has not been a lot sold on which a single shilling has been expended by way of settlement, nor upon which there has been a settler placed; so that those proprietors who have expended money in making settlements have no cause of complaint."

Complaints had been made to the home government, of which Mr. Stuart had informed the governor, that a large quantity of the land disposed of had been bought for trifling sums by the governor and other officials of the island. The truth of this charge was acknowledged by the governor, for he says in the letter from which we have quoted so largely: "That the officers of the government have made purchases is certain, and that I have made some myself is also as certain; but I should be glad to know who would be an officer of government if, by being such, he was deprived of his privileges as a citizen."

Mr. Stuart writes the governor on the twenty-ninth of June, 1783, that he received, on the twenty-second of April, three letters from him, dated respectively, thirtieth November, first and seventh December, 1782, and in reference to the sales of land which had been effected, remarks: "The time of the sale, in the midst of a distressful war, when there could be neither money nor purchasers; the rigid condition of obliging the proprietors to pay their quitrents in the island, and not giving at least a twelvemonth's notice of the sale in England, as well as in the island, are everywhere urged and admitted as sound arguments against the confiscation of lands in an infant colony, and I must frankly confess that they have too much force in them to be totally denied."

Whilst it is impossible to deny that Governor Patterson had ample governmental authority to dispose of the lands, yet his doing so before he had any evidence whatever that the advertisements sent had obtained the desired publicity, or even that his letters had reached their destination, was, to say the least, a most unreasonable proceeding, and constituted sufficient ground of grave complaint against his conduct. That as an intending purchaser he had a material interest in bringing the lands speedily to the hammer, cannot be denied; and that after so many years had elapsed since the act and the treasury minute by which a sale of the townships whose quitrents were in arrears was rendered legal, he should have chosen a period for the sale when, according to his own confession, capitalists might not be disposed to give a guinea for the island, seems to import that the governor had, in the conduct of the business, consulted his own interest rather than that of the proprietors. This impression is deepened by the proceedings which followed.

It has been already stated that, on receiving from England the act which was intended to restore the property sold to the original holders, he had delayed to submit it to the house of assembly. Believing that the present house would pass the act in question, in the event of his being again ordered to submit it for their approval, he resolved dissolution of the house, and to exert his influence in obtaining one better suited to his purpose. He accordingly carried out his resolution early in 1784, and, in March following, a general election took place, and the legislature met soon after. It is a most significant indication of the state of public opinion at this time, in reference to the governor's conduct in so hastily disposing of the lands, that the new house, instead of approving of the governor's conduct, resolved to present a complaint against him to the King, and was actually engaged in framing it, when a dissolution, by command of the governor, again took place. His Excellency, appreciating the importance of the crisis to himself personally, determined to leave no means untried to secure an assembly favorable to his views. The danger was imminent; for the recent proceedings were adopted by the house in ignorance of the views of the home government as to the governor's conduct, which he had carefully concealed, and which were known only to the council, who were bound by oath to secrecy. He expected an order from England to submit the dreaded act to the house, and was most desirous that, before that could be done, the forthcoming house should pledge itself to an approval of the sales of 1781, and thus neutralize the effect which a knowledge of the intended disapproval of the previous assembly might produce on the home government.

Circumstances favored his design. New York having been evacuated by the British troops, many of them had resolved to settle in the island. A large number of loyalists were now leaving the States and settling in Nova Scotia. Efforts were made by the governor to induce some of them to settle in the island. In addressing Mr. Stuart in 1783, he says, in reference to this subject: "I do not as yet hear, notwithstanding my efforts, of any of the loyalists coming this way. They have all gone to Nova Scotia, through the influence of Mr. Watson. I will not, however, as yet despair of having a part. I am sending a person among them on purpose, and at my own expense, to carry our terms and to invite some of the principal people to our lands. If they will but come,—and depend on the evidence of their own senses,—I am certain they will prefer this island to any of the uncultivated parts of Nova Scotia. It is exceedingly unlucky that my despatches of last November did not reach you in time. Had the proprietors sent an agent to New York, offering liberal terms to the loyalists, they would have reaped more benefit thereby than by all the memorials they will ever deliver to government." We find, by a letter from Mr. Stuart to the governor, dated a month later than that from which a quotation has just been given, that the proprietors were sensible of the importance of presenting inducements to the loyalists, for they subscribed liberally to a fund raised for the purpose of conveying them to the island. Orders were issued to the governor to apportion part of the land to the loyalists; the attorney general was to make out the deeds of conveyance without any expense to the proprietors, who were to be exonerated from the quitrents of such shares of their land as were granted to the loyalists. In consequence of these arrangements, a considerable number of loyalists were induced to come to the island, to whom the governor paid due attention, and whose votes he had no difficulty in securing at the coming election. In order to complicate matters still more, and throw additional obstacles in the way of the much dreaded act, he took care that not a few of the allotments made to the refugees should be on the lands sold in 1781.

Being thus fortified for the coming battle, he determined to risk another election in March, 1785, when he secured the return of a house bound to his interests, which Mr. Stewart, of Mount Stewart—on whose testimony implicit reliance can be placed—assures us "was not accomplished without a severe struggle, much illegal conduct, and at an expense to the governor and his friends of nearly two thousand pounds sterling." The time of the assembly was, to a considerable extent, taken up during the session by proceedings which had a tendency to produce a favorable impression as to the governor's acts. Not a word was said in the house regarding the proceedings of 1781; but, when the house met in the following year, the governor determined that a measure should be adopted which would frustrate any attempt to render the sales of 1781 futile. To effect this object, he caused a measure to be introduced entitled "An act to render good and valid in law all and every of the proceedings in the years one thousand seven hundred and eighty and one thousand seven hundred and eighty-one, which in every respect related to or concerned the suing, seizing, condemning, or selling of the lots or townships hereinafter mentioned, or any part thereof." This act was adopted without scruple by the assembly, but was disallowed by His Majesty; and, affording as it did convincing proof of the governor's determination to act in opposition to his instructions, led to his being superceded in his office.

Mr. Stuart, the London agent for the island, fought at all times resolutely for the governor, using all the means in his power to place his character and transactions in a favorable light before the government and proprietors. Having obtained information from reliable sources as to the intentions of the government in reference to the governor, he addressed a letter to him on the 19th of June, 1786, informing him of the decision as to his recall. This manuscript communication, now before us, is especially interesting and valuable, as showing that, after its receipt, Governor Patterson could not have been mistaken as to the nature of the recall, and as accounting for some of his subsequent proceedings. Mr. Stuart says: "Your brother will have acquainted you with the caballing and intrigueing of your opponents to effect your removal, and of the invincible silence, or rather sullenness, of office with regard to their real and ultimate intentions towards you. Mr. Nepean, I think, has indeed opened himself at last, and given a pretty plain clew to their disposition not to support you. He told your brother very lately that Lord Sydney had sent you the King's leave of absence. This is surely a plain indication, especially after you were required to answer charges, and those answers still remain unheard and undecided upon, although your brother has made repeated application, and even memorialized the council for a hearing. The real cause and design of this extraordinary and unfair step neither your brother nor I has yet been able to develop. Mr. Nepean endeavored to gloss it over by many specious assurances and declarations that it proceeded from no hostile intentions, but was meant only to afford you an opportunity of effectually vindicating your conduct, and refuting the many accusations which had been sent home against you; in which event, he said, you would return to your government with additional honor and support. He may think these will pass as very plausible motives; but what as to their reality? I can only construe it as a measure, of great and unnecessary severity,—I might say injustice. It is not customary to call home governors until their conduct has been investigated and adjudged. They may put what construction they please upon the gentle terms, 'leave of absence,' but if you think it incumbent to accept this leave of absence, it must appear in the eyes of the world as an absolute recall. This is an event, my dear friend, which I have long dreaded; and what adds inexpressibly to the poignancy of my present feelings, is that I know not how to offer you advice in a situation of so much delicacy; for if you disobey this insidious order, your character may suffer in the public estimation, and if you obey it, your fortune may eventually be materially injured. It is indeed a cruel alternative, but it is a case in which you alone can be a competent judge.

"This business has been managed with so much secrecy, or, at least, it has been so studiously concealed from your friends, that we have not been able to learn when your leave of absence was sent out, or whether, indeed, it be yet gone. In case of your removal, your brother has picked up some intimation that Colonel Fanning, Lieutenant Governor of Nova Scotia, is likely to be your successor. In the present temper and disposition of office, I fear that your brother's *succession* would be more difficult than to sustain you in the government. I am exceedingly anxious to learn the fate of the quitrent bill. I hope the assembly may have passed it in some shape, and that the sales have been revoked. This is intelligence which should have arrived *ere* this time. I fear that your long silence and delay on this head is construed into contumacy and resistance. Your enemies here are busy and fertile in their insinuations."

Anxious to serve his friend the governor, Stuart, under pressure from that gentleman's brother, addressed a letter on the twenty-sixth of February, 1786, to Lord Sydney, though doubtful of the propriety and policy of the act, in which he states that he received a letter from the governor, intimating that he (the governor) was aware that reports had been circulated in England grossly misrepresenting his motives in having purchased some of the lots escheated under the quitrent act of 1774,—the governor declaring that his sole motive in making these purchases was to secure to himself a part of the very old arrears due to him for salary,—an act which he conceived to be strictly legal,—and stating that he had bought the lands at their full value. The governor was prepared, as stated in his letter, to restore what he had bought on his being reimbursed the amount of the purchase-money, with interest, agreeably to their lordships' resolution in 1783.

Stuart's letter, from which we have quoted so largely, was received by the governor on the tenth of October, 1786, and it is extremely probable that it was by the same mail that he also received official information of his having been superceded in the government of the island, and commanded to submit to the assembly the act rendering the sales of 1781 voidable,—of which another copy was now sent,—which had come to his hands two years previously, but with regard to which no action had been yet taken. The governor, as if sensible of his extreme folly in disregarding the royal instructions, submitted the measure to the house of assembly; and the bill was read for the first time on the first of November, and for the second, on the tenth of the same month; but it was subsequently decently interred by a house which was guided by the significant nods of the governor. But, in order to conciliate the home government, his excellency caused a private bill to be introduced, providing for the restoration of the escheated land to the proprietors, but so contrived that, even if carried out, the heavy payments required to be made counterbalanced any benefits that could be derived from its adoption. When the character of this measure became known to the proprietors, they brought a criminating complaint against the superceded governor and the council, which, on being investigated by the committee of privy council, led to the dismissal of the members of council implicated, as well as that of the attorney general. No further action against Governor Patterson was deemed necessary, as he had been already dismissed.

Early in November, Lieutenant-Governor Fanning arrived from Nova Scotia to assume the government of the island; but Mr. Patterson refused to give up the reins of office, on the ground that the season was too far advanced for his return to England,—the appointment of Fanning being regarded by Patterson as only intended to supply his place during his own temporary absence. Mr. Stewart, of Mount Stewart, asserts that Patterson *affected* ignorance of the nature of the recall respecting whose import, as being absolute and final, no reasonable doubt could exist; but in this we can prove he was mistaken, from the terms in which the appointment was conveyed to Fanning by Lord Sydney,—a document which Mr. Stewart evidently had not seen, and which proves that Patterson was not destitute of a very plausible if not solid reason for holding his post till the weather admitted of his leaving the island. Lord Sydney, addressing Fanning, in a despatch dated the thirtieth of June, 1786, says: "The King having thought it necessary to recall Lieutenant-Governor Patterson, of the Island of Saint John, in consequence of some complaints which have been exhibited against him, that an inquiry should be made into his conduct, His Majesty, from the opinion which he is pleased to entertain of your ability and discretion, and with a view to give you an early proof of his royal approbation of your services, has been pleased to appoint you to carry on the public service of the island *during Lieutenant-Governor Patterson's absence*, or until some determination shall have taken place respecting his proceedings.

"As it is His Majesty's desire that Lieutenant-Governor Patterson should be relieved in time to enable him to return to England in the course of the autumn, His Majesty trusts that you will lose no time in repairing to Saint John, and in settling such arrangements with the said lieutenant-governor, previous to his departure, as may be necessary for your carrying on the business of the island." Thus Patterson's retention of office till the spring does not seem in the circumstances unreasonable; but Mr. Stewart, in his account of the island, informs us that his continuance in it was contrary to the desire of the inhabitants generally, who, during the winter, did not fail to present addresses to Fanning, calling upon him to assume the government to which, according to his commission, he had been appointed. On the arrival of Fanning, Patterson addressed the following letter to Lord Sydney, the Colonial Secretary:—

"Island of Saint John, 5th November, 1786.

"My Lord,—Lieutenant-Governor Fanning arrived here yesterday, and by him I have been honored by your lordship's letter of the thirtieth June, saying that many representations have been made to the King of improper proceedings in the exercise of the powers with which I have been vested, and that it is His Majesty's pleasure that I should repair to England as soon as may be, to give an account of my conduct; also commanding me to deliver to Lieutenant-Governor Fanning such papers and documents as may be necessary to enable him to carry on the public service during my absence.

"I have received His Majesty's commands with the utmost veneration and respect, and nothing gives me so much pain as when I have it not in my power to carry them into immediate execution.

"Such papers and documents as appear in the least necessary towards carrying on the present service shall be delivered without loss of time; but there are unsurmountable reasons why I cannot this winter quit this island. The season is too far advanced to leave a possibility of arranging my little matters so as to prevent total ruin in my absence. Besides, my lord, if the charges are such as I have already answered, my *ipse dixit* will add but little weight to my defence, and I have no further proof to offer. If there have been any new charges sent from hence, the evidence to disprove them cannot be had in England; therefore, my going home without them would only prove a useless trouble to your lordship and to myself. It is an unspeakable grief of heart to me that I am under the necessity so long of lying under the appearance of having proved unworthy of my station. All my labors for thirty years have been in search of reputation, and I have gained it everywhere but where most I wished. Be assured, my lord, it will be my pride and glory if I can restore confidence among the council of my royal master. I hope and trust your lordship will feel my situation as I do myself, and that in justice you will order me copies of my crimes, so as to have them by the first of spring; and be assured that I shall, as soon after the receipt of them as possible, with every anxious and eager hope, pay instant obedience to the royal mandate.

"Were it even possible for me, at so few days' notice, to quit the island, even with the total ruin of my family, I should be obliged to accumulate ruin on ruin by being obliged to stay a whole season in England to wait for evidence from home, and in place of expediting, it must delay my hearing. But if I cannot go from hence prepared to answer my accusers, after my arrival my fate may be soon decided; and if I have not been guilty of what will deprive me of my liberty, I may return in the course of the summer to cultivate my farm.

"His Majesty is full of justice. He is the father of his people, and therefore cannot wish the ruin of a subject, much less of an old and faithful servant. Then I doubtless shall have justice. I wish no more. Afford me only an opportunity of clearing my character, and I shall instantly resign. I have long and anxiously wished to do it, and most certainly shall the moment I can with honor.

"I cannot even guess at the nature of my present accusations; but be they what they may, I wish to meet them; and I shall do so, my lord, with a confidence and certain knowledge that they are as unfounded as the last. I know I have done no wrong, and therefore court inquiry; but I also know my enemies, and must go prepared among them. A conscious rectitude of heart forms, my lord, arms of adamant,—a shield which admits no fear.

"I am, my lord, &c.,

"Walter Patterson."

But Patterson had a large number of friends in the island who backed him in his opposition to Fanning; and the council, consisting of men of his own selection, and the assembly being ready to act according to his dictation, he was in hopes that representations proceeding from these sources would secure his restoration to a position to which he was now clinging with tenacity. During the winter the government of the island remained in this anomalous condition; but early in April following, Governor Fanning issued a proclamation notifying his appointment, and calling on all loyal inhabitants to recognize his title to the governorship. But Patterson issued, on the following day, a counter proclamation, declaring that he was the accredited representative of His Majesty, and enjoining the people to pay no attention to the pretensions of a usurper.

A correspondence passed between the rivals. From manuscript copies, now before us, it appears that Patterson and Fanning had entered into an agreement on the seventh of November, 1786, by which the latter gentleman's appointment was to remain in abeyance for some time. Patterson, on the arrival of Fanning, had intimated his intention of meeting the assembly as governor; but Fanning contended that Patterson had promised to give up the government after the legislative business which he wished transacted was finished. This was emphatically denied by Patterson, who asserted that the command was, by mutual consent, to remain with him till the weather permitted his departure from the island, or more distinct orders were received from England, to which representations of the state of matters were forwarded by both parties. On the 17th of February, Patterson addressed a bitter letter to Fanning, complaining of his violation of the agreement solemnly made between them, in which he wrote: "Was it consistent with that engagement that your warrant was exhibited to a large company at your own table, and afterwards to the public by one of that company, in order to prove your right to the command? Was it consistent with that engagement that my avowed and notorious enemies were almost constantly adopted as your confidential friends? You will not be surprised at my faith in you being put to a severe trial when I heard that the court of justice was disturbed, and a copy of your warrant there read by a gentleman very much in your confidence, questioning the judges as to your right of command, and calling on all His Majesty's subjects on their allegiance to assert your right; and when I have been told that the son of that gentleman, in the same open court, said to the commanding officer that, if it had not been for his detachment, you should long ago have had the government,—meaning that he and his friends would by violence have wrested it from me. I have also been informed that officers of the government refuse paying any attention to my orders, and quote your commission and yourself as the reason of such disobedience."

Notwithstanding the intense fermentation occasioned by this unseemly dispute, the public peace was not disturbed. As was generally anticipated, on the arrival of the spring mail, the conduct of Patterson was rebuked by the home government, and he was peremptorily commanded to transfer the permanent command to Fanning,—a change which, Mr. Stewart says, was "agreeable to the island in general." [F] Patterson soon left the island for Quebec, but returned in a few months, and exerted himself to the utmost in obstructing the operations of the government; but, after two years' residence, and bitter opposition to the administration of his successor, he left the island and returned to England, cherishing the hope of enlisting the sympathy and support of the proprietors resident there,—a hope which was doomed to be disappointed.

Fidelity to historical accuracy compels us to say that a charge affecting the moral character of the late governor had been made, in which the wife of one of his friends was implicated. That charge, whether true or false, was doubtless forwarded to English headquarters, where, if supported by satisfactory evidence, it was certain to have no small influence in determining the fate of Patterson as governor, and may account for the mysterious silence of officials (as complained of by Mr. Stuart) when pressed for information with regard to the reasons by which government was influenced in dismissing him from a post which he had held for sixteen years. In one of Patterson's private memorandum books, now before us, there are some curious entries, in his own handwriting, with regard to that charge, in which he summarises various arguments which might be urged against the probability of its truthfulness, but which neither affirm nor deny its validity. If these notes had not been made by his own hand, and the pronoun *I* had not been once inadvertently used, they might be supposed to have been the production of one on whom was devolved the legal defence of the governor.

When Patterson arrived in London, he found the friends who had formerly used their influence in his favor extremely cool; and thus all hope of his restoration to the governorship was blighted. The large sums he had expended in the election of a house favorable to his views, and the impossibility of saving any part of his annual income (five hundred pounds sterling), without sacrificing the becoming dignity of his post, added to the circumstance that his wife and family had to be maintained in England during the whole period of his incumbency, rendered his means extremely limited. Being pressed by his creditors, his extensive and valuable property in the island was sold—under hard laws, which had been enacted under his own administration—at nominal prices. It need therefore excite no surprise that he never returned to a scene invested with so many painful recollections.

But the question occurs: what became of the escheated lands which were ordered to be restored to the original proprietors? After the proceedings already recorded, no determined effort to obtain the property was made by the original holders, with regard to whose claims to restitution no doubt could now exist. The assembly did, indeed, pass an act in 1792, by which the old proprietors were permitted to take possession of their property; but eleven years having elapsed since the sales took place, and complications of an almost insuperable nature having in consequence ensued, the government deemed it inexpedient to disturb the present holders, more particularly as not a few of them had effected a compromise with the original grantees, which entitled them to permanent possession. Hence the act referred to was disallowed, and thus a subject which had for years agitated the community was permitted to remain in continued abeyance.

CHAPTER III.

Proprietors indifferent to their engagements—Extent to which settlement was effected—Complaints of the People of nonfulfilment of engagements—Character of the Reply—The influence of the Proprietors with the Home Government—The Duke of Kent—Proposal in 1780 to name the Island New Ireland—The name adopted—Formation of Light Infantry, and Volunteer Horse—Immigration of Highlanders—Memoir of General Fanning.

As proof that the great body of the proprietors were utterly indifferent to the engagements they contracted when they obtained their lands, it is only necessary to state that in only ten of the sixty-seven townships into which the island was divided were the terms of settlement complied with, during the first ten years which had elapsed since possession was granted. In nine townships settlement was partially effected, and in forty-eight no attempt whatever at settlement seems to have been made. In 1797, or thirty years after the grants were issued, the house of assembly, sensible of the necessity of taking action for the more effectual settlement of the island, passed a series of resolutions,—founded on a deliberate and painstaking investigation of all the townships,—which were embodied in a petition to the home government, praying that measures should be taken to compel proprietors to fulfil the conditions on which the land had been granted. The assembly drew attention to the following facts: That, on twenty-three specified townships, consisting of four hundred and fifty-eight thousand five hundred and eighty acres, not one settler was resident; that on twelve townships the population consisted only of thirty-six families, which, on an average of six persons to each family, numbered in the aggregate two hundred and sixteen souls, who thus constituted the entire population of more than half of the island. On these and other grounds, it appeared to the house that the failure of so many of the proprietors in implementing the terms and conditions of their grants was highly injurious to the growth and prosperity of the island, ruinous to its inhabitants, and destructive of the just expectations and views of the government in its settlement. The house contended that the long forbearance of the government, towards the proprietors who had failed to do their duty, had no other effect than to enable them to speculate on the industry of the colony. The house was of opinion that the island, if fully settled, was adequate for the maintenance of half a million of inhabitants, and it prayed that the proprietors should be either compelled to do their duty, or that their lands should be escheated, and granted to actual settlers.

The petition embodying these views was forwarded to the Duke of Portland,—the colonial secretary at the time,—and the force of its facts and arguments seems to have been felt by the government, for a despatch was sent to Governor Fanning, intimating that measures would be adopted to rectify the grave evils enumerated in the petition. The process of escheat was not, however, acceptable to the proprietors who had done their duty by settling their lands, for the obvious reason, that in the event of free grants being made of the forfeited property, the tenants on the already-settled laud would prefer to give up their farms and become proprietors. In conformity with the promise made by government, Governor Fanning, in his speech to the assembly in November, 1802, said that he had the satisfaction to inform them, on the highest authority, that the public affairs of the island had been brought under the consideration of His Majesty's ministers in a manner highly favorable to the late humble and dutiful representations made on behalf of the inhabitants, respecting the many large, unsettled, and uncultivated tracts of land in the island. In order to give effect to the measures which had been adopted by His Majesty's ministers, it would be necessary that the government of the island should be prepared to adopt, when circumstances should render it advisable, the requisite and legal steps for effectually revesting in His Majesty such lands as might be liable to be escheated. The house, in their reply to the address, requested a more explicit statement from his excellency as to the information which he had received on this important subject; to which his excellency replied, that he had already presented all the information which it was in his power to furnish. It does indeed seem strange that the governor should have been instructed to refer officially to measures which "*had been adopted*" by the home government for the rectification of an admitted evil, and yet was apparently unable to explain the character of these measures for the guidance of the assembly in a branch of legislation which they were unequivocally invited to adopt. Such mysterious reticence was in direct opposition to ordinary governmental procedure in similar cases. But the local government, never dilatory in business connected with escheat, prepared a bill entitled "An act for effectually revesting in His Majesty, his heirs and successors, all such lands as are, or may be, liable to forfeiture within this island," which was passed by the assembly and assented to by the governor on the second of April, 1803. It did seem a mockery of the assembly when that bill was, contrary to the expectations of the people, disallowed by the home government, without any reason assigned. A committee on the state of the colony accordingly drew up a strong and spirited remonstrance, in which they boldly said:

"It appears to the committee, and they have the strongest reason to believe, that the royal *assent* to the said act for reinvesting His Majesty with such lands as are or may be liable to forfeiture within this island, has been graciously approved by His Majesty." They then expressed their conviction, which was well founded, that the formal royal allowance had been withheld by means of unfounded representations of interested individuals in England. The committee sent these resolutions to William and Thomas Knox, the agents for the island in London, with instructions to use their utmost efforts to give effect to the remonstrance; and the house of assembly also presented an address to the lieutenant-governor, complaining of the efforts that had been made to render His Majesty's intentions abortive, requesting him to transmit their petition and resolutions to Lord Castlereagh, and duplicates to the Earl of Liverpool, president of the Committee of the Privy Council for Trade and Plantations. The house also appointed a committee, consisting of Holland, Macgowan, Stewart, Palmer, and Macdonald, to draw up a new bill, substantially the same as the former, which was duly passed. Nothing was wanting on the part of the assembly to neutralize the influence brought to bear in London in order to frustrate their intentions; and if the British government had not on this occasion lost its usual character for consistency and adherence to principles, so explicitly enunciated, the royal intentions, as intimated by the lieutenant-governor, would have been honestly carried out. The period was one of great political excitement in London. Lord Hobart, through whom the governor had received a solemn promise that the evil complained of would be rectified, had given place in the colonial secretaryship to the exciteable Castlereagh, and the solemn obligations of office appear to have been forgotten in the political fermentation of the moment. It would be difficult to point out, in the history of the British colonial administration, another instance where the dictates of political consistency and honor were so flagrantly disregarded as in the case under review.

The influence exerted on government by the proprietors resident in London seemed irresistible, and was such as no government of our time could tolerate. The key to their power seems to be found in the circumstances that they were, for the most part, men in intimate social relations with parties in office, and, moreover, mainly consisted of officers who were supposed to have rendered good service in time of war, and whose complaints or representations, therefore, commanded at all times the royal consideration and sympathy. The proprietors, besides, cultivated the good-will and friendship of the under-secretaries, and other secondary government officials, who kept them informed of what was going on, and contributed in many indirect ways to promote their views. Mr. Stuart, in his letters to Governor Patterson,—who was by no means distinguished for the *suaviter in modo*,—frequently urged him to write certain persons in the government offices in a conciliatory and friendly manner, as he was convinced that they could exert no small influence in behalf of his interests. The proprietors not only succeeded in preventing the resolutions commended by the Duke of Portland from leading to any practical result, but also in obtaining, in 1802, an important reduction in the quitrents which remained unpaid, and which now amounted to the large sum of fifty-nine thousand one hundred and sixty-two pounds sterling; the sum due on some of the townships being actually more than their estimated value. In order to discriminate between the proprietors who had exerted themselves to carry out the terms of their grants, and those who had not, the government divided the commutation into four classes, requiring from the proprietors who had on their property the necessary number of settlers only five years' quitrents, instead of thirty-two years',—namely, from 1769 to 1801,—and making a proportionate deduction in the case of the four other classes. But as evidence of the determination of many of the landowners not to conform to the law, and their confidence in their own power to set the regulations of government at defiance,—as they had hitherto systematically done,—it may be here stated, that even the reduced amount does not seem to have been paid; and it was mainly in consequence of such daring and long-continued violation of obligation that the people, from time to time, in paroxysms of just indignation, demanded the establishment of courts of escheat.

In 1794, Prince Edward—afterwards Duke of Kent, and father of Her Majesty the Queen—arrived in Halifax. In that year two provincial companies were raised for the protection of the island, and when His Royal Highness became commander-in-chief of the forces in British North America, he ordered new barracks to be erected at Charlottetown, and defensive works for the protection of the harbor to be constructed. The Duke never visited the island, but its inhabitants were duly sensible of the practical interest he took in its welfare; and having determined that its name should be changed, on account of the mistakes incident to other towns bearing the same designation, a local act was introduced in 1798, which changed the name to Prince Edward Island, which act received the royal allowance on the first of February, 1799. We find that in the year 1780, an act for altering the name of the island from Saint John to that of New Ireland was passed in the assembly with a suspending clause. In a letter addressed by Mr. Stuart to governor Patterson, dated the third of March, 1781, he says: "Your passing an act to change the name of the island is considered as a most unprecedented instance of irregularity. The reasons you give why it should be changed are admitted to be of some force, but they insist upon it that you ought, in common decency, to have set forth those reasons in a petition to the King, instead of passing a presumptuous act which is neither warranted by law nor usage." This act was, of course, disallowed; but the governor did not lose sight of the hint as to petitioning, as appears from a passage in another letter from Stuart to Governor Patterson, dated, October, 1783, in which he says: "I am not unmindful of your petition for changing the name of the island, but I keep it back till we shall have carried points of more importance. When they are accomplished, I shall bring it forward." Had the first application been made by petition to the King, it is extremely probable that the proposed change of name would have been adopted.

Besides the two companies mentioned, a light infantry company and three troops of volunteer horse were formed in the island, who were handsomely clothed and mounted at their own expense, and armed at the expense of the government; at this time every man from sixteen to sixty years of age was subject to the militia laws. These wise precautions prevented any hostile descent on the island during the war, and tended to infuse a spirit of self-reliance and patriotic ardor into the community.

If the reduction of the quitrents failed as an inducement to the proprietors to pay what was now really due to government, it did not fail to lead to brisk business in the sale of property, for from the commutation to the year 1806, nearly a third of the entire land in the island had been transferred by purchase to persons, many of whom were really determined, by industry and strict regard to law, to make the venture permanently profitable.

The year 1803 was remarkable in the history of the island for a large immigration of highlanders from Scotland. The Earl of Selkirk brought out to his property about eight hundred souls. They were located on land north and south of Point Prim, which had been previously occupied by French settlers, but a large portion of which was now again covered with wood, and thus rendered difficult of cultivation. Many of his lordship's tenants became successful settlers.

Lieutenant-General Fanning's connection with the island, as governor, terminated in 1804. During his administration the island did not make any remarkable progress in its various interests; but Mr. John McGregor,—a native of the island, and of whom we shall have more to say by-and-bye,—in his work on British North America, has hardly done the general justice, in representing him as of very "obscure origin, and owing his future to circumstances, the advantages of which he had the finesse to seize." General Edmund Fanning was a native of America, and was born in the Province of New York, on the twenty-fourth of April, 1739. He was the son of James Fanning, a captain in the British service, and of his second wife Mary Smith, daughter of Colonel William Smith, who for some time administered the government of New York, and was sole proprietor of Smith Town, on Long Island. The paternal grandfather of General Fanning came to America, from Ireland, with Earl Bellemont, in 1699.

Captain James Fanning, having disposed of his commission while in England, returned to New York in 1748, when his son Edmund, then in the ninth year of his age, was sent to a preparatory school, and thence removed to Yale College, New Haven, where, after going through the regular course of collegiate studies, he received the degrees of Bachelor and Master of Arts; and in 1774 he was honored by the University of Oxford, England, with the degree of Doctor of Civil Law. From college he proceeded to North Carolina, where, after studying two years under the attorney general of that province, he was, in 1762, admitted to the bar. He was successful in his profession; but the troubles of the eventful period in America which followed the passing of the Stamp Act by the British Parliament, induced him to enter the civil and military service of his country. In 1765 he was appointed by Governor Tryon of North Carolina one of the Judges of the Supreme Court in that province in the room of Mr. Justice Moore, who was dismissed from office upon the supposition of his favoring the public commotions at the time existing in North Carolina. In 1768 he raised, at the request of Governor Tryon, a corps of eight hundred provincials to oppose and put down a body of insurgents who styled themselves regulators, whose object was to rescue from trial and punishment leading rebels. In 1771 he was again called upon by Governor Tryon to raise and embody a corps of provincials to suppress an insurrection in North Carolina, and was second to Governor Tryon at the battle of Allamance, in which action, the insurgents, to the number of twelve thousand, were totally defeated.

In the year 1773 Colonel Fanning went to England, strongly recommended to His Majesty's ministers for his services in North Carolina. Having applied for the office of Chief Justice of Jamaica, he received a letter from Lord Dartmouth, then secretary of state for the American department, stating that it was impossible in this case to comply with his wishes, but that he should have the first vacant post that might be deemed worthy of his services. Having received this assurance, he returned to America. Two months after his arrival at New York, he was appointed to the office of surveyor general of that province, the annual fees of which were said to be worth two thousand two hundred pounds sterling. But in the following year Colonel Fanning was driven from his house in New York, and took refuge on board the Asia, ship of war. He afterwards served in the army, having raised a regiment called "The King's American Regiment." During the war he was twice wounded. There is ample proof that he discharged his military duties with courage and ability.

On the 24th of February, 1783, Colonel Fanning was appointed Lieutenant-Governor of Nova Scotia, an appointment which he accepted with a promise from Lords Sydney and North that it should lead to something better. Subsequently John Parr was appointed Lieutenant-Governor of Nova Scotia, and, as previously stated, Governor Fanning was ordered to relieve Governor Patterson, of Prince Edward Island, which he did in the confident expectation that he should succeed to the government of Nova Scotia on the retirement or death of Parr. In 1791 Fanning was informed of the death of Parr by a letter from Richard Buckeley, president of the council of Nova Scotia, who concluded by saying, "as the government of this province, by His Majesty's late instructions, devolves on you, as senior lieutenant-governor, I accordingly give you early notice of the vacancy." This information was received too late in the autumn to admit of Governor Fanning's proceeding to Halifax, and while making preparations for going thither, he was informed that the position was conferred on Mr. Wentworth,—intelligence which caused him great disappointment, as he had well-founded expectations of succeeding to the government of Nova Scotia. The governor applied immediately for leave of absence, but was politely refused, on the ground that his absence might, in time of war, prove dangerous to the island. After repeated applications, he at last received a letter from Lord Hobart, dated the 6th of May, 1804, granting him liberty to return to England after the arrival of Colonel DesBarres, and informing him that His Majesty had directed that, in consideration of his long and faithful services, a provision at the rate of five hundred pounds sterling should be made for him yearly in the estimates of the island. Addresses were presented to the governor before his departure, by the council, the respective counties, and the grand jury of the Island. In 1816 General Fanning closed his accounts at the audit office, when His Majesty's ministers, to mark their approval of his administration of the government of the island, directed a retrospective increase of his salary from the period of his appointment to the colony, in 1786, to that of his retirement. General Fanning died at his residence in Upper Seymore Street, London, on the 28th of February, 1818, in the seventy-ninth year of his age.

Here we introduce to our readers the Rev. Theophilus DesBrisay, who, by royal warrant, dated the twenty-first day of September, 1774, was appointed to "the parish of Charlotte." Mr. DesBrisay was the son of the gentleman who has been mentioned as administrator of the island during the absence of Governor Patterson. He was born in Thurles, in the County of Tipperary, Ireland, on the ninth of October, 1754, arrived in the island in the year 1775, and was rector of Charlotte Parish till his death, which occurred on the fourteenth of March, 1823. He was the only protestant clergyman on the island till the year 1820; was a man of sterling character, and a faithful servant of the Divine Master. Like Bishop McEachern and others, he was subjected, in the faithful discharge of his sacred duty, to privations of which the present generation have no adequate conception. [G]

CHAPTER IV.

Colonel F. W. DesBarres, successor to General Fanning—His character as a Governor—Succeeded by Charles Douglas Smith—His character as displayed in his opening address—Proclamation of immunity from Proprietory conditions—Oppressive measures in regard to Quitrents—John McGregor, Sheriff—Public meetings called in the Counties—Tyranny of the Governor exposed—Arrival of Colonel Ready, and departure of Smith.

In July, 1805, Colonel Joseph F. W. DesBarres arrived in the island for the purpose of succeeding Governor Fanning. He was a man well advanced in life, and had held for some time the position of Lieutenant-Governor of Cape Breton, when that island was a separate province. His administration was notable for the occurrence of three important events, namely, the official announcement to the assembly that the act of 1803, which was intended to invest in the Crown the lands on which arrears had not been paid, was disallowed; the passing of the important resolutions of the assembly, to which reference has been already made, condemning the disallowance as grossly unjust, and in direct opposition to a settled and declared imperial policy; and the declaration of war by the United States against Great Britain. Colonel DesBarres is said to have been a man of cultivated mind, who, during his administration, strictly adhered to the official line of duty; and if he did not originate, during the eight years he was in office, any measure which could be regarded as of striking public utility, he gave no evidence of a selfish or tyrannical disposition, which is more than could be affirmed of his successor, Charles Douglas Smith,—a brother of Sir Sydney Smith,—who succeeded DesBarres in 1813. The assembly met in November of the same year. The address which the governor delivered on that occasion was such as indicated the temper of the man: it was dictatorial and insolent in its tone. He prorogued the house in January, and indicated his estimate of the utility of the popular branch of the legislature by not again convening it till July, 1817. Its proceedings in that year were not satisfactory to the governor, who was determined to shackle the members and prevent them from adopting any measures which did not accord with his own notions of propriety. His excellency accordingly dissolved the house, and a new one was convened in 1818, which, proving quite as refractory as the previous one, was also suddenly dissolved, and another elected in 1820.

On the eighth of October, 1816, the governor had published a proclamation in which he intimated that the King had graciously resolved to extend to the proprietors of land in the island immunity from certain forfeitures to which they were liable by the conditions of their original grants, and also to grant the remission of certain arrears of quitrent, and fix a scale for future payment of quitrent. But the governor, before the amount of quitrent to be exacted had been determined by the home government, directed the acting receiver general to proceed, in January, 1818, to enforce payment of the arrears which had occurred between June, 1816, and December, 1817, on the old scale. Much distress was occasioned by these proceedings; and on the matter being represented to the home government, orders were issued to discontinue further action, and to refund the money exacted above the rate of two shillings for every hundred acres. It was at the same time intimated that the new rate would be rigidly exacted in future; but the years 1819, 1820, and 1821 passed over without any public demand being made. Several proprietors, during that period, had offered payment to the acting receiver general, by whom they were informed that he had no authority to receive it. The impression was therefore prevalent that no further quitrent would be demanded, more especially as payment was not exacted in the neighboring provinces of Nova Scotia and New Brunswick. But on the twenty-sixth of June, 1822, the following notice was posted up in Charlottetown by John Edward Carmichael, the receiver general: "This office will be kept open from the first to the fourteenth of July, ensuing, for the payment of all arrears of quitrent due and payable within this island. Office hours, from ten till two o'clock." This demand not being peremptory in its terms, was disregarded by many who saw it, and the great body of proprietors in the country never heard of the notice.

In December, 1822, the acting receiver general posted up another notice, intimating that payments must be made by the fourteenth of January; but no steps were taken to give due publicity to the notice throughout the island, neither was any warning given to the proprietors as to the consequences of nonpayment. In January a distress was taken on the lands of two of the principal proprietors on townships thirty-six and thirty-seven. Immediately after doing this, the officers proceeded to the eastern district of King's County, which was one of the most populous on the island, and astonished the people by demanding instant payment, or promissory notes payable in ten days, on pain of having their land and stock disposed of by public sale. This district was inhabited by highlanders, who spoke no other language than their native Gaelic. Men who would have faced an open foe in the field, with the courage characteristic of the Celtic race, had a profound respect for law, and dread and horror of the bailiff; and, in order to pay the demand so suddenly and unexpectedly made, many of the poor fellows loaded their carts with such produce as they could collect, and began a journey of from fifty to sixty miles to Charlottetown, in the depth of winter, in order to redeem the notes which they had given to the heartless myrmidons of the law. The sudden influx of grain into the market thus produced, caused a great decline in prices. This, with the suffering occasioned by the long journey, roused public indignation, and the people resolved to hold meetings in the respective counties, and take measures for their own protection against the tyranny to which they were subjected. At this time, John McGregor, subsequently Secretary to the Board of Trade in London, and M.P. for Glasgow, was high sheriff of the island, and a requisition was immediately drawn up and presented to him. It began in the following terms: "We, His Majesty's loyal subjects, freeholders and householders in different parts of this island, in the present alarming and distressing state thereof,—threatened at this time with proceedings on the part of the acting receiver general of quitrents, the immediate effect whereof cannot fail to involve a great part of the community in absolute ruin,—feel ourselves irresistably impelled—when the island has been nearly three years deprived of that constitutional protection and support which might be expected from our colonial legislature—to call upon you, as high sheriff of the island, to appoint general meetings of the inhabitants to be held in the three counties into which this island is divided, that they may have an opportunity, according to the accustomed practice of the parent country, of consulting together for the general benefit, and joining in laying such a state of the colony at the foot of the Throne, for the information of our most gracious Sovereign, as the present circumstances thereof require." The requisition was signed by forty individuals, and the sheriff appointed the meetings to be held at certain specified dates at Charlottetown, St. Peter's, and Princetown.

This very legitimate procedure on the part of the people did not accord with Governor Smith's notions of propriety, and he deemed it proper to remove Mr. McGregor from the office of sheriff, and to confer it on his late deputy, Mr. Townshend. On the eighteenth of February, the Hilary term of the supreme court commenced, and Mr. Townshend, at the request of the governor, struck out the name of John Stewart from the panel. During the term, petitions were presented to the grand jury, complaining of the conduct of the acting receiver general and his deputies, and true bills were found against the latter; but no trial took place in consequence of the interference of the governor.

On the sixth of March, the first meeting called by the sheriff took place at Charlottetown. Considering the deep snow on the ground and the state of the roads, it was numerously attended, and the proceedings were conducted with the utmost order and regularity. A number of resolutions were passed, which were embodied in an address to the King, containing grave charges against the governor. It was said that, though he had resided on the island for ten years, he had only been once absent from Charlottetown, when he ventured to drive eighteen miles into the country, thus failing to make himself acquainted with its actual condition. He was charged with illegally constituting a court of escheat in 1818, and, in violation of his own public proclamation of the 8th of October, 1816, harassing by prosecution the tenants of township number fifty-five. He was charged with refusing to receive an address from the house of assembly in answer to his speech at the opening of the session in November, 1818, though he had appointed an hour for that purpose. In addition to this public insult, he was accused of sending a message, on the fifteenth of December, to the assembly, requiring both houses to adjourn to the fifth of January following; and before the business in which they were then occupied was finished, and when the lower house was on the point of adjourning, in accordance with the said message, it was insulted by Mr. Carmichael, the lieutenant-governor's son-in-law and secretary, who, advancing within the bar, addressed the speaker loudly in these words: "Mr. Speaker, if you sit in that chair one minute longer, this house will be immediately dissolved," at the same time shaking his fist at the speaker; and while the house was engaged in considering the means of punishing this insult, the lieutenant-governor sent for the speaker, and, holding up his watch to him, said he would allow the house three minutes, before the expiration of which, if it did not adjourn, he would resort to an immediate dissolution; and this extraordinary conduct was soon after followed by a prorogation of the legislature, in consequence of the house having committed to jail the lieutenant-governor's son for breaking the windows of the apartment in which the house was then sitting. The lieutenant-governor was also charged with screening Thomas Tremlet, the chief justice of the island, from thirteen serious charges preferred against him by the house. He was also accused of degrading the council by making Mr. Ambrose Lane, a lieutenant of the 98th regiment, on half pay, and then town major of Charlottetown, a member of it, without having any claim to the position, save that of having recently married a daughter of the lieutenant-governor. Another member was a Mr. William Pleace, who came to the island a few years previously as a clerk to a mercantile establishment; from which trust he was dismissed, and then kept a petty shop of his own, where he retailed spirits. These were some of the charges brought against the governor, and the address concluded with the following words: "That your Majesty's humble petitioners regret much the necessity they are under of approaching your Majesty's sacred person in the language of complaint now submitted to your paternal consideration, and humbly trust, on a full review thereof, your Majesty will be satisfied that the further continuance of Lieutenant-Governor Smith in the command of your Majesty's island must be distressing to its inhabitants, and, by preventing the usual course of legislative proceedings, greatly impede its prosperity." The addresses, adopted by the other counties were similar to that of which we have just given a sketch.

One of the accusations brought against the governor, which has not yet been mentioned, was, that he permitted, as chancellor of a court over which he himself presided, heavy and vexatious additions to the fees since the appointment of Mr. Ambrose Lane as registrar and master. On the fourteenth of October, the lieutenant-governor, on pretence that this charge was a gross libel and contempt of the court of chancery, commenced proceedings before himself—on the complaint of his son-in-law—against the members of the committee appointed by Queen's County to manage the address to the King, who were all served with an attachment, and subsequently committed to the custody of a sergeant-at-arms. The object of these proceedings was evidently to get hold of Mr. Stewart, in order to prevent him from going to England with the petitions,—of which the lieutenant-governor had determined to get possession. Mr. Stewart only got notice of the governor's intentions two hours before officers arrived at his house on purpose to take him into custody; but he escaped to Nova Scotia with the petitions, and thence proceeded to England. Had Stewart been taken into custody, there would, doubtless, have been a rebellion in the island, for the people were exasperated. Chagrined beyond measure at Stewart's escape, the lieutenant-governor determined to lay a heavy fine on the other members of the committee, and sequestrators were appointed to enter upon their property and secure the amount; but being now alarmed at unmistakeable symptoms of a popular tumult, he prudently ordered proceedings to be delayed till his judgment could be enforced. The defence was ably conducted by Messrs. Binns and Hodgson.

On Saturday morning, the twenty-sixth of July, 1823, appeared the first number of the *Prince Edward Island Register*, printed and edited by James D. Haszard, in which newspaper all the proceedings to which we have alluded were published. For the publication of these, Mr. Haszard was served with an order to appear at the bar of the court of chancery, being accused as guilty of a contemptuous libel against the court and the officers of the court. Mr. Palmer was agent for the prosecutor. Mr. Haszard was asked if he would disclose the authors of the publication complained of,—which he agreed to do. The parties were Messrs. Stewart, McGregor, Mabey, Dockendorff, Owen, and McDonald. Addressing himself to Mr. Haszard, the chancellor said: "I compassionate your youth and inexperience; did I not do so, I would lay you by the heels long enough for you to remember it. You have delivered your evidence fairly, plainly, clearly, and as became a man; but I caution you, when you publish anything again, keep clear, sir, of a chancellor! Beware, sir, of a chancellor!" And with this solemn admonition, Mr. Haszard was dismissed from the bar.

But the rule of the chancellor was destined not to be of much longer duration; for on Thursday, the twenty-first of October, 1824, His Excellency Colonel Ready, accompanied by Mr. Stewart, arrived in a brig from Bristol, after a passage of twenty-eight days. "He was loudly cheered on landing by a great concourse of spectators, and was received on the wharf by a guard of the 81st regiment and a number of the most respectable inhabitants." A public meeting of the inhabitants, called by the sheriff, Mr. William Pope, was held for the purpose of voting an address to the lieutenant-governor. Colonel Holland, Mr. Hodgson, and Mr. Binns were appointed to prepare it. "We feel," said the inhabitants, "the utmost confidence that the harmony which ought always to exist between the government and the people is perfectly established, and that your excellency will believe that loyalty, obedience to the laws, and a love of order is the character of the inhabitants of Charlottetown. We cannot omit on this occasion to express our unfeigned gratitude and thanks for the attention which His Majesty has been graciously pleased to pay to the interests of this colony, in confiding its government to your excellency's hands, and to add our most fervent wishes that your administration of it may be long and happy." The town was illuminated in the evening, and, to the credit of the inhabitants of Charlottetown, the exuberance of joy and festivity on the occasion was not marred by any impropriety, or insult to the man who had exercised his functions with a harshness and tyranny which made him the most unpopular governor who ever ruled on the island. The new governor was entertained at dinner in the Wellington Hotel. John Stewart was chairman, and the Honorable George Wright croupier. It is only fair to say, that an address was presented to the late governor, previous to his embarkation for England, signed by the members of council, principal officers of government, and two justices of the peace. Considering the character of Governor Smith's administration, there is a spice of humor in the following portion of his reply: "I assure you I must ever feel a high interest in the prosperity of a colony whose welfare, it is well known to many of you, I have unceasingly watched over. It is my confident hope, as well as my fervent wish, that the island may continue to flourish under my successor, aided as he will be by the same support and advice from which I have myself so much and so generally benefited."

CHAPTER V.

Governor Ready desires to govern constitutionally—Energetic legislation—George Wright, Administrator—Change in the mode of paying Customhouse Officials—Fire in Miramichi—Petitions of Roman Catholics to be relieved from civil disabilities—Proceedings of the Assembly touching the question—Dispute between the Council and Assembly—Catholic Emancipation—The Agricultural Society—Death of George the Fourth—Cobbett on Prince Edward Island—Colonel Ready succeeded by A. W. Young—The Census—Death of Governor Young—Biographical Sketch of him.

Governor Smith delighted in autocratical rule, and had not called an assembly together since 1820; but Governor Ready, wishing to govern the island in a more constitutional manner, summoned, on his accession to office, a new house, which met in January, 1825, and proceeded to business with some degree of spirit and earnestness. Acts were passed for the encouragement of education, for regulating juries and declaring their qualifications, for regulating the fisheries, for limiting and declaring the jurisdiction of justices of the peace, for empowering the governor to appoint commissioners to issue treasury notes to the extent of five thousand pounds, and for increasing the revenue by taxation. Another session of the house was held in October of the same year, when the house displayed equal energy and diligence in transacting the public business. John Stewart was speaker, and the members elected for Charlottetown were Robert Hodgson and Paul Mabey. Mr. Samuel Nelson was an unsuccessful candidate for the town. He had been accused of not signing the address to the King, praying for the recall of Governor Smith. In his reply to that charge, Mr. Nelson stated a fact which shows the inherent meanness of the late governor in his treatment of the people. "Governor Smith," said Mr. Nelson, "never did anything for me. On the contrary, he broke me as a captain in the militia, and when I was putting a porch to my door he *sent a peremptory demand to pull it away*."

The governor returned to England towards the close of the year, on private business, and during his absence the government was administered by the Honorable George Wright.

The officers of customs received in this year official instructions from the lords commissioners to discontinue the exaction of fees after the fifth of January ensuing, as fixed salaries were to be granted to them,—a regulation which extended to all the colonies.

In this year, eighteen vessels arrived at the island from Great Britain, and one hundred and twenty-eight from the British colonies. There were imported fifty-four thousand gallons of rum, two thousand five hundred gallons of brandy, three thousand gallons Geneva, and two thousand gallons of wine, which, for a population of about twenty-three thousand, was a large supply. The imports were valued at £85,337, and the exports at £95,426.

In the autumn of 1825 an extensive and most destructive fire took place in Miramichi, which swept over an immense area, destroying timber, farm steadings, and cattle. Many of the unfortunate inhabitants perished in the flames, and hundreds were left destitute. A liberal collection was made in the island for the relief of the suffering, and a vessel chartered to convey produce to the scene of the disaster.

The governor returned from England towards the close of the year 1826, and again assumed the reins of government. The house met in March following. In his opening address, the governor congratulated the house on the improvements recently made in the internal communications of the country,—the western line of road being completed up to Princetown, and surveys having been made for extending the line to Cascumpec and the North Cape. His excellency also referred to the advantages which would accrue from the establishment of an agricultural society. Among other useful measures passed during the session was one for ascertaining the population of the island, and for authorizing the formation of a fire engine company for Charlottetown.

During the last session a petition was presented by the Roman catholics of the island, praying that they should be relieved from those civil disabilities under which they suffered. Consideration of the important subject was at that time deferred on account of the advanced period of the session. The subject was now brought up by Mr. Cameron, in a temperate and sensible speech, in which he stated that, notwithstanding the predictions of persons hostile to the prayer of the petitioners, not a single petition was presented to the house against the proposed change. Mr. Cameron concluded by proposing the following resolution: "*Resolved*, that it is the opinion of this house that the right of voting at elections of members to serve in the general assembly ought to be extended to His Majesty's subjects of the Roman catholic religion within the island, and that the election laws should be altered conformable to this resolution." A long and animated discussion took place, in which the attorney general, Dr. McAulay, Mr. Hodgson, and others supported it; and Mr. Campbell, Mr. McNeill, and Mr. Montgomery led in opposition. On the question being put, the votes were equal; but the speaker, Mr. Stewart, gave the casting vote against the resolution, on the ground that the question had not been settled in England. The speaker was one of the most enlightened men in the assembly, and his decision on this occasion cannot be said to have been in accordance with his general character. Had the resolution passed, the assembly would have had the honor of being in advance, on this question, of the parliament of Great Britain. As subjects of the Crown, the Roman catholics, in asking to have a voice in the election of the legislature,—whose laws they were bound to obey in common with protestants,—claimed no favor, but a right which ought never to have been withheld, and the subsequent concession of which experience has proved to be as satisfactory in practice as it is equitable in principle. On the presentation of the petition in 1825, a voluminous and very able correspondence was carried on in the columns of the *Register*, in the conduct of which the best talent in the island, on both the catholic and protestant sides, was enlisted. Theological questions, that had no bearing on the subject in dispute, were, unhappily, imported into the controversy; and, whatever difference of opinion may exist as to the discussion in its religious aspect, there can be none as to the fact of every argument advanced against the Roman catholic's right to be put on an equal footing with the protestant in all matters appertaining to civil and religious liberty, being completely demolished by the accomplished advocates of the Roman catholic claims. While the elaborate communications to which we have referred were imbued on both sides with considerable bitterness, yet, to the credit of the island combatants, it may be truly said that such bitterness was sweetness itself compared with the venom characteristic of similar controversies, as carried on at this period in other places. Fidelity to historical accuracy, at the same time, constrains us to state that, while on the part of catholics, as the aggrieved party, whose rights were tyranically and persistently disregarded, paroxysms of irritation were the natural result of oppression, no such apology can to the same extent be offered in behalf of their opponents.

In October, 1825, the council passed a resolution to the effect that they would not in future be disposed to give their assent to any bill for appropriating money, unless the sums and services therein contained should be submitted in separate resolutions for their concurrence. This resolution was not agreeable to the assembly, who claimed the sole right of originating all money bills, and who denied the right of the council to alter or amend them. This difference of opinion led to a protracted controversy. In May, 1827, the council sent a message to the assembly, in which the question was elaborately argued, to which the assembly returned an equally elaborate reply. The dispute resulted, in 1827, in the council agreeing to the two principal bills of supply, and rejecting an *ad valorem* duty bill; but in the following session—that of 1828—the appropriation bill was rejected by the council, which obliged the governor to confine the expenditure of the year to purposes of necessity. In meeting the house, in 1829, the governor expressed the hope that the unfortunate dispute of the last session would be brought to an amicable adjustment, and recommended a system of mutual compromise as the most effectual mode of securing that object. Although the council had resolved to transact no further business with the assembly until the latter body expunged a previous resolution from their journals containing certain imputations on the council, yet the house had refused to do so. Business communication was, however, resumed, and continued as if nothing had happened.

On the sixth of January, 1825, died Benjamin Chappell, late postmaster of the island, in the eighty-seventh year of his age. He and his brother William emigrated from England in the year 1775. They owned one of the first packets that sailed between Charlottetown and the mainland. He saw the country in its rude and wilderness state, and was an attentive observer of all the vicissitudes it underwent in its gradual progress towards improvement, and few took a deeper interest in its prosperity. He was a man of sterling piety, actively devoted to the cause of religion, and may with truth be considered the founder of the present Methodist establishment of the island. He was personally known and beloved by John Wesley, who was in the habit of corresponding with him for many years; and it afforded Mr. Chappell much delight to detail to his friends many interesting anecdotes that grew out of his intimacy with that great and good man. He was brought up to the millwright business, and was well acquainted with machinery in all its extensive branches. He was a man of intelligence and strong mind, and, with a perfect knowledge of his own business, possessed a great deal of useful information. If a life of consistent piety, as expressed in the virtues that dignify human nature, can endear a man to society, the memory of Benjamin Chappell will be long and affectionately cherished in the island.

In the session of 1829 a select committee of assembly, for preparing a specific plan on which a bill might be founded for promoting classical education, presented their report, recommending the establishment of a classical academy in Charlottetown, to be designated the "Central Academy," vesting the management in a patron and nine trustees. Two masters were to be employed, each to receive a salary of one hundred and fifty pounds a year; and no religious test was to be permitted. A bill in conformity with these recommendations was accordingly introduced and sanctioned.

The most important act passed in the session of 1830 was one "for the relief of His Majesty's Roman catholic subjects." The agitation for the removal of the disabilities under which the Roman catholics suffered in the old country resulted in catholic emancipation; and the British government recommended the adoption of similar measures in the colonies, which recommendation weakened unreasonable opposition to the change. The act now passed provided that all statutes which imposed on Roman catholics civil or political disabilities should be repealed, and that all civil and military offices and places of trust or profit should be as open to them as to other portions of the King's subjects.

The agricultural society, which had been for some time in operation in the island, was active in accomplishing the beneficent purposes for which it was established: it encouraged improved stock by an annual exhibition and premiums, and imported seeds. District societies were formed at Saint Eleanor's and Princetown. The governor took a practical interest in the operations of the society, of which the Honorable George Wright was president; the Honorable T. H. Haviland, vice-president; and Mr. Peter MacGowan, secretary and treasurer.

In August, 1830, intelligence of the death of King George the Fourth, which had occurred on the twenty-sixth of June, reached the island. The reign of His Majesty lasted about ten years and a half; but, including his regency, he was at the head of the government more than nineteen years. He was succeeded by William the Fourth.

The ignorance which in our days prevails in the old country respecting the American colonies is not quite so deplorable as that which existed at the period of the island history at which we have now arrived. It may amuse the reader to learn what the celebrated Cobbett thought at this time of Prince Edward Island, as a home for emigrants, and of the kind of business that was prosecuted there: "From Glasgow," wrote Cobbett, "the sensible Scots are pouring out amain. Those that are poor, and cannot pay their passage, or can rake together only a trifle, are going to a rascally heap of sand, rock and swamp, called Prince Edward Island, in the horrible Gulf of Saint Lawrence; but when the American vessels come over with indian corn and flour and pork and beef and poultry and eggs and butter, and cabbages, and green pease, and asparagus for the soldier, and other tax-eaters that we support upon that lump of worthlessness,—for the lump itself bears nothing but potatoes,—when these vessels return, the sensible Scots will go back in them for a dollar a head, and not a man of them will be left but bed-ridden persons." If such are the doctrines which were taught to the people of Britain by men like Cobbett, what must have been the depth of ignorance respecting the North American colonies which pervaded the masses? The very articles which the islanders were prepared to export to the states, if an inlet for them were permitted, were the articles which the foolish grammarian imagined they were importing. He little thought that in the capital of this island of "rock" a cargo of whinstones would be very acceptable, and find ready sale.

In September, 1831, Colonel Ready was relieved from the government of the island by the arrival of Lieutenant-Colonel A. W. Young. The departure of Colonel Ready was deeply regretted by the people. His administration was distinguished by activity, energy, and usefulness, constituting a striking contrast to that of his predecessor. During his retention of office there was a large increase of the population. From the year 1829 to 1831, eighteen hundred and forty-four emigrants had arrived, and new life was infused into the commerce and agriculture of the island.

In January, 1832, Governor Young met the house of assembly for the first time. There was a dread of cholera, now raging in Europe, which led to the passing of a measure in the assembly "to prevent the spread of infectious diseases." A day of fasting was appointed in the month of May, and, happily, the island was not visited by a pestilence which, in other places, laid tens of thousands in the grave. In this year an act was also passed to provide for the conveyance of the mails between Charlottetown and Pictou, by a steam vessel, a grant of three hundred pounds yearly having been voted for that purpose. The service was accordingly performed by the Steamer *Pocahontas*, which ran twice a week to Pictou,—the cabin passage-money being twelve shillings currency. In the following year the census was taken, from which it appeared that the population of the island, which, in 1827, had been twenty-three thousand, had increased to thirty-two thousand. An act was also passed in this year by which the duration of the assembly was reduced from the period of seven to that of four years.

In May, 1834, Governor Young went to England, whence he returned in September, as Sir Aretas W. Young. In June of the same year died John Stewart, of Mount Stewart, at the age of seventy-six. He came to the Island in 1778. He was speaker of the house of assembly for a number of years, and was one of the most useful public men of his day. We have read much of his private and official correspondence, which has led us to form a high opinion of his integrity, industry, and zeal. His book on the island, published in 1806, is a reliable work, so far as facts are concerned, though not written with the grace and freedom which distinguished the letters of his contemporary, John Stuart, the London agent of the island.

A general election took place towards the close of 1834, and the new house met in January, 1835. A dispute arose between the assembly and the council, respecting the revenue bills, which led to the necessary supplies not being granted, but after a short interval the governor convoked the assembly in April, and as the result of a previous informal conference between the disputants, it was arranged that the revenue bill should be separated from the appropriation bill,—as a solution of the difficulty,—and thus the dispute terminated. In consequence of the illness of his excellency, the session of one week's duration was prorogued by a commission, who were desired to express to the assembly his excellency's pleasure at the satisfactory termination of its labors.

On Tuesday, the first of December, 1835, His Excellency Sir Aretas William Young died at his official residence in Charlottetown. At the age of seventeen he obtained an ensigncy, by purchase, in Podmore's regiment, and a company, by purchase, in the 13th foot, in 1796. He served with the 13th regiment, in Ireland during the rebellion, and was present with that corps, under the command of Sir Charles Colville, in every memorable action fought in Egypt under the gallant Sir Ralph Abercrombie, in 1801, for which he received a medal. He was subsequently employed for several years in Sicily and Gibralter, as aide-de-camp to General the Honorable Henry Edward Cox, the commander-in-chief in the Mediterranean. He was promoted, in 1807, to be major in the 97th regiment, then commanded by Lieutenant-General Sir James Lyon, and served with the 4th division, under Lieutenant-General Sir Lowry Cole, in the Peninsular campaigns of 1808, and in subsequent years was engaged in the battles of Vimiera, Talavera and Busaco, and in the first siege of Badajoz. Whenever the division was in movement, the light companies were entrusted to his charge, and during a part of the retreat of the army from the frontiers of Portugal to the lines of Torres Vedras, these companies were embodied under his command as a light battalion.

In an affair with the enemy at Tobral, near Lisbon, his horse was shot dead under him; and it has been remarked by a distinguished general officer that, on every occasion, in every difficulty and in many hours of trial, the example he set, the steps he trod, led the men cheerfully and fearlessly to do their duty. The 97th, owing to its thinned ranks, having been ordered to England, he was promoted, in 1813, to a lieutenant-colonelcy in the 3rd West India Regiment, stationed at Trinidad; and, with five companies of that corps, was sent to join the expedition against Guadaloupe in 1815, and received one of the badges of the Order of Merit, presented by Louis the Eighteenth. On his return to Trinidad, he was selected by Sir James Leith to command the troops in Granada; and, on leaving the regiment in 1815, received a letter, accompanied with a piece of plate, from the officers, expressive of their unfeigned feelings of regard and esteem for the comfort and happiness experienced under his command. On his being ordered back to Trinidad, in 1816, he was voted the thanks of the council and assembly of Granada, with a sword valued at one hundred guineas. During the absence, in 1820, of Governor Sir Ralph

Woodford from Trinidad, he administered the government for four months; and in consideration of the advantage which the community had derived during that period by his being a member of the council, was requested still to continue a member,—to which he acceded, subject to the approval of the commander of the forces, who, in giving his consent, remarked, that in whatever situation Lieut.-colonel Young might be placed, the public service would be benefited. In 1823, in again giving up the government, which he had held for two years,—during a second absence of the same governor,—he was presented with four addresses, namely, one from the council, one from the Board of Cabildo,—with a vote of one hundred and fifty guineas to purchase a sword, and with the request that he would sit for his portrait, to be placed in their hall as a token of their sense of the efficient manner in which he had presided over that board, and to record their opinion of the moderation, steadiness, and ability which, on all occasions, marked his administration; one from the inhabitants, with a piece of plate, to record their gratitude for the integrity and impartiality of his government; and one from the colored inhabitants, acknowledging their deep sense of the prudence, moderation, and humanity which distinguished his administration of the government.

On the final disbandment of the 3d West India Regiment, in the beginning of 1825, he was waited on by a deputation of the inhabitants of Trinidad, with a farewell address, and with the request of his acceptance of a piece of plate of the value of two hundred and fifty sovereigns. He was appointed in 1826 to the newly-created office of His Majesty's Protector of Slaves in the colony of Demerara,—the arduous duties of which he conscientiously performed for five years. He retired from the army, by the sale of his commission, in May, 1826, and was allowed by His Majesty, on the recommendation of the commander-in-chief, to retain the local rank of lieutenant-colonel in the West Indies, in consideration of the value of his services, and of the zeal, intelligence, and gallantry with which he had discharged every duty. He was gazetted, as already stated, to be governor of Prince Edward Island, on the twenty-fifth of July, 1851; and in consequence of the favorable opinion entertained by the King of his merits, communicated in a despatch from Lord Stanley, His Majesty conferred on him, on the ninth of July, 1834, the honor of knighthood.

At the period of his death he was in the fifty-eighth year of his age, and had thus terminated an honorable career of forty-one years in the King's service.

CHAPTER VI.

George Wright, Administrator—Court of Escheat refused—Central Academy—Severe Frost in September—Death of William the Fourth—Educational Condition of the Island—Forcible Resistance to Rent-paying—Rebellion in Canada—Able Report of Committee of Legislature on Land Question—The Coronation of Queen Victoria—Mechanics' Institute formed—Lord Durham on Land Question—The formation of an Executive, separate from a Legislative Council ordered—Mr. Cooper a delegate to London.

On the death of Governor Young, the Honorable George Wright was sworn in as administrator of the government until the appointment of a new governor. In February, 1836, Colonel Sir John Harvey was appointed governor, and arrived in the island in August, when the usual addresses of welcome were presented. There had been a popular agitation for some time for the establishment of a court of escheat, and despatches were received from the colonial secretary intimating that the prayer of certain petitions, presented to His Majesty on the subject, could not be granted. As we intend to devote, at a more advanced stage of the narrative, a chapter to the elucidation of the land question, we refrain at present from any lengthened remarks on the subject.

In January of this year the Central Academy was opened. Its first teachers were the Rev. Charles Loyd and Mr. Alexander Brown, formerly teacher of the grammar school. Mr. Loyd, having retired on account of ill health, was succeeded by the Rev. James Waddell, son of the Rev. John Waddell, of Truro, N. S.

The governor made a tour through the island for the purpose of becoming acquainted with its principal inhabitants, and observing its capabilities and resources. He was received everywhere with that degree of respect to which his position entitled him; and, in replying to the numerous addresses presented, expressed himself as highly gratified by the hospitality of the people, and the indications of progress manifested.

On the seventh of September, 1837, a frost of unprecedented severity for the season set in, by which the potato crop was greatly injured, and cereals were much damaged. Thus the prospect of a plentiful harvest was blighted in a night throughout the entire island. The loss thus sustained was referred to by the governor on opening the assembly in the spring following; and he called attention to the expediency of granting pecuniary aid for the purpose of supplying seed-grain and potatoes to such of the sufferers as required them.

In March, 1837, Colonel Sir J. Harvey, after being promoted to the rank of major general, was appointed Governor of New Brunswick, for which province he left towards the close of May. After the departure of the governor, the Honorable George Wright, as senior member of the council, took the oath of office, as administrator of the government until the arrival of Sir Charles Augustus FitzRoy, who was appointed to succeed Sir John Harvey. The new governor arrived in June.

On the twentieth of June, William the Fourth died. Intelligence of His Majesty's death reached the island towards the close of July. On the twenty-first of July, Queen Victoria was proclaimed in London.

The first official visitor of schools was appointed this year, in the person of Mr. John McNeill, who, in his report for the year, gave the number of schools in the three counties as fifty-one, and the number of scholars as fifteen hundred and thirty-three. In his report, Mr. McNeill gives us an interesting peep at the educational condition of the country at this period, specifying the various causes to which the extreme deficiency of the educational machinery was attributable. In many of the settlements the inhabitants were poor, and having to struggle with numerous difficulties in procuring subsistence for their children, their education was regarded as a matter of secondary importance. Little encouragement was, in most cases, held out to teachers of character and qualification, and the precarious mode in which their salaries were paid operated powerfully as a bar in the way of educational advancement. Hence it not unfrequently happened, when the necessary literary attainments were wanting, that it was only persons of shipwrecked character, and blasted prospects in life, who had assumed the important office of schoolmaster. "I must also mention," reported Mr. McNeill, "another practice which is too prevalent in the country, and which, I conceive, is exceedingly injurious to the respectability of the teacher in the eyes of his pupils, and, consequently, hurtful to his usefulness,—that is: receiving his board by going about from house to house; in which case he is regarded, both by parents and children, as little better than a common menial." Mr. McNeill's suggestions, by way of reformation, were judicious and well put. He held the situation of visitor for ten years, and seems to have been well qualified for the post. When he vacated the situation, in 1847, there were one hundred and twenty schools, of all grades, and over five thousand scholars.

The new governor visited all the principal districts of the island, and, as the result of his inquiries and observations, addressed a circular to the proprietors of land, in which he advocated the granting of important concessions to the tenantry, with a view of allaying the agitation for escheat, and removing any just grounds of complaint. The governor stated to the proprietors that it was impossible for any one, unacquainted with the local circumstances of a new colony, to form a correct estimate of the difficulties and privations which the past settlers on wilderness lands had to encounter. He said it was a long series of years before he could obtain from the soil more than a bare subsistence for himself and his family, notwithstanding the most unwearied perseverance and industry. It ought not, therefore, to be matter for surprise that, although he might be ready and willing to pay a fair equivalent, either in rent or otherwise, for the land occupied, he should feel dismayed at the prospect of being deprived of the hard-earned fruits of the labor of the earliest and best years of his manhood, whether from an accumulation of heavy arrears of rent, which he was unable to realize from the land, or from the refusal of the proprietor to grant him a tenure of sufficient endurance to ensure to his family the profits of his industry; and this, probably, in the decline of life, with a constitution broken, and health impaired by incessant toil. In these circumstances it could not be matter for surprise that he should be discontented with his lot, or that he should instil hostile feelings into the minds of his family, and be ready to lend a willing ear to proposals, however fallacious, which held out a hope of relief.

After alluding to the fact, that the high sheriff of King's County had been recently resisted by a considerable body of armed men, while engaged in enforcing an execution on a judgment obtained in the supreme court for rent, and had his horses barbarously mutilated, he recommended, as a remedy for the evil, that land-agents should have a discretionary power to relieve tenants of arrears of rents, in cases where it was impossible they could ever pay them; and that long leases should be granted at the rate customary in the colony, the rent to be payable in the productions of the soil at the market prices. He also recommended that, in cases where long leases were objected to, the tenants should be allowed to purchase the fee simple at twenty years' purchase, or that payment for their improvements, at a fair valuation, should be ensured on the expiration of their terms.

The governor forwarded a copy of the circular containing these reasonable suggestions to the secretary of state for the colonies. This mode of dealing with the tenantry, it may be here remarked, had already, in numerous instances, been acted upon with the best results, so that the efficiency of the change recommended in securing harmony between landlord and tenant had been most satisfactorily tested.

Towards the close of 1837, a rebellion broke out in Canada. The insurgents mustered in considerable numbers, but without sufficient organization, and their leaders—utterly incompetent and cowardly—were the first to escape after a few shots were fired. The militia of the island offered their services in vindication of the King's authority; but the troops in Canada were quite sufficient to extinguish the rebellion, ere it had attained to any formidable dimensions.

The colonial secretary, Lord Glenelg, transmitted to the governor the copy of a memorial from the proprietors of land, protesting against the royal assent being given to an act of the legislature of the island for levying an assessment on all lands in the island, and demanding an opportunity of stating their objections to it, by their counsel, before the judicial committee of the privy council. This document was referred to a joint committee of the legislative council and assembly, who, in April, 1838, produced an able and elaborate report in justification of the law. The committee, of which T. H. Haviland, R. Hodgson, John Brecken, Joseph Pope, Edward Palmer, and others were members, showed that the local expenditure of the government for the last twelve years had been £107,643, of which £27,506 had been expended on roads and bridges, to the great advantage of the property of the memorialists; £13,556 on public buildings and wharfs; and £66,562 for other local purposes. And of these large sums, the whole amount contributed by the proprietors of the soil had been only £7,413, leaving the balance of £100,000 to be borne by the resident consumers of dutiable articles. The committee fortified their position by extracts from despatches sent by Lords Stanley and Glenelg, and completely justified the imposition of a tax of four shillings currency on wilderness lands. The report, when printed, occupied upwards of five newspaper columns, set in minion type, and bore striking evidence of the industry and ability of its framers.

It appears from a despatch from Lord Durham, then governor general of British North America, which we found at Government House in Charlottetown, and which was not published either at the time or subsequently, that Lord Glenelg forwarded this able report, along with other documents bearing on the subject of escheat, in September, 1838, to his lordship, for the purpose of obtaining his special opinion on the subject, for the guidance of the home government. It is scarcely necessary to premise, before giving this important state document, that Lord Durham is considered the highest authority on those colonial subjects of which he treats in his celebrated report,—a document which will stand for successive generations as a lasting monument of his ability as a statesman, and which has been and is now recognized as embodying the most masterly exposition of colonial questions which has ever been published.

"Castle of Saint Lewis, Quebec,

8th October, 1836.

"My Lord,—I have had the honor of receiving your despatch of the fifth October, whereby you desire that I will express to you my judgment on the whole subject of escheat in the Island of Prince Edward. After perusing the voluminous documents with your lordship's despatch, I do not feel that it is in my power to add anything to the very full information on the subject which these documents comprise. The information before me is now so ample that upon no matter of fact can I entertain a doubt. Nearly the whole island was alienated in one day by the Crown, in very large grants, chiefly to absentees, and upon conditions of settlement which have been wholly disregarded. The extreme improvidence—I might say the reckless profusion—which dictated these grants is obvious: the total neglect of the government as to enforcing the conditions of the grants is not less so. The great bulk of the island is still held by absentees, who hold it as a sort of reversionary interest which requires no present attention, but may become valuable some day or other through the growing want of the inhabitants. But, in the meantime, the inhabitants of the island are subjected to the greatest inconvenience—nay, the most serious injury—from the state of the property in land. The absent proprietors neither improve the land themselves, nor will let others improve it. They retain the land and keep it in a state of wilderness. Your lordship can scarcely conceive the degree of injury inflicted on a new settlement hemmed in by wilderness land, which has been placed out of the control of government, and is entirely neglected by its absent proprietors. This evil pervades British North America, and has been for many years past a subject of universal and bitter complaint. The same evil was felt in many of the states of the American Union, where, however, it has been remedied by taxation of a penal character,—taxation, I mean, in the nature of a fine for the abatement of a nuisance. In Prince Edward Island this evil has attained its maximum. It has been long and loudly complained of, but without any effect. The people, their representative assembly, the legislative council, and the governor have cordially concurred in devising a remedy for it. All their efforts have proved in vain. Some influence—it cannot be that of equity or reason—has steadily counteracted the measures of the colonial legislature. I cannot imagine it is any other influence than that of the absentee proprietors resident in England; and in saying so I do but express the universal opinion of the colony. The only question, therefore, as it appears to me, is whether that influence shall prevail against the deliberate acts of the colonial legislature and the universal complaints of the suffering colonists. I can have no doubt on the subject. My decided opinion is, that the royal assent should no longer be withheld from the act of the colonial legislature.

"At the same time, I doubt whether this act will prove a sufficient remedy for the evil in question. It was but natural that the colonial legislature—who have found it impossible as yet to obtain any remedy whatever—should hesitate to propose a sufficient one. Undeterred by any such consideration,—relying on the cordial coöperation of the government and parliament in the work of improving the state of the colonies,—I had intended, before the receipt of your lordship's despatch, and still intend, to suggest a measure which, while it provides a sufficient remedy for the evil suffered by the colonists, shall also prove advantageous to the absent proprietors by rendering their property more valuable. Whether the inhabitants of Prince Edward Island prefer waiting for the now uncertain results of a suggestion of mine, or that the act which they have passed should be at once confirmed, I cannot tell; but I venture earnestly to recommend that Her Majesty's government should be guided by their wishes on the subject; and in order to ascertain these, I propose to transmit a copy of the present despatch to Sir Charles FitzRoy, with a request that he will, after consulting with the leading men of the colony, address your lordship on the subject.

"With respect to the terms proposed by the proprietors, I am clearly of opinion that any such arrangement would be wholly inadequate to the end in view.

"I am, &c.,

"Durham.

"Lord Glenelg."

The reference in the closing paragraph of the despatch is evidently to a memorandum of terms proposed by the proprietors for the sale and settlement of land in the island, and forwarded to Lord Genelg by Mr. G. R. Young, their talented solicitor and counsel, in January, 1838.

The very decided opinion expressed by Lord Durham led to the confirmation by Her Majesty of the act passed in 1837 for levying an assessment on all lands in the island, which confirmation was effected at a meeting of the privy council, held on the twelfth of December, 1838; but his lordship's despatch was not communicated to the assembly by the governor. Its publication would have gratified the inhabitants of the island, and mightily strengthened the agitation which had been prosecuted for so many years with so comparatively little success.

Lord Durham, in his report, has repeated many of the arguments contained in the despatch which we have given, and the valuable evidence given by John W. Le Lacheur, Robert Hodgson,—now Sir Robert,—Sir Charles FitzRoy, George Wright, Thomas Haviland, John Lawson, and G. R. Goodman is published as a portion of the appendix to His Lordship's report,—evidence which presents a clear and most reliable account of the land question, and exhibits within a moderate compass, with startling effect, the evils which had their origin in the reckless disposal of the island to non-resident proprietors, who disregarded the conditions on which it had been granted.

The coronation of Her Majesty the Queen took place on the twenty-eighth of June, and the event was celebrated in Charlottetown in a manner becoming the loyalty of the inhabitants. The prison doors were thrown open and the debtors set free. A plentiful repast was provided for the poorer classes, of which they joyfully availed themselves. The city was illuminated in the evening, and large bonfires kindled. At a county meeting, held in the court-house, a congratulatory address to the Queen was adopted, and forwarded to London by the governor.

Towards the close of the year 1838, a Mechanics' Institute was established in Charlottetown, mainly through the instrumentality of Mr. Charles Young,—now the Honorable Judge Young, LL. D. The introductory lecture, which was subsequently published in the *Gazette*, was delivered by that gentleman. The Lieutenant-governor, Lady Mary FitzRoy, the chief justice, and a large number of the leading people of the town were present. A course of lectures was thus inaugurated which for many years furnished entertainment and instruction to those who availed themselves of the privilege of attendance. In Charlottetown, as well as in other towns, there is a good deal of latent talent which might be beneficially elicited in the delivery of lectures during the winter evenings. It not unfrequently happens that lecture-committees apply for lecturers in quarters where more able ones than can be found with themselves do not exist.

"'Tis distance lends enchantment to the view."

In the year 1838, the chief of the Micmac tribe presented a petition to the governor, praying for a grant of land to his tribe, which he represented as consisting of five hundred souls. This number seems to have been exaggerated; for the governor, in writing to Lord Glenelg, in reply to an application for information, states that the number of Indians on the island did not exceed two hundred. The governor recommended a grant of Lennox Island—the property of Mr. David Stewart—to the tribe.

Two sessions of the assembly were held in 1839. Whilst the first was proceeding with the public business, a despatch arrived ordering the governor to form an executive, separate from a legislative council. He immediately prorogued the house, and made the necessary nominations to both the councils. The house again met in March, in order to complete the business which remained unfinished at the recent prorogation. During the short interval which had elapsed since the termination of the late session, intelligence had reached the governor that active measures had been taken by the State of Maine to enforce by arms their alleged claims to the territory in dispute between that state and the province of New Brunswick. The season of the year did not admit of any active assistance being rendered in the emergency; but the island authorities determined to respond to the feelings and sentiments expressed by the council and assembly of the neighboring province of Nova Scotia.

W. Cooper was the speaker of the house of assembly in 1839, and was sent as a delegate to London on the land question. Three propositions were made on the subject, namely, the establishment of a court of escheat; the resumption by the Crown of the rights of the proprietors; and a heavy penal tax on wilderness land. The home government rejected the project of escheat, and did not feel at liberty to recommend the advance of two hundred thousand pounds from the treasury. With respect to the third proposal, Lord John Russell, the colonial secretary, expressed his unwillingness to adopt it at the moment, so soon after the imposition of a tax of the same description, and until it had been clearly proved that no remedy was to be expected from the imposition of that tax, and from the disposition of the proprietors to come to an equitable arrangement with the tenantry. The colonial secretary declined to discuss the question with Mr. Cooper, and made his decision known, through the governor of the island, in a despatch dated the seventeenth of September, 1839, in which he expressed his approval of the terms proposed by the proprietors, through their agent, Mr. Young, recommending them as the basis on which Her Majesty's government desired that the question should be arranged.

CHAPTER VII.

Marriage of the Queen—Education in 1842—Foundation-stone of the Colonial Building laid—The Governor withdraws his patronage from Public Institutions—Dispute between the Governor and Mr. Pope—Election disturbances in Belfast—The Currency Question—Responsible Government discussed—Governor Huntley succeeded by Sir Donald Campbell—Earl Grey's reason for withholding Responsible Government—The death of Sir Donald Campbell—Ambrose Lane, Administrator—Sir A. Bannerman, Governor—Responsible Government introduced—Temperance movement—The loss of the "Fairy Queen"—Dissolution of the Assembly—Governor Bannerman succeeded by Dominick Daly—The Worrell Estate bought by the Government—J. Henry Haszard perishes in the Ice Boat—Census of 1855—A loan wanted—The Imperial Guarantee promised, but not given—Resolutions praying for a Commission on the Land Question—Charles Young, Administrator—Biographical Sketch of Bishop McDonald,—Death of James Peake.

In February, 1840, the Queen was united in marriage to Prince Albert, of Saxe-Coburg-Gotha, and in November of the same year the Princess Royal was born. Intelligence of an attempt to assassinate the Queen reached the Island towards the end of July. The culprit was a lad named Edward Oxford, a servant out of place. As Her Majesty, accompanied by Prince Albert, was proceeding in a carriage for the purpose of paying a visit to the Duchess of Kent, at her residence in Belgrave Square, they were fired upon by Oxford, who held a pistol in each hand, both of which he discharged. The shots did not, however, take effect, and it was subsequently discovered that the youth was insane.

The governor, Sir Charles A. FitzRoy, having been appointed to the West Indies, he was succeeded by Sir Henry Vere Huntley, who arrived in November, 1841, and received the usual welcome. In March of the year following died the Honorable George Wright. He had been five times administrator of the government, a duty which devolved upon him as senior member of the council, to which he had been appointed in 1813. He also, for many years, filled the office of surveyor-general. He appears to have discharged his duties conscientiously, and his death was regretted by a large circle of friends.

In February, 1842, Mr. John McNeill, visitor of schools, presented his report, which furnished interesting facts respecting the progress of education in the island. In 1833 the number of schools was seventy-four,—in 1841 they had increased to one hundred and twenty-one. While the number of schools had increased in this ratio, the number of children attending them had in the same period been more than doubled.

Total Population.	No. of Schools.	No. of Scholars.	Average Attendance in each school.
In 1833—32,293	74	2176	29.4
In 1841—74,034	121	4356	36

In November, 1842, Mr. John Ings started a weekly newspaper, designated *The Islander*, which fully realized in its conduct the promises made in the prospectus. For thirty-two years it continued an important public organ, when, for reasons into which it is not our business to inquire, it was discontinued.

In March, 1843, a serious disturbance took place in township forty-five, King's County, when a large assemblage of people forcibly reinstated a person named Haney into the possession of a farm from which he had been legally ejected. The dwelling-house of a person employed by the proprietor to protect timber was also consumed by fire, resulting from the torch of an incendiary. Energetic measures were adopted to enforce the majesty of the law.

On the sixteenth of May, 1843, the corner stone of the colonial building was laid by the Governor, Sir Henry Vere Huntley. A procession was formed at government house, and moved in the following order: masons, headed by a band of music; then followed the governor on horseback, surrounded by his staff; after whom came the chief justice, the members of the executive and legislative councils, the building committee, the various heads of departments, the magistracy,—the members of the Independent Temperance Society bringing up the rear. Having, with trowel and mallet, gone through the ceremony, His Excellency said: "The legislature having granted means for the erection of a provincial building, and the corner stone having been now laid, I trust that a new era of prosperity will open in this colony, and am satisfied that the walls about to rise over this stone will resound with sentiments expressive of British feeling, British principles, and British loyalty." A royal salute was then fired, and three hearty cheers for the Queen were given by hundreds who had collected to witness the proceedings. The design was drafted by Isaac Smith, President of the Mechanics' Institute, and the building was to be composed of freestone, imported from Nova Scotia,—the estimated cost being nearly eleven thousand pounds currency.

At the annual meeting of the Central Agricultural Society, a letter was read from Mr. T. H. Haviland, intimating that in consequence of recent public measures with relation to government house, the governor withdrew his name from the public institutions of the island, and that consequently he ceased to be the patron of the agricultural society. It seems that the governor deemed the action of the assembly, in reference to government house, illiberal in a pecuniary sense; but that was a very insufficient reason for a step so fatal to his excellency's popularity and usefulness. The committee, with a negative sarcasm which the governor must have felt keenly, simply passed a resolution expressing regret that any public measures—in reference to government house—over which the society had no control, should have been deemed by his excellency a sufficient reason for the withdrawal of his name as patron of the society; and a resolution was passed, at the annual meeting, soliciting the honor of His Royal Highness Prince Albert's patronage, which, it is unnecessary to add, was readily granted.

In 1846 a dispute arose between the governor and Mr. Joseph Pope, which excited considerable interest at the time, and which resulted in a correspondence between the colonial office and the governor. It seems that Mr. Pope had opposed strenuously, as an influential member of the house of assembly,—he was then speaker,—a proposal to add five hundred pounds to the governor's annual salary, and this generated in the mind of his excellency a very undignified feeling of hostility to Mr. Pope, who had only exercised a right which could not be legitimately called in question. Writing to Mr. Gladstone, then colonial secretary, the governor said of Mr. Pope: "As for any support from Mr. Pope, I am quite satisfied that in all his private actions, since the time of my persisting in reading the speech, at the opening of the session of 1845, respecting the debt he had accumulated, he has been my concealed enemy." The governor resolved to get quit of Mr. Pope, as an executive councillor, and proceeded, in utter disregard of his instructions, to effect that object by suspending that gentleman from his seat at the board, without any consultation with other members of the council, assigning to Mr. Gladstone, as his reason for dispensing with the usual forms, that he had learnt from good private sources that the council, if consulted, would have dissuaded the suspension of Mr. Pope, and would have recommended the commencement of proceedings, by referring the question to Her Majesty's government. This reason could not prove satisfactory to the colonial secretary, and the governor was ordered to bring the case before the executive council, in which Mr. Pope was to be reinstated as a member; and if they should advise his suspension, then, but not otherwise, he was to be suspended from his office as an executive councillor, until Her Majesty's pleasure was known. Copies of the despatches in which charges were brought against Mr. Pope were ordered to be sent to himself, to which he had an opportunity of replying; but, in the meantime, he prudently tendered his resignation to the governor, in a long communication, in which he gave his reasons for so doing, and in which he embodied a reply to the governor's charges, and condemned his gubernatorial action in very plain and energetic terms.

The legislature met for the first time in the new colonial building in January, 1847. An election for the district of Belfast was ordered to be held on the first of March. There were four candidates in the field: Messrs. Douse and McLean on one side, and Messrs. Little and McDougall on the other. A poll was opened at Pinette. The chief supporters of the two former gentlemen were Scotchmen, and of the two latter, Irishmen. A riot ensued, in which a man named Malcolm McRae was so severely injured that he died. Several others lost their lives in this disgraceful scene. Dr. Hobkirk testified before the executive council that from eighty to a hundred persons were suffering from wounds received in the contest. A large force was sent to the locality, and, on the nineteenth of March, Messrs. Douse and McLean were returned without opposition. There is not now a more peaceful locality in the island than that in which the riot took place; national prejudice and political rancor are lost in kindly fellowship.

Messrs. Charles Hensley, Daniel Hodgson, and George Birnie having been appointed by the governor commissioners to examine into all matters connected with the state of the currency of the island, presented their report in February, 1847,—a report which was creditable both to their industry and judgment. It appears from a letter addressed by Mr. Robert Hodgson, then attorney general, to the commissioners, that the legal currency of the island was the coinage of the United Kingdom of Great Britain and Ireland, and the Spanish milled dollar, which was valued at five shillings sterling,—the debtor having the option of paying in either of these descriptions of money. The commissioners drew attention to the fact, that the currency of the island was greatly depreciated, and that the process of depreciation was going on, which was proved by the circumstance that the Halifax bank note of a pound, which twelve months previously, would purchase no more than twenty-three shillings of the island currency, was now received and disbursed at the treasury for twenty-four shillings. This depreciation the commissioners attributed to an extensive issue of unconvertible paper, both notes and warrants, combined with a growing distrust of the economical administration of the finances of the colony, arising from the continued excess of the expenditure over the receipts of revenue for some years past. They therefore recommended the reversal of the order of procedure, by diminution of outlay, the increase of revenue, the gradual abolition of notes, and the restraining of the issue of warrants to the amount required yearly for the public service. They also alluded to the advantages that would result from the establishment of a substantial bank, issuing notes payable on demand, and affording other facilities for the commercial and agricultural operations of the island. The commissioners concluded their report by expressing their deliberate opinion that whilst a paper circulation, based on adequate and available capital, was, under prudent management, of the utmost benefit to a commercial and agricultural population, and would contribute largely to its prosperity, unconvertible paper was a curse and a deception,—a delusive and fictitious capital, which left no solid foundation to rest upon in any time of reverse and difficulty. They also expressed the hope that on no pretext should a permanent debt be established in the colony, as the evil effects of such a burden would not be confined to the additional charge upon the revenue, but would necessitate the absorption of capital which might be more beneficially employed in commerce, manufactures, or agricultural improvement.

The subject of responsible government was discussed at length in the assembly during the session of 1847, and an address to the Queen on the subject was adopted by the house, in which it was represented that the lieutenant-governor or administrator of the colony should be alone responsible to the Queen and imperial parliament for his acts, that the executive council should be deemed the constitutional advisers of the representative of Her Majesty, and that when the acts of the administrator of the government were such as the council could not approve, they should be required to resign. The house recommended that four members of the executive council should be selected from the lower branch of the legislature, such members being held responsible to the house for the acts of the administrator of the government. As the local resources of the assembly did not admit of retiring pensions being provided for the officers who might be affected by the introduction of the system of departmental government, it was suggested that the treasurer, colonial secretary, attorney general, and surveyor general should not be required to resign, but that they should be required to give a constitutional support to the measures of government. In closing the session, the governor intimated his intention of giving the address which had been voted by the house his cordial support.

As the governor's term of office was about to expire, a petition was got up by his friends, praying for his continuance in office. This movement stimulated a counter movement on the part of an influential section of the community, who were antagonistic to the governor, and, consequently, a counter petition was framed, and a subscription set on foot to pay the expenses of a deputation to convey the petition to England. The deputation consisted of the following gentlemen: Mr. Joseph Pope, speaker of the house of assembly, Mr. Edward Palmer, and Mr. Andrew Duncan, a prominent merchant. The main grounds on which the continuance in office of the governor was objected to were the following:—That he had recently coalesced with parties who had been unremitting in their endeavors to bring his person and government into contempt; that he had shown a disinclination to advance the real interests of the colony, by withdrawing his patronage and support from all public societies in the island, because the legislature had declined to accede to his application for an increase of salary from the public funds; that on one occasion, through the colonial secretary, he publicly denounced every member of society who would dare to partake of the hospitality of a gentleman—a member of the legislative council—who was then politically opposed to him; that he had, on various occasions, improperly exercised the power given to him by the Queen, by appointing parties totally unqualified by education and position to the magistracy; that on a late occasion he had personally congratulated a successful political candidate at government house, with illuminated windows, at a late hour of the night, in presence of a large mob, who immediately after proceeded through the town, and attacked the houses of several unoffending inhabitants. This formidable catalogue of complaints was calculated to produce a most unfavorable impression on the home government, as to Sir Henry Vere Huntley's competency to govern the colony. But the home government had come to a determination on the subject before the arrival of the deputation. "I regret to say," wrote Lord Grey, then the colonial secretary, addressing the governor on the twelfth of August, "that having carefully reviewed your correspondence with this office, I am of opinion that there is no special reason for departing in your case from the ordinary rule of the colonial service, and I shall, therefore, feel it my duty to recommend that you be relieved in your government on the termination of the usual period for which your office is held."

Sir Donald Campbell, of Dunstaffnage, was appointed to take the place of Governor Huntley. He arrived in Charlottetown early in December, and as belonging to an ancient highland family, was greeted with more than ordinary enthusiasm.

When in London, the speaker of the house of assembly and Mr. Palmer called the attention of Earl Grey to the state of the currency, and his lordship subsequently addressed a despatch to the lieutenant-governor on the subject. He alluded to the practice of the local government issuing treasury warrants for small sums of money, and treasury notes for still smaller sums, for the purpose of meeting the ordinary expenses of the government, as tending to depreciate the currency below its nominal value. Two remedies presented themselves: first, whether it would be proper to endeavor to restore this depreciated currency to its original value; or, secondly, whether it would not be better to fix its value at its present rate, taking the necessary measures for preventing its further depreciation. He recommended the latter course, as more injustice was usually done by restoring a depreciated currency to its original value than by fixing it at the value which it might actually bear. To prevent further depreciation, he recommended that the legislature should pass a law enacting that the existing treasury warrants should be exchanged for treasury notes to the same amount, and that these notes should be declared a legal tender; that it should not be lawful to make any further issue of treasury notes, except in exchange for the precious metals, the coins of different countries being taken at the value they bore in circulation, and that the treasury notes should be made exchangeable at the pleasure of the holders for coin at the same rate. In order to enable the colonial treasurer, or such other officer as might be charged with the currency account, to meet any demands which might be made upon him for coin in exchange for treasury notes, it might be necessary to raise a moderate sum by loan, or otherwise, for that purpose. Though these suggestions were not entirely carried out, yet an act was passed in the session of 1849, which determined the rates at which British and foreign coins were to be current, and how debts contracted in the currency of the island were to be payable.

The year 1848 was not remarkable for any historic event in the island,—the taking of the census being the most noteworthy, when the population was ascertained to be 62,634. But it was a most memorable year in the history of Europe, for in that year Louis Philippe, the King of the French, vacated the throne, and fled to England for protection, an event which occasioned a general convulsion on the continent of Europe.

The attention of the assembly was called to the evils which resulted from elections taking place in the island on different days, which presented an opportunity to the evil-disposed to attend in various districts, and create a disturbance of the public peace. A measure was accordingly introduced and passed, which provided for the elections taking place in the various electoral districts on the same day,—an antidote to disorder which has operated admirably, not only in Prince Edward Island, but in all places where it has been adopted.

During summer, the governor—in order to become acquainted with the state of the country—paid a visit to the various sections of the island, and was well received. He was entertained at dinner by the highland society, and the whole Celtic population rejoiced in the appointment of one of their countrymen to the position of lieutenant-governor.

In January, 1849, a public meeting was held in Charlottetown, for the purpose of forming a general union for the advancement of agricultural pursuits. The chair was occupied by Sir Donald Campbell, and resolutions were adopted, and a subscription begun to carry out the object of the meeting.

Earl Grey transmitted a despatch to the governor in January, 1849, stating the reasons why the government did not accede to the desire, so generally expressed, to have responsible government introduced. He stated that the introduction of the system had, in other cases, been postponed until the gradual increase of the community in wealth, numbers, and importance appeared to justify it. He referred to the circumstance that Prince Edward Island was comparatively small in extent and population, and its commercial and wealthy classes confined almost entirely to a single town. While its people were distinguished by those qualities of order and public spirit which formed the staple foundation of all government, in as high a degree as any portion of their brethren of British descent, yet the external circumstances which would render the introduction of responsible government expedient were wanting,—circumstances of which time, and the natural progress of events, could alone remove the deficiency. For these reasons Earl Grey concurred with his predecessor, Mr. Gladstone, that the time for a change had not yet arrived. He, at the same time, expressed his conviction that the existing system of administration was compatible with the complete enjoyment by the inhabitants of the colony of the real benefits of self-government.

The colonial secretary thought that the period had come when the assembly of the island should undertake to provide for the civil list. He accordingly addressed a despatch to the governor, intimating that the home government was willing to provide the salary of the governor, which it proposed to increase to fifteen hundred pounds sterling a year, provided the other expenses of the civil government were defrayed from the funds of the island. To this proposal the house expressed its willingness to accede, provided that all revenues arising from the permanent revenue laws of the colony were granted in perpetuity, all claim to the quitrents and crown lands abandoned, and a system of responsible government conceded. The home government, in reply, expressed its willingness to accede to the wishes of the assembly on all these points, with trifling modifications, save the granting of responsible government, in the present circumstances of the island. The governor, therefore, deemed it the best course to dissolve the assembly and convene a new one, which met on the fifth of March, 1850. In the reply to the governor's speech, the assembly inserted a paragraph, in which want of confidence in the executive council was emphatically expressed. Mr. Coles also moved a resolution in the house, embodying the reasons of the assembly for its want of confidence, and refusing to grant supplies till the government should be remodelled, or in other words, responsible government conceded. The governor proposed to meet the views of the house so far, on his own responsibility, as to admit into the executive council three gentlemen possessing its confidence in room of three junior members of the council. This proposal was not deemed acceptable. The house then adopted an address to the Queen, in which its views were set forth. The house contended that, in taking measures to secure responsible government, the governor would be only acting in accordance with the spirit of his instructions, and that as all the members of the executive council had resigned, there was no impediment to the introduction of the desired change. The house was prorogued on the twenty-sixth of March, but again summoned on the twenty-fifth of April. Whilst the house granted certain limited supplies, it refused to proceed to the transaction of the other business to which its attention was called in the governor's opening speech. No provision was made for the roads and bridges, and other services, and the governor, in his answer to the address of the house in reply to his closing speech, said: "I should fail in the performance of my duty, if I did not express my disapprobation of your premeditated neglect of your legislative functions."

The governor transmitted an able despatch to the colonial secretary, in 1849, on the resources of the island, which Lord Grey appreciated highly; but the career of the baronet as a governor was destined to be of short duration, for he died in October of the following year, at the comparatively early age of fifty years. In Sir Donald Campbell were united some of the best qualities of a good governor. He was firm and faithful in the discharge of duty; at the same time of a conciliatory and kindly disposition.

The Honorable Ambrose Lane, who had been formerly administrator during Governor Huntley's temporary absence, was again appointed to that office till the arrival of Sir A. Bannerman, the new lieutenant-governor. His excellency arrived at Charlottetown on the eighth of March, having crossed the strait in the ice-boat. The legislature assembled on the twenty-fifth of March, 1851. In the opening speech the governor informed the house that responsible government would be granted on condition of compensation being allowed to certain retiring officers. The house acceded to the proposal, and a new government—sustained by a majority of the assembly—was accordingly formed in April,—the leaders being the Honorable George Coles, president, and the Honorable Charles Young, attorney general. The Honorable Joseph Pope was appointed to the treasurer-ship, and the Honorable James Warburton to the office of colonial secretary. Besides an important act to commute the Crown revenues of the island, and to provide for the civil list in accordance with the suggestions of the home government, a measure was in this year passed for the transference of the management of the inland posts, and making threepence the postage of ordinary letters to any part of British America, and a uniform rate of twopence to any part of the island. This year was also memorable in the annals of the island, in consequence of a violent storm which swept over it on the third and fourth of October, by which seventy-two American fishing vessels were seriously damaged or cast ashore.

The governor, in opening the session of 1852, stated that he had much pleasure in visiting many parts of the island; but that he observed with regret the educational deficiency which still existed, and which the government would endeavor to assist in supplying, by introducing a measure which, he hoped, would receive the approval of the house. An act for the encouragement of education, and to raise funds for that purpose by imposing an additional assessment on land, was accordingly passed, which formed the basis of the present educational system.

In April, 1853, the Honorable Charles Young and Captain Swabey—the former attorney general, and the latter registrar of deeds and chairman of the Board of Education—resigned their seats as members of the executive council. Mr. Joseph Hensley was appointed to the office of attorney general, and Mr. John Longworth to that of solicitor general, in place of Mr. Hensley. Mr. Young's resignation was mainly owing to the approval, by a majority of his colleagues in the government, of an act to regulate the salaries of the attorney general and solicitor general, and clerk of the Crown and prothonotary, for their services, to which he and other members of the government had serious objections, which they embodied in a protest on the passing of the bill.

The temperance organizations in the island were particularly active at the period at which we have arrived. A meeting was held in Charlottetown, for the purpose of discussing the propriety and practicability of abolishing by law the manufacture and sale of intoxicating liquors. There would be consistency in prohibiting the manufacture and importation of intoxicating liquors, as well as the sale of them. But the Maine law, which permits the importation of liquor into the state, whilst it prohibits its sale, is a useless anomaly. Let anyone visit Portland—where he might expect to see the law decently enforced—and he will find in one, at least, of the principal hotels in the city, a public bar-room in which alcoholic liquors of all kinds are openly sold; and, if he chooses to begin business in the liquor line, he can, for thirty dollars, procure a license from one of the officials of the United States government, for that purpose. The United States law sanctions the importation and sale of intoxicating drinks; the Maine state law forbids the sale ostensibly, whilst it is really permitted. The temperance movement has effected a vast amount of good, but coercion is not the means by which it has been accomplished.

During the session of 1853, an act to extend the elective franchise was passed, which made that privilege almost universal. The house was dissolved during the summer, and at the general election which ensued the government was defeated. A requisition was in consequence addressed to the governor by members of the assembly, praying for the early assembling of the house, in order that, by legal enactment, departmental officers might be excluded from occupying seats in the legislature, to which request the governor did not accede.

On the seventh of October, 1853, a sad catastrophe took place in the loss of the steamer *Fairy Queen*. The boat left Charlottetown on a Friday forenoon. Shortly after getting clear of Point Prim, the vessel shipped a sea which broke open the gangways. When near Pictou Island the tiller-rope broke, and another heavy sea was shipped. The rope was, with the assistance of some of the passengers, spliced; but the vessel moved very slowly. The captain and some of the crew got into a boat and drifted away, regardless of the fate of the female passengers. Among the passengers were Mr. Martin I. Wilkins, of Pictou, Mr. Lydiard, Mr. Pineo, Dr. McKenzie, and others. After having been subjected to a series of heavy seas, the upper deck, abaft the funnel, separated from the main body of the vessel, and providentially constituted an admirable raft, by which a number of the passengers were saved, among whom were Messrs. Wilkins, Lydiard, and Pineo, who landed on the north side of Merigomish Island, after eight hours of exposure to the storm and cold. Dr. McKenzie,—an excellent young man,—other two males, and four females perished.

In opening the assembly of 1854, the governor referred in terms of congratulation to the prosperous state of the revenue. On the thirty-first of January, 1850, the balance of debt against the colony was twenty-eight thousand pounds. In four years it was reduced to three thousand pounds. The revenue had increased from twenty-two thousand pounds, in 1850, to thirty-five thousand in 1853, notwithstanding a reduction in the duty on tea, and two thousand eight hundred pounds assessment imposed for educational purposes.

The new house having declared its want of confidence in the government, a new one was formed, of which the leaders were the Honorables J. M. Holl and Edward Palmer; but there was a majority opposed to it in the upper branch, which, to some extent, frustrated the satisfactory working of the machine. The house was prorogued in May; and, in opposition to the unanimous opinion of his council, the governor dissolved the assembly,—the reason assigned for this course of procedure being, that the act passed for the extension of the franchise had received the royal assent, and that for the interest of the country it was necessary to have a house based on the new law. An appeal to the country was certain to ensure the defeat of the government; and the governor was accused of desiring to effect that object before his departure from the island,—for he had been appointed to the government of the Bahamas. It is only due to Governor Bannerman to state that he had anticipated difficulties, which constrained him to consult the colonial secretary as to the most proper course of action, and that he received a despatch, in which the duke said: "I leave it with yourself, with full confidence in your judgment, to take such steps in relation to the executive council and the assembly as you may think proper before leaving the government." We may be permitted to say that it is only in very rare and exceptional cases that either a British sovereign or a royal representative can be justified in disregarding the advice of constitutional advisers; and the case under notice does not seem, in any of its bearings, to have been one in relation to which the prerogative should have been exercised.

Dominick Daly, Esq., succeeded Governor Bannerman, and arrived on the island on the twelfth of June, 1854, and was received by all classes with much cordiality: addresses poured in upon his excellency from all parts of the island. A few days after the arrival of the new governor the election took place, and was, as anticipated, unfavorable to the government, which, to its credit, resigned on the twentieth of July,—intimation to that effect having been communicated to the governor by the president of the executive council, John M. Holl. A new government was formed, and the house assembled in September, in consequence of the ratification of a commercial treaty between the British and United States governments, and the withdrawal of the troops from the island,—circumstances which required the immediate consideration of the assembly. The session was a short one, the attention of the house being directed exclusively to the business for the transaction of which it had met. An act was immediately passed to authorise free trade with the United States, under the treaty which had been concluded. The measure opened the way for the introduction into the island, free of duty, of grain and breadstuffs of all kinds; butter, cheese, tallow, lard, etc., in accordance with a policy which has been found to operate most beneficially in the countries where it has been adopted. Great Britain declared war in this year against Russia; but, beyond the withdrawal of the troops and the advance of the prices of breadstuffs and provisions, the island was not affected by its prosecution.

The Worrell Estate, consisting of eighty-one thousand three hundred and three acres, was purchased by the government at the close of the year 1854,—the price paid for the property being twenty-four thousand one hundred pounds, of which eighteen thousand pounds were paid down, and the balance retained till the accuracy of its declared extent was ascertained.

In the session of 1855 a considerable amount of legislative business was transacted, including the passing of an act for the incorporation of Charlottetown, an act for the incorporation of the Bank of Prince Edward Island, and an act to provide a normal school for the training of teachers. In proroguing the assembly, the governor referred in terms of condemnation to any further agitation of the question of escheat, as successive governments were opposed to every measure which had hitherto passed relating to the subject, in the wisdom of which opposition the governor expressed himself as fully concurring. He approved of the active measures which had been taken under the Land Purchase Bill, and expressed his conviction that similar measures only required the cordial co-operation of the tenantry to secure an amount of advantage to themselves which no degree of agitation could obtain. The island had contributed two thousand pounds to the Patriotic Fund, which had been instituted to relieve the widows and children of soldiers who fell in the Crimean war; and the governor expressed Her Majesty's satisfaction with the generous sympathy thus evinced by the people and their representatives.

In the month of March, 1855, a distressing occurrence took place. The ice-boat from Cape Tormentine to the island, with Mr. James Henry Haszard, Mr. Johnson, son of Dr. Johnson, medical students, and an old gentleman—Mr. Joseph Weir, of Bangor—as passengers, had proceeded safely to within half a mile of the island shore, when a severe snow-storm was encountered. The boat, utterly unable to make headway, was put about, drawn on the ice, and turned up to protect the men from the cold and fury of the storm. Thus they were drifted helplessly in the strait during Friday night, Saturday, and Saturday night. On Sunday morning they began to drag the boat towards the mainland, and, exhausted,—not having tasted food for three days,—they were about ceasing all further efforts, when they resolved to kill a spaniel which Mr. Weir had with him, and the poor fellows drank the blood and eat the raw flesh of the animal. They now felt a little revived, and lightened the boat by throwing out trunks and baggage. Mr. Haszard was put into the boat, being unable to walk; and thus they moved towards the shore, from which they were four or five miles distant. On Monday evening Mr. Haszard died from exhaustion. They toiled on, however, and on Tuesday morning reached the shore, near Wallace, Nova Scotia, but, unfortunately, at a point two miles from the nearest dwelling. Two of the boatmen succeeded in reaching a house, and all the survivors, though much frost-bitten, recovered under the kind and judicious treatment which they received.

The census taken in 1855 declared the population of the island to be seventy-one thousand. There were two hundred and sixty-eight schools, attended by eleven thousand pupils. The Normal School was opened in 1856 by the governor, and constituted an important addition to the educational machinery of the island.

During the session of 1855 an act was passed to impose a rate or duty on the rent-rolls of the proprietors of certain rented township-lands, and also an act to secure compensation to tenants; but the governor intimated, in opening the assembly in 1856, that both acts had not received Her Majesty's confirmation, at which, in their reply to the speech, the house expressed regret,—not hesitating to tell His Excellency that they believed their rejection was attributable to the influence of non-resident proprietors, which had dominated so long in the councils of the Sovereign. Mr. Labouchere, the colonial secretary, in intimating the decision of the government in reference to the acts specified, stated that whatever character might properly attach to the circumstances connected with the original grants, which had been often employed against the maintenance of the rights of the proprietors, they could not, with justice, be used to defeat the rights of the present owners, who had acquired their property by inheritance, by family settlement, or otherwise. Seeing, therefore, that the rights of the proprietors could not be sacrificed without manifest injustice, he felt it his duty steadily to resist, by all means in his power, measures similar in their character to those recently brought under the consideration of Her Majesty's government. He desired, at the same, time, to assure the house of assembly that it was with much regret that Her Majesty's advisers felt themselves constrained to oppose the wishes of the people of Prince Edward Island, and that it was his own wish to be spared the necessity of authoritative interference in regard to matters affecting the internal administration of their affairs.

With regard to the main object which had been frequently proposed by a large portion of the inhabitants, namely, that some means might be provided by which a tenant holding under a lease could arrive at the position of a fee-simple proprietor, he was anxious to facilitate such a change, provided it could be effected without injustice to the proprietors. Two ways suggested themselves: first, the usual and natural one of purchase and sale between the tenant and the owner; and, secondly, that the government of the island should treat with such of the landowners as might be willing to sell, and that the state, thus becoming possessed of the fee-simple of such lands as might thus be sold, should be enabled to afford greater facilities for converting the tenants into freeholders. Such an arrangement could not probably be made without a loan, to be raised by the island government, the interest of which would be charged upon the revenues of the island. Mr. Labouchere intimated that the government would not be indisposed to take into consideration any plan of this kind which might be submitted to them, showing in what way the interest of such loan could locally be provided for, and what arrangements would be proposed as to the manner of disposing of the lands of which the fee-simple was intended to be bought.

In 1856 the legislature presented an address to the Queen, suggesting the guaranty of a loan for the purchase of township lands, with a view to the more speedy and general conversion of leaseholds into freehold tenures. In answering this address, the colonial secretary intimated that the documents sent to him appeared to Her Majesty's government to afford a sufficient guaranty for the due payment of the interest, and for the formation of a sinking-fund for the payment of the principal of the loan; and that they were prepared to authorise a loan of one hundred thousand pounds, sterling, to be appropriated, on certain specified conditions, to the purchase of the rights of landed proprietors in the island. It will be afterwards seen that good faith was not kept with the people of the island in this matter.

The question as to whether the Bible ought to be made a text-book in the public schools of the island had been freely discussed since the opening of the Normal School, in October, 1856, when the discussion arose in consequence of remarks made by Mr. Stark, the inspector of schools. Petitions praying for the introduction of the Bible into the Central Academy and the Normal School were presented at the commencement of the session of 1858, and the question came before the house on the nineteenth of March, when Mr. McGill, as chairman of the committee on certain petitions relating to the subject, reported that the committee adopted a resolution to the effect that it was inexpedient to comply with the prayer of the several petitions before the house asking for an act of the legislature to compel the use of the protestant Bible as a class-book in mixed schools like the Central Academy and Normal School, which were supported by protestants and catholics alike,—the house feeling assured that so unjust and so unnecessary a measure was neither desired by a majority of the inhabitants of the colony, nor essential to the encouragement of education and religion. The Honorable Mr. Palmer moved an amendment, to the effect that it was necessary to provide by law that the holy Scriptures might be read and used by any scholar or scholars attending either the Central Academy or Normal School, in all cases where the parents or guardians might require the same to be used. The house then divided on the motion of amendment, when the numbers were found equal; but the speaker gave his casting vote in the negative. Mr. McGill being one of the prominent public men opposed to the principle of compulsion in religious matters, was at this time subjected to much unmerited abuse, emanating from quarters where the cultivation of a better spirit might be reasonably expected.

The quadrennial election took place in June, 1858, when the strength of the government was reduced to such a degree as to render the successful conduct of the public business impossible. The government dismissed the postmaster and some of his subordinates from office, which occasioned a large county meeting in Charlottetown, at which resolutions condemnatory of the action of the government and expressive of sympathy for and confidence in the ability and fidelity of the officials were passed. The principal speakers were Mr. William McNeill, Colonel Gray, Honorable E. Palmer, and W. H. Hyde. When the house met, it was found that parties were so closely balanced that the business of the country could not be transacted on the basis of the policy of the government or opposition. The house failed to elect a speaker,—the parties nominated having refused to accept office in the event of election. A dissolution consequently took place, and a new election was ordered. The contest at the polls resulted in the defeat of the government, who resigned on the fourth of April, and a new government was formed, of which the leaders were the Honorable Edward Palmer and the Honorable Colonel Gray.

On the morning that the *Islander* published the names of the new government, it also announced the death of Duncan McLean, who for nine years edited that paper, and who had, just before his death, been appointed Commissioner of Public Lands. Mr. McLean was a well-informed and vigorous writer; and, although his pen was not unfrequently dipped in political gall, yet he was genial and kindly in private life, and was a man who never nourished his wrath to keep it warm, or allowed it to extend beyond the political arena. Mr. McLean had a large circle of friends who deeply regretted his death.

The governor, in the opening speech of the session, intimated that he had received communications from Her Majesty's government on the subject of a federal union of the North American Provinces. He also stated that it was not the intention of the home government to propose to parliament the guaranteeing of the contemplated loan. He also informed the house that he had some time previously tendered his resignation of the lieutenant-governorship of the island, that his services were to be employed in another portion of the colonial possessions, and that his successor had been appointed.

Colonel Gray submitted to the house a series of resolutions, which were adopted with certain modifications, praying that Her Majesty would be pleased to direct a commission to some discreet and impartial person, not connected with the island or its affairs, to inquire into the existing relations of landlord and tenant, and to negotiate with the proprietors for such an abatement of present liabilities, and for such terms for enabling the tenantry to convert their leaseholds into freeholds as might be fairly asked to ameliorate the condition of the tenantry. It was suggested in these resolutions that the basis of any such arrangement should be a large remission of arrears of rent now due, and the giving every tenant holding under a long lease the option of purchasing his land at a certain rate at any time he might find it convenient to do so.

The legislative council, of which the Honorable Charles Young, LL. D., was president, adopted an address praying that the Queen would be pleased to give instructions that an administration might be formed in consonance with the royal instructions when assent was given to the Civil List Bill, passed in April, 1857. The council complained that the principle of responsible government was violated in the construction of the existing executive council, which did not contain one Roman catholic, though the population of that faith was, according to the census of 1855, thirty-two thousand; that not one member of the legislative council belonged to the executive; that persons were appointed to all the departmental offices who had no seats in the legislature, and who were, in consequence, in no way responsible to the people; and as all persons accepting office under the Crown, when members of the assembly, were compelled to appeal to their constituents for re-election, this statute was deliberately evaded, and no parliamentary responsibility existed.

In replying to the address of the legislative council, in a counter-address, the house of assembly contended that there was no violation of the principle of the act passed in 1857; that the prejudicial influence of salaried officers having seats in the assembly was condemned by the people at the polls, as indicated by the present house, where there were nineteen for, to eleven members opposed to the principle. As evidence of public opinion on the subject, it was further stated, that when the commissioner of public lands, after accepting office in the year 1857, appealed to the people, he was rejected by a large majority; that the attorney general and registrar of deeds, at the general election in June last, were in like manner rejected; and that at the general election in March last, the treasurer and postmaster-general were also rejected,—the colonial secretary being the only departmental officer who was able to procure a constituency.

On the nineteenth of May, Lieut. Governor Daly prorogued the house in a graceful speech. He said he could not permit the last opportunity to pass without expressing the gratification which he should ever experience in the recollection of the harmony which had subsisted between the executive and the other branches of the legislature during the whole course of his administration, to which the uninterrupted tranquillity of the island during the same period might in a great measure be attributed. The performance of the important and often anxious duties attached to his station had been facilitated and alleviated by the confidence which they had ever so frankly reposed in the sincerity of his desire to promote the welfare of the community; and notwithstanding the peculiar evils with which the colony had to contend, he had the satisfaction of witnessing the triumph of its natural resources in its steady though limited improvement. In bidding the house and the people farewell, he trusted that the favor of Divine Providence, which had been so signally manifested towards the island, might ever be continued to it, and conduct its inhabitants to the condition of prosperity and improvement which was ever attainable by the united and harmonious cultivation of such capabilities as were possessed by Prince Edward Island.

Sir Dominick Daly having left the island in May, the Honorable Charles Young, president of the legislative council, was sworn in as administrator. Mr. George Dundas, member of parliament for Linlithgowshire, was appointed lieutenant-governor, and arrived in June, when he received a cordial welcome. Amongst the numerous addresses presented to the governor was one from the ministers of the Wesleyan Conference of Eastern British America, assembled in Charlottetown, who represented a ministry of upwards of a hundred, and a church-membership of about fifteen thousand.

General Williams, the hero of Kars, visited the island in July, and received a hearty welcome from all classes. He was entertained at supper served in the Province Building. The Mayor of Charlottetown, the Honorable T. H. Haviland, occupied the chair, having on his right hand Mrs. Dundas and General Williams, and on his left, Mrs. E. Palmer and the Lieutenant-governor. The Honorable Mr. Coles acted as croupier.

On the thirtieth of December, 1859, at Saint Dunstan's College, died the Right Reverend Bernard Donald McDonald, Roman catholic bishop of the island. He was a native of the island, having been born in the parish of Saint Andrew's in December, 1797. He obtained the rudiments of an English education in the school of his native district,— one of the very first educational establishments then existing on the island. He entered, at the age of fifteen, his *alma mater*,—the Seminary of Quebec. Here he remained for ten years, during which time he distinguished himself by his unremitting application to study, and a virtuous life. It was then that he laid the foundation of that fund of varied and extensive learning—both sacred and profane—which rendered his conversation on every subject agreeable, interesting, and instructive. Having completed his studies, he was ordained priest in the spring of 1824, and he soon afterwards entered on his missionary career. There being but few clergymen on the island at that time, he had to take charge of all the western parishes, including Indian River, Grand River, Miscouche, Fifteen Point, Belle Alliance, Cascumpec, Tignish, etc. In all these missions he succeeded, by his zeal and untiring energy, in building churches and parochial houses. In the autumn of 1829 he was appointed pastor of Charlottetown and the neighboring missions. In 1836 he was nominated by the Pope successor to the Right Reverend Bishop MacEachern, and on the fifteenth of October of that year was consecrated Bishop of Charlottetown in Saint Patrick's Church, Quebec.

The deceased prelate was charitable, hospitable, and pious. Having few priests in his diocese, he himself took charge of a mission; and besides attending to all his episcopal functions, he also discharged the duties of a parish priest. He took a deep interest in the promotion of education. He established in his own district schools in which the young might be instructed, not only in secular knowledge, but also in their moral and religious duties, and encouraged as much as possible their establishment throughout the whole extent of his diocese. Aided by the co-operation of the charitable and by the munificent donation of a gentleman, now living, he was enabled to establish in Charlottetown a convent of ladies of the *Congregation de Notre Dame*,—which institution is now in a flourishing condition, affording to numerous young ladies, belonging to Charlottetown and other parts of the island, the inestimable blessing of a superior education. But the educational establishment in which the bishop appeared to take the principal interest was Saint Dunstan's College. This institution, which is an ornament to the island, the lamented bishop opened early in 1855. The care with which he watched over its progress and provided for its wants, until the time of his death, was truly paternal. Long before he departed, he had the satisfaction of seeing the institution established on a firm basis and in a prosperous condition.

In the year 1856 the bishop contracted a cough, and declining health soon became perceptible. He, however, continued to discharge his duties as pastor of Saint Augustine's Church, Rustico, until the autumn of 1857, when, by medical advice, he discontinued the most laborious portion of them. Finding that his disease—chronic bronchitis—was becoming more deeply seated, he went to New York in the summer of 1858, and consulted the most eminent physicians of that city, but to little or no purpose. His health continuing to decline, he set his house in order, and awaited the time of his dissolution with the utmost resignation. About two months before his death he removed from Rustico, and took up his residence in Saint Dunstan's College, saying that he wished to die within its walls. On the twenty-second of December he became visibly worse, and on the twenty-sixth he received the last sacraments. He continued to linger till the thirtieth, when he calmly expired, in the sixty-second year of his age.

The lieutenant-governor was instructed by the home government that, in the event of the absence of harmony between the legislative council and the assembly, he should increase the number of councillors, and thus facilitate the movements of the machine. Five additional members were accordingly added to the council. During the session, several acts were passed relating to education, including one which provided for the establishment of the Prince of Wales College.

The governor laid before the house a despatch, which he had received from the colonial secretary, the Duke of Newcastle, relative to the subject of the proposed commission on the land question. His grace had received a letter, signed by Sir Samuel Cunard and other proprietors, in which, addressing his grace, they said: "We have been furnished with a copy of a memorial, addressed to Her Majesty, from the house of assembly of Prince Edward Island, on the questions which have arisen in connection with the original grants of land in that island, and the rights of proprietors in respect thereof. We observe that the assembly have suggested that Her Majesty should appoint one or more commissioners to inquire into the relations of landlord and tenant in the island, and to negotiate with the proprietors of the township lands, for fixing a certain rate of price at which every tenant might have the option of purchasing his land; and, also, to negotiate with the proprietors for a remission of the arrears of rent in such cases as the commissioners might deem reasonable; and proposing that the commissioners should report the result to Her Majesty. As large proprietors in this island, we beg to state that we shall acquiesce in any arrangement that may be practicable for the purpose of settling the various questions alluded to in the memorial of the house of assembly; but we do not think that the appointment of commissioners, in the manner proposed by them, would be the most desirable mode of procedure, as the labors of such commissioners would only terminate in a report, which would not be binding on any of the parties interested. We beg, therefore, to suggest that, instead of the mode proposed by the assembly, three commissioners or referees should be appointed,—one to be named by Her Majesty, one by the house of assembly, and one by the proprietors of the land,—and that these commissioners should have power to enter into all the inquiries that may be necessary, and to decide upon the different questions which may be brought before them, giving, of course, to the parties interested an opportunity of being heard. We should propose that the expense of the commission should be paid by the three parties to the reference, that is to say, in equal thirds; and we feel assured that there would be no difficulty in securing the adherence of all the landed proprietors to a settlement on this footing. The precise mode of carrying it into execution, if adopted, would require consideration, and upon that subject we trust that your grace will lend your valuable assistance.

"If the consent," said the colonial secretary, "of all the parties can be obtained to this proposal, I believe that it may offer the means of bringing these long pending disputes to a termination. But it will be necessary, before going further into the matter, to be assured that the tenants will accept as binding the decision of the commissioners, or the majority of them; and, as far as possible, that the legislature of the colony would concur in any measures which might be required to give validity to that decision. It would be very desirable, also, that any commissioner who might be named by the house of assembly, on behalf of the tenants, should go into the inquiry unfettered by any conditions such as were proposed in the assembly last year."

The proposal of the colonial secretary, as to the land commission, came formally before the house on the thirteenth of April, when Colonel Gray moved that the house deemed it expedient to concur in the suggestions offered for their consideration for the arrangement of the long pending dispute between the landlords and tenants of the island, and, therefore, agreed to the appointment of three commissioners,—one by Her Majesty, one by the house of assembly, and the third by the proprietors,—the expense to be divided equally between the imperial government, the general revenue of the colony, and the proprietors; and that the house also agreed, on the part of the tenantry, to abide by the decision of the commissioners, or the majority of them, and pledged themselves to concur in whatever measures might be required to give validity to that decision. Mr. Coles proposed an amendment, to the effect that there were no means of ascertaining the views and opinions of the tenantry upon the questions at issue, unless by an appeal to the whole people of the colony, in the usual constitutional manner, and that any decision otherwise come to by the commissioners or referees appointed should not be regarded as binding on the tenantry. On a division, the motion of Colonel Gray was carried by nineteen to nine. It was then moved by Mr. Howat, that the Honorable Joseph Howe, of Nova Scotia, should be the commissioner for the tenantry, which was unanimously agreed to.

During this session, that of 1860, the assembly agreed to purchase the extensive estates of the Earl of Selkirk; and the purchase of sixty-two thousand and fifty-nine acres was effected, at the very moderate rate of six thousand five hundred and eighty-six pounds sterling,—thus enabling the government to offer to industrious tenants facilities for becoming the owners of land which was then held by them on lease.

On the fourth of May, 1860, died Mr. James Peake, at Plymouth, England. From the year 1823 until 1856, Mr. Peake was actively engaged in mercantile pursuits on the island. He was a successful merchant, and for some years held a seat in Her Majesty's executive council. Of a kind find generous disposition, he did not live to himself, but was ever ready to extend a helping hand to industrious and reliable persons, who might need aid and encouragement. He was highly esteemed as a liberal, honorable man. His integrity and enterprise placed him in the front rank as a merchant. "None," said the *Islander*, "was more deservedly respected, and by his death the world has lost one who was an honest and upright man."

CHAPTER VIII.

Arrival of the Prince of Wales—His Reception—The British Colonial Secretary expresses satisfaction with the Assembly's proceedings in regard to the Land Commission—The Report of the Commissioners—Its cardinal points presented—Their views with regard to Escheat and other subjects—The case of the Loyalists and Indians. Remarks on the Report: its merits and its defects. The evils incident to the Land Question fundamentally attributable to the Home Government—The Immigrants deceived—The misery consequent on such deception—The burden of correction laid on the wrong shoulders—Volunteer Companies—General Census—Death of Prince Albert—The Duke of Newcastle and the Commissioners' Report.

The Prince of Wales having, in compliance with an invitation from the Canadian parliament, resolved to visit British North America, he was invited by the authorities to pay a visit to Prince Edward Island. Having signified his intention of doing so, suitable preparations were made for his reception. His Royal Highness having proceeded to Newfoundland, and thence to Nova Scotia and New Brunswick, he, after a short stay in these colonies, arrived in Charlottetown, in the ship *Hero*, on Thursday, the tenth of August, about twelve o'clock, m. On the *Hero* swinging to her anchors, the lieutenant governor, attended by Colonel Gray, stepped into a barge and proceeded on board the ship. After a short interval, his excellency returned, and intimated that the royal party would disembark in half an hour. The governor received His Royal Highness as he stepped on the pier, and, in the name of the colonists, welcomed him to the island. The governor then presented the mayor to the Prince, and the recorder and city council, collectively. A guard of honor, consisting of a detachment of the 62nd regiment, and a body of volunteers, lined the way from the landing place to the royal carriage, into which, amidst the cheers of the people, the Prince stepped, inviting the governor to occupy the vacant seat. The procession was then formed, headed by an escort of volunteer cavalry, commanded by Major Davies. Immediately in advance of the first carriage walked the mayor, supported by the recorder and the city treasurer, and after the carriages, the procession was composed of the judges, the executive council, the members of both branches of the legislature, the clergy, the public officers, the city councillors, the committee of management, the members of the bar and other gentlemen, the troops, and societies and associations. There were four triumphal arches through which the procession passed. These were erected at the public expense. On passing through Rochfort Square, the procession halted for a moment opposite a platform, on which were assembled upwards of a thousand children, neatly attired, and belonging to the sabbath schools. When the carriage of the Prince reached the platform, a thousand youthful voices united in singing the national anthem, when the emotion of the Prince was such that he actually shed tears.

At the door of Government House, His Royal Highness was received by Mrs. Dundas, and conducted to the drawing-room, where the members of the executive council were presented by the governor. Rain, which had threatened all day, now began to descend; but there was a pleasant interval in the afternoon, during which the Prince rode, taking the Saint Peter's and Malpeque roads, and returning in time for dinner, at half-past seven o'clock. There was a general illumination in the evening, the due effect of which was marred by heavy rain. But the following day was a splendid one. His Royal Highness, in the uniform of a colonel, held a levee in the forenoon, after which he inspected the volunteers, to the number of about four hundred and fifty men, in front of Government House. They were commanded by Major the Hon. T. H. Haviland, who was complimented on the appearance of the force. Major Davies' troop of cavalry also received its share of royal commendation.

His Royal Highness drove to the Colonial Building for the purpose of receiving the addresses of the executive council and of the corporation of the city. He was received by Mr. Palmer and the Mayor, at the entrance. Two large stands had been erected for the accommodation of ladies wishing to witness the interesting ceremony. The civic and executive addresses were respectively read by the Recorder and the Honorable Edward Palmer. We may be permitted to say that these addresses, in point of good taste and expression, were far above the average of such compositions. To these addresses the Prince made suitable replies. In the afternoon His Royal Highness took another ride into the country, making a brief halt at the farm of Mr. H. Longworth, whence he obtained an extensive view of Charlottetown and the harbor.

In the evening there was a ball in the Colonial Building, which was attended by a numerous and brilliant assemblage, and where His Royal Highness danced with much spirit, remaining till after three o'clock.

On Saturday the prince departed from the island, where he had produced a most favorable impression,—leaving one hundred and fifty pounds to be disposed of in charity, according to directions communicated to the lieutenant-governor and his lady.

On the sixteenth of June, 1860, the Duke of Newcastle addressed a despatch to the lieutenant-governor, expressing his sense of the promptitude and completeness with which the house of assembly had given its support to the plan devised in the hope of terminating the differences on the question of land, by which the island had been so long agitated, and intimating that a commission would be forwarded, under the royal sign manual, containing the appointment of the Honorable Joseph Howe, Mr. John Hamilton Gray, and Mr. John William Ritchie, as commissioners,—Mr. Howe being the representative of the tenants, Mr. Gray of the Crown, and Mr. Ritchie of the proprietors. The commissioners accordingly opened their court at the Colonial Building, on the fifth of September, 1860,—Mr. Gray presiding. There appeared at the court, as counsel for the government of the colony, on behalf of the tenantry, Mr. Samuel Thomson, of Saint John, N. B., and Mr. Joseph Hensley; and for the proprietors, Mr. R. G. Haliburton and Mr. Charles Palmer. Mr. Benjamin DesBrisay was appointed clerk to the commissioners. On the first day, the court was addressed by counsel representing the various interests, and on the succeeding days, a very large number of witnesses were examined, for the purpose of eliciting information for the guidance of the court in coming to a decision. After the evidence had been heard, the court was addressed by counsel.

The report of the commissioners was dated the eighteenth of July, 1861; and, as any history of the island would be incomplete without an outline of its contents, the writer will now proceed to give such outline, which, whilst it presents leading facts and arguments adduced, will not, it is hoped, be open to the charge of undue prolixity.

As we have, in the course of the narrative, given an incidental sketch of the history of the land question, we shall pass over that portion of the commissioners' report which is occupied with facts that have already been partially submitted, and to which we must again refer at a more advanced stage of the narrative, and give the substance of the remedies which the commissioners proposed for existing evils. The commissioners expressed the hope that they might be regarded as having entered upon the discharge of their duties, not only with a high appreciation of the honor conferred by their appointment, but also with a due sense of the grave responsibilities which they assumed. When they commenced their labors there was a general impression that the act of the provincial legislature, which made their award binding on all parties concerned, would receive the royal assent; and, although the decision of the colonial secretary—not to submit that act for Her Majesty's approval—somewhat relieved them from the weight of responsibility necessarily involved in the preparation and delivery of a judgment beyond appeal, they still felt that, as their award was to affect the titles of a million of acres, and the rights and interests of eighty thousand people, a hasty decision would not be a wise one, and that the materials for a judgment ought to be exhausted before the report was made.

By traversing the island and mixing freely with its people, the commissioners had become familiar with its great interests and general aspects. By holding an open court in all the shire towns, they had given to every man on the island, however poor, an opportunity to explain his grievances, if he had any. By bringing the proprietors and tenants face to face before an independent tribunal, mutual misunderstandings and exaggerated statements had been tested and explained, and the real condition of society and the evils of the leasehold system had been carefully contemplated from points of view not often reached by those whose interests were involved in the controversy. The evidence collected, though not under oath,—the commissioners not being vested with power to administer oaths,—was most valuable in aiding them to form a correct estimate of the evils of which the people complained.

The documentary history of the question extended over nearly a century of time, and was to be found in the journals of the Legislature, in the newspaper files of the colony, and in pamphlets more or less numerous. The amount of time and money wasted in public controversy no man could estimate; and the extent to which a vicious system of colonization had entered into the daily life of the people, and embittered their industrial and social relations, it was painful to record.

The commissioners felt that as the case of Prince Edward Island was exceptional, so must be the treatment. The application of the local government for a commission, and the large powers given to it by the Queen's authority, presupposed the necessity of a departure from the ordinary legal modes of settling disputes between landlords and tenants, which the experience of half a century had proved to be inadequate.

Finding that it was impossible to shut out of their inquiry, while on the island, the questions of escheat, quitrents, and fishery reserves,—the claims of the descendants of the original French inhabitants, Indians, and loyalists,—they thought it quite within the range of their obligations to express their opinions freely upon these branches of the general subject.

The question of escheat, though apparently withdrawn from the scope of their inquiry by despatches from the colonial office,—received long after the opening of the commission,—could not be put aside. The discussion of the question was forced upon them from the day the court opened until it closed. The commissioners, therefore, thought it comported with their duty to express the conclusions at which they had arrived.

In considering the best mode of quieting the disputes between the proprietors and their tenants, and of converting the leasehold into freehold tenures, the commissioners remarked that the granting of a whole colony in a single day, in huge blocks of twenty thousand acres each, was an improvident and unwise exercise of the prerogative of the Crown. There was no co-operation on the part of the proprietors in peopling the island. Each acted on his own responsibility, and while a few showed energy in the work, the great body of the grantees did nothing. The emigrants sent out by the few were disheartened by the surrounding wilderness owned by the many, who made no effort to reclaim it, or were tempted to roam about or disregard the terms of settlement by the quantity of wild land, with no visible owner to guard it from intrusion. By mutual co-operation and a common policy, the proprietors might have redeemed the grants of the imperial government from the charge of improvidence. The want of these indispensible elements of success laid the foundation of all the grievances which subsequently afflicted the colony.

The commissioners regarded the land purchase act as embodying the most simple and efficacious remedy for existing evils. Under that act the Worrell and Selkirk estates had been purchased,—covering about one hundred and forty thousand acres, by which signal advantages were secured, the proprietors being dispossessed by their own consent, the tenants being enabled to purchase their holdings and improvements, not necessarily at a price so high as to represent the rents stipulated to be paid, but at the lowest price which the expenses of management, added to the aggregate cost of the estate, would warrant; and the wild lands were at once rescued from the leasehold system, and were subjected to the wholesome control of the local government, to be hereafter disposed of in fee simple, at moderate prices, as they are in all the other North American provinces. The commissioners unanimously recommended the application to the whole island of the principles embodied in the land purchase act, under modifications which appeared to be essential to their more extended adoption.

With respect to escheat, the commissioners reported that there was no light in which the present escheat of the titles, on the ground of the conditions of the original grants having been broken, could be viewed, which would not exhibit consequences most disastrous to the island. They therefore reported that there should be no escheat of the original grants for non-performance of conditions as to settlement.

The commissioners recommended that the imperial parliament should guarantee a loan of one hundred thousand pounds, so that the money could be borrowed at a low rate of interest. With the command of such a fund, the government would be in a condition to enter the market, and to purchase, from time to time, such estates as could be obtained at reasonable prices. They did not doubt that many of the proprietors would be glad to sell, and the competition for the funds at the disposal of the government would so adjust the prices that judicious purchases could be made without any arbitrary proceedings or compulsory interference with private rights. The commissioners felt that it might be beyond their duty to make such a suggestion, but they hoped Her Majesty's government would regard the case of Prince Edward Island as exceptional, its grievances having sprung from the injudicious mode in which its lands were originally given away.

Assuming that the imperial parliament guaranteed a loan, there remained to be considered the nature of the security which would be offered. Although it was not improbable that doubts might have arisen as to the ability of the colony to repay so large an amount, a glance at its financial position would show that the required relief might be given without the risk of any loss to the mother country. The commissioners showed that the revenue of the island had increased from seventeen thousand pounds in 1839, to forty-one thousand in 1859,—more than doubling itself in twenty years. It seemed apparent, therefore, that without disturbing the tariff or reducing the ordinary appropriations, in five years the natural increase of population, trade, and consumption would give six thousand pounds a year, or a sum sufficient to pay the interest on a hundred thousand pounds, at six per cent. As it was not improbable that five years would be required to purchase the estates, and expend the loan to advantage, it might happen that the revenue would increase as fast as the interest was required, without any increase in the tariff, or diminution of the appropriations. But it might be reasonably assumed, when a new spirit was breathed into the island, and its population turned to the business of life, with new hopes and entire confidence in the future, that trade would be more active, and the condition of the people improve. The very operation of the loan act might therefore supply all the revenue required to meet the difference; but if it should not, an addition of two and a half per cent, upon the imports of the island, or a reduction of the road vote for two or three years, would yield the balance that might be required.

In making their calculations, no reference was made to the fund which would be at once available from the payment of their instalments by the tenants who purchased. Two thousand five hundred pounds had been paid by the tenants on the Selkirk estate in the first year after it was purchased. Guided by the experience thus gained of the disposition and of the resources of the tenantry, it was deemed by the commissioners fair to conclude that if such a sum could be promptly realized from sales of land, admitted to be among the poorest in the island, the local government might fairly count upon the command of such an increase, from the re-sale of the estates they might purchase, as would enable them to keep faith with the public creditor, without any risk of embarrassment.

In considering the remedies to be applied, three conclusions forced themselves on the commissioners: that the original grants were improvident and ought never to have been sanctioned; that all the grants were liable to forfeiture for breach of the conditions with respect to settlement, and might have been justly escheated; and that all the grants might have been practically annulled by the enforcement of quitrents, and the lands seized and sold by the Crown, at various times, without the slightest impeachment of its honor. But whilst this opinion was firmly held, still, the Sovereign having repeatedly confirmed the original grants, it was impossible to treat the grantees in any other manner than as the lawful possessors of the soil.

Assuming, then, the sufficiency of the original grants, and the binding authority of the leases, the commissioners were clearly of opinion that the leasehold tenure should be converted into freehold. It was, they said, equally the interest of the imperial and local governments that this should be done, that agrarian questions should be swept from the field of controversy, that Her Majesty's ministers might be no longer assailed by remonstrance and complaint, and that the public men in the island might turn their attention to the development of its resources.

Assuming, therefore, that a compulsory compromise was inevitable, the question arose: upon what terms should the proprietors be compelled to sell, and the tenants be at liberty to purchase?

In answer to this important question, the commissioners awarded that tenants who tendered twenty years' purchase to their landlords, in cash, should be entitled to a discount of ten percent., and a deed conveying the fee-simple of their farms. Where the tenant preferred to pay by instalments, he should have that privilege; but the landlord would not be bound to accept a less sum than ten pounds at any time; nor should the tenant have a longer time than ten years to liquidate the debt. The tenants whose lands were not worth twenty years' purchase, and who therefore declined to pay that amount, might tender to their landlords what they considered the value of their farms. If the landlord declined to accept the amount offered, the value should be adjusted by arbitration. If the sum tendered was increased by the award, the tenant was to pay the expenses; if it was not, they should be paid by the landlord. It was provided that the rent should be reduced in proportion to the instalments paid; but no credit should be given for any such instalments until the three years arrears allowed by the commissioners' award were paid, nor while any rent accruing after the adjustment of the value of the farm remained due. Proprietors who held not more than fifteen thousand acres, or such as desired to hold particular lands to that extent, were not to be compelled to part with such lands under the award. Leases under a term of less than forty years were not affected by the award.

With regard to arrears of rent due, it was awarded by the commissioners that a release of all arrears, beyond those which had accrued during the three years preceding the first of May, would be for the benefit of both landlords and tenants.

With regard to the case of the descendants of the loyalists who sought homes in Prince Edward Island after the confiscation of their properties in the old revolted colonies, the commissioners considered that they had claims on the local government. His Majesty's government, in 1783, felt the full force of the claims of their ancestors, and was sincere in its desire to make a liberal provision for them; but the rights which they had then acquired, when the proprietors had engaged to make certain grants of land for their benefit, were, unfortunately, not enforced. The commissioners recommended that the local government should make free grants to such as could prove that their fathers had been lured to the island under promises which had never been fulfiled.

With regard to the claims of the descendants of the original French inhabitants, the commissioners, with every desire to take a generous view of the sufferings of persons whose only crime was adherence to the weaker side in a great national struggle, could not, after the lapse of a century, rescue them from the ordinary penalties incident to a state of war.

The Indian claims were limited to Lennox Island, and to grass lands around it; and as it appeared by evidence that the Indians had been in uninterrupted occupancy of the property for more than half a century, and had built a chapel and several houses on the island, the commissioners were of opinion that their title should be confirmed, and that this very small portion of the wide territory their forefathers formerly owned should be left in the undisturbed possession of this last remnant of the race.

The commissioners closed their report by expressing their conviction that, should the general principles propounded be accepted in the spirit by which they were animated, and followed by practical legislation, the colony would start forward with renewed energy, dating a new era from the year 1861. In such an event, the British government would have nobly atoned for any errors in its past policy, the legislature would no longer be distracted with efforts to close the courts upon proprietors, or to tamper with the currency of the island; the cry of tenant-rights would cease to disguise the want of practical statesmanship, or to over-awe the local administration; men who had hated and disturbed each other would be reconciled, and pursue their common interests in mutual co-operation; roads would be levelled, breakwaters built, the river-beds dredged, new fertilizers applied to a soil annually drained of its vitality; emigration would cease, and population attracted to the wild lands would enter upon their cultivation, unembarrassed by the causes which perplexed the early settlers. Weighed down by the burden of the investigation, the commissioners had sometimes felt doubtful of any beneficial results; but they now, at the close of their labors, indulged the hope that, if their suggestions were adopted, enfranchised and disenthralled from the poisoned garments that enfolded her, Prince Edward Island would yet become the Barbadoes of the Saint Lawrence.

Our limits will not admit of a more extended account of the commissioners' report, which constitutes a most important portion of the annals of the island. We hope we have succeeded in giving the kernel of it. It is impossible for any candid person to rise from the perusal of the document, as well as of the voluminous body of facts and evidence on which it is based, without the conviction that the work was committed to men whose experience and acquirements eminently fitted them for the onerous duty entrusted to them, and without feeling that they were inspired with the desire to do justice to all the interests involved. They condemned—and most justly—the imperial government, which had originally granted the land in such enormous quantity to each grantee, on the ground of public services, the merits of which it was most difficult for the commissioners to estimate. To say the truth, in the case of many of the grantees, it would require a microscope of no ordinary power to detect their existence. The conditions attached to the grants were deliberately disregarded by the bulk of the proprietors, who, up to the time the commission was appointed, continued to wield an amount of influence in the councils of successive Sovereigns, which successfully frustrated every effort made by the people to obtain justice. The emigrants who left their native land were under the impression that they were to be conducted to a country where they might speedily attain, by moderate industry, to independence; where advantages were to be obtained which could not be got in other portions of the vast continent of America. In four years from the date of the original grants a third of the land was to be actually settled; within ten years there was to be a settler to every hundred acres of land; as evidence that there was to be no lack of protestant clergymen, one hundred acres were allotted for a church and glebe; and as a guaranty that the schoolmaster would be found at home, thirty acres were allotted to him in this prospectively populous and happy island. The honor of the British government was committed as a guaranty for the realization of these brilliant promises. But during the first ten years the terms, as to population, were complied with in ten townships only, nine being partially settled, and forty-eight utterly neglected. The proprietors, knowing that they could get the British government to do what they pleased, petitioned, in the year after the grants were made, for a separate government, and the expense was to be met by the quitrents, which, however, they took good care not to pay; and as a reward for the concession of a separate government, Britain had to pay for the maintenance of the civil establishment of the island. Thirty years after the grants were made, the assembly passed resolutions which set forth clearly the extent to which the obligations under which the proprietors had come were disregarded, and petitioned that they might be compelled to fulfil the conditions on which they had obtained the land, or that it should be escheated and granted in small tracts to actual settlers. In shameful violation of the principles of national honor and justice, the representations of the people, through their representatives, were disregarded, in consequence of the influence brought to bear, by the grantees, on a weak and incompetent government; and thus there was on the part of Britain a flagrant breach of faith with the immigrants who had been tempted to leave their native country, trusting to guarantees the violation of which was never suspected. The people of the island continued for ninety years to protest against the injury under which they suffered, till at last a commission was appointed. Credit must be given to the commissioners for the thoroughness of their investigation, for the reliability of their facts, and for the impartiality and general soundness of their awards. Yet the report seems to lack necessary pungency and power in dealing with the iniquity of successive governments in failing to make compensation to the island immigrants and their successors for injuries persistently inflicted, and borne with a degree of patience that excites our wonder. Instead, however, of such injuries generating sympathy or admiration, leading to a rectification of admitted evils, the only result was a flow of official twaddle about the sacred rights of property, and the duty of obedience to imperial edicts relating to the soil,—edicts of which any civilized country might well be ashamed, and to which no parallel can be found in the voluminous annals of the colonial possessions of an empire on which the sun never sets. While immigrants to other portions of America obtained good land in fee-simple for the merest trifle, and were working their way to competence and independence, the farmers of Prince Edward Island, weighed down by rent, were doomed to clear the forest and improve the land, finding themselves in many cases, in their old age, no richer than on their arrival in the country, with no prospect before their families but hard work, and with no hope of a permanent or adequate return. Happily, the fearful difficulties encountered by the early settlers do not exist—at least in the same degree—now; and by dint of economy, hard work, and self-denial, not a few have attained to comparative comfort and independence. The commissioners say: "the grievances of the island have sprung from the injudicious mode in which the lands were originally given away." That is only half the truth. The Crown had the abstract right to grant the land in blocks of twenty thousand acres each; but the Crown had not the right, after the conditions on which the land had been allotted were published, and its good faith had been committed to the fulfilment of these conditions by the owners on pain of forfeiture, to permit their violation without the infliction of the penalty. Thousands, on the faith of these conditions being honestly implemented, had staked their prospects in life. The original immigrants would not have come to Prince Edward Island as tenants while they might have obtained free land elsewhere, unless compensatory advantages had been offered. These advantages were implied in the conditions of settlement attached to the grants. When, therefore, the British government permitted the violation of the contract, they broke faith with the immigrants, and became morally and constitutionally responsible for the consequences of such violation. The remedy was in the hands of the Crown. The original proprietors having failed to keep their engagements, the clear and honest duty of the Crown was to declare the land of such proprietors escheated, and, as compensation to the emigrants, to make moderate free grants to them of a portion of it. Instead of adopting this manly and honest course, the Crown ignored the injury inflicted on the tenants, and allowed the proprietors to retain their land in a wilderness state, thus causing long-continued misery and bitterness in the island, and almost permanently obscuring the lustre of one of the brightest gems in the

British colonial diadem. The charge of indifference to the just complaints of the people cannot be brought against the successive local legislatures and governments of the island. Law after law was enacted, and petition after petition was laid at the foot of the throne. The people met in masses and prayed for relief. Verily, there was no lack of importunity; but the official ear—always open to the complaints and representations of many landholders and their satellites, who were ever sensitive to the imaginary rights, but totally oblivious of the real duties of property—was conveniently deaf to the groans of an oppressed people. Year after year passed without any effectual remedy being applied, and the original proprietors either died or transferred their property to others; and for a long period, before the appointment of the commission, the answer to all applications to the colonial office for escheat was the melancholy chant of *too late! too late!* Father Time and his progeny proscription now presented barriers which were deemed insuperable. Every successive minister for the colonies became expert at counting on his fingers the number of years that had elapsed since the British government broke faith with the people of Prince Edward Island, and re-echoed the chant, "Too late! too late!" It must be conceded that, after the lapse of so long a period, it was impossible, without positive injury to proprietors who were in no way responsible for existing evils, to escheat the land, and the views taken by the commissioners on this point must commend themselves to every unprejudiced mind; but, admitting all this, the question occurs, was it too late *to fix blame in the proper quarter*, and to repair the damage sustained by the island? Certainly not. We think it must be regarded as a radical defect in the report of the commissioners that no pointed answer was given to that question. It was unfortunately too late to make compensation to those who first came to the country on the faith of imperial pledges which were not redeemed, and who, after a life of toil, had passed the bourne whence no traveller returns, leaving an inheritance of difficulty and trouble to their sons and daughters; but it was not too late to make honorable compensation to the latter, and, at the same time, justice to the present owners of the soil, by buying the land with money out of the public treasury of the mother country, and giving it to those whose just claims had been so long criminally disregarded. Whilst in the plainest terms the commissioners admitted that the island grievances sprung from the injudicious mode in which the lands were originally given away, they did not press for due compensation being made by the country whose rulers had produced these grievances, but recommended that the imperial government should guarantee a loan for the purchase of the land of one hundred thousand pounds, on the production, by the island authorities, of most satisfactory security for the payment of principal and interest. In plain English, the aggrieved parties were made practically responsible for oppression in the production of which they had no hand, and for which, therefore, they could in no legitimate sense be held responsible. On the assumption that the British government were not accountable, the award of the commissioners was admirable; but, assuming their responsibility, the cost of rectification was recommended to be borne by the wrong parties.

Let it not be for a moment supposed that it is intended by these remarks to foster discontent in the island, to weaken the bonds which unite it to the old country, or to generate a spirit of disloyalty to the Crown or dissatisfaction towards good landlords. Were the writer inspired by so criminal a desire, his efforts would fail in the production of any such consequences. The people have learned to put no confidence either in governments or princes; but, under Almighty favor, by economy, temperance, and hard work, to trust to their own efforts in sweeping from the island the remnants of a pernicious system, and of attaining that measure of independence and prosperity to which such formidable obstacles have been presented, but the ultimate realization of which the capabilities of the island warrant. Since the island became British property, not a petition or complaint has been laid at the foot of the throne which has not breathed the most devoted loyalty; and the people, under trials which might have tested the patience of Job, have borne them with a degree of meekness and patience to which few parallels can be produced; and at this moment the beloved Queen of Great Britain has not more sturdy, faithful, and resolute defenders of her throne and person than the inhabitants of Prince Edward Island. Loyalty must be indigenous to a soil where, under such adverse conditions, it has taken such deep root and flourishes.

In the very year when the commissioners were prosecuting their inquiries, Prince Edward Island responded to the call for a defensive force by organizing twenty companies of volunteers, mustering upwards of a thousand men, showing a degree of loyalty, zeal, and energy in that direction inferior to no other portion of the Queen's dominions.

A general census of the island was taken in 1861. The population was then—as certified in the most accurate returns—eighty thousand eight hundred and fifty-six, including three hundred and fifteen Indians. The churches numbered one hundred and fifty-six; schoolhouses, three hundred and two; and public teachers, two hundred and eighty. There were eighty-nine fishing establishments on the island, which produced twenty-two thousand barrels of herrings and gasperaux, seven thousand barrels of mackerel, thirty-nine thousand quintals of codfish, and seventeen thousand gallons of fish-oils. There were one hundred and forty-one grist-mills, one hundred and seventy-six saw-mills, and forty-six carding-mills; fifty-five tanneries, manufacturing one hundred and forty-three thousands pounds of leather.

The executive government having, in 1861, appointed commissioners to superintend the collection of products and manufactures of the island for the London exhibition of 1862, the duty was judiciously performed, and the articles forwarded to the exhibition under the charge of Mr. Henry Haszard, the secretary to the commissioners.

A profound sensation was caused in the island by intelligence of the seizure of Messrs. Mason and Slidell, civil servants of the Southern States, when under the protection of the English flag, on their passage from Havana to England on board the steamship *Trent*. A remonstrance was forwarded by the British government to that of the Northern States; and the act of the commander of the *San Jacinto*—the American vessel by which the outrage was committed—having been disapproved of by the American government, the Southern commissioners were set at liberty, and the dispute happily terminated.

On the eighth of January, 1862, intelligence of the death of His Royal Highness Prince Albert reached the island. He died at Windsor Castle on the fourteenth of December, 1861, in the forty-second year of his age. Official intimation of his death was communicated to the lieutenant-governor by the Duke of Newcastle, and His Excellency ordered that forty-two minute-guns should be fired from Saint George's Battery at twelve o'clock, noon; and Her Majesty's faithful subjects were enjoined to put themselves into mourning. The life of the departed Prince was one of singular purity and usefulness, and his memory will forever stand honorably associated with that of Queen Victoria, than whom a more virtuous and beloved Sovereign never swayed a British sceptre. An address of condolence to Her Majesty was adopted by the legislature.

In answer to a despatch from the governor to the colonial secretary, requesting that he should be favored with a copy of the land commissioners' report, His Excellency received a despatch from the Duke of Newcastle, dated the seventh of February, 1862, accompanied by a copy of the report, which was anxiously desired by the people. His Grace said that he was desirous of expressing his appreciation of the painstaking, able, and impartial report which the commissioners had furnished,—a report which would derive additional weight from its unanimity, and which was the result of an investigation so complete that it had exhausted the material for inquiry into the facts of the case. The difficulties that remained were those which were inherent in the subject, and which had, for a long course of years, baffled every attempt at solution. His Grace, at the same time, held out no hope—for reasons which he did not state—that the loan of one hundred thousand pounds, in order to buy the estates of Prince Edward Island from their present owners, would be guaranteed. Mr. Labouchere, the colonial minister, suggested such a loan in 1855, and it was warmly advocated by Lord Stanley in 1858, when he held that office; and the people of the island had fair ground for additional complaint against the home government, when that government did not condescend even to state manfully the reasons for such a point-blank refusal, more especially as the commissioners had advocated *most earnestly* the imperial guaranty of such a loan,—such recommendation being one of the cardinal points in their award. The duke further intimated in the despatch that there appeared to be insuperable objections to that multiplicity of separate land arbitrations which would be the effect of the alternative measure alluded to in the commissioners' report. Shorn of the vital portions of the award, which were thus politely ignored, the report was divested, to a large extent, of its immediate practical value; and the official compliment paid to the commissioners was but very poor compensation for the rejection of incomparably the most important portions of an award which had been arrived at after a painstaking and complete investigation, in the conduct of which was enlisted an amount of patience, impartiality, discrimination, and ability which it would be difficult to match. The secret of the mild manner in which imperial delinquencies, in the treatment of Prince Edward Island, were touched upon in this production may probably be found in a due appreciation by the commissioners of governmental sensitiveness on the point, producing the conviction that to ask for more than would probably be granted would injure—rather than promote—just claims to compensation.

The assembly met in February, and adopted a resolution, by a vote of twenty-three to six, pledging itself to introduce a measure to confirm the award of the commissioners in all its provisions. The action of the assembly in thus, without hesitation, honorably abiding by the award of the commissioners, without cavil or complaint, was highly creditable to its character; but the award did not meet with the same degree of approval at the hands of the landowners who were parties to the appointment of the commission. The Duke of Newcastle addressed a despatch to the governor, dated the fifth of April, 1862, enclosing a draft bill, drawn up by the proprietors, for settling the differences between landlords and tenants on certain townships, in the preamble of which it was stated that the commissioners, in providing that the value of land should be ascertained by arbitrators, to be appointed by the landlords and tenants, exceeded the authority intended to be given to them by the assembly and the proprietors, and if their suggestion were adopted, disputes and litigation between the landlords and tenants would ensue. Thus these gentlemen completely ignored the award of the commissioners, and proposed to substitute a remedy of their own. In thus acting, they had the support of the colonial secretary, for although, in the despatch by which the draft bill was accompanied his Grace did not express positive approval of the landowners' proposals, he, nevertheless, stated that it would give him great pleasure if Sir Samuel Cunard's anticipations as a proprietor were realized in reference to the bill.

Two acts had been promptly passed by the assembly on the land question,—one to give effect to the report of the commissioners, and another to facilitate the operation of the award in cases of anticipated difficulty; and the local government framed a minute in which they affirmed, in reference to the landlords' proposed bill, that they could not believe that the legislature would sanction any measure bearing on the land question which might differ essentially from the principles embodied in the commissioners' report. They asserted that the assembly deemed the government pledged to carry out the award of the commission, and they denied that the charge preferred in the preamble of the proprietors' bill, that the commissioners had exceeded their commission, could be substantiated. From the language of the commission, the government argued that the powers conferred upon them were unlimited,—amply sufficient to empower them to define any mode of settlement of a purely equitable character. By a passage contained in a despatch of the colonial secretary, he seemed to apprehend that the arbitration system prescribed by the commissioners would necessitate a multiplicity of separate local arbitrations, which would constitute insuperable objections against this mode of adjustment. The government, however, did not anticipate that many of these arbitrations would take place in the practical working of the system. In their opinion, two or three cases on a township would have the effect of establishing a scale of prices which would become a standard of value. The minute—a temperate and well-reasoned document—concluded with an expression of the hope that the bills passed by the house of assembly would receive the royal sanction. They reminded the colonial secretary that the differences which the commissioners were appointed to determine had, for half a century, exerted a most baneful influence upon the colony, and that the people hailed with much satisfaction the prospect of having them adjusted. Should anything occur to prevent such adjustment, the consequences would be of a very serious nature, and result in causing much anxiety to Her Majesty's ministers, and also to the local government.

To this minute, which was dated the twenty-second of July, 1862, the Duke of Newcastle replied in a despatch of the ninth of August, following. He expressed regret that he could not concur in the views of the government. The main questions which the commissioners were appointed to decide were: first, at what rate tenants ought to be allowed to acquire freehold interests in their property; and, next, what amount of arrears of rent should be remitted by the landlords. On the first and most important of these questions, the commissioners professed themselves unable to come to any conclusion, and, instead of deciding it, they recommended, virtually, that it should be decided by other arbitrators, to be hereafter nominated. This, however, he said, was not what they were charged to do: they were authorized by the proprietors to make an award themselves, but they were not authorized to transfer the duty of making that award to others. The trust confided to them was a personal one. The proprietors relied on the skill, knowledge, and fairness of the three gentlemen appointed in 1860; and they could not, therefore, be called upon, in deference to these gentlemen's opinion, to confide their interests even to arbitrators specially designated in the award, much less to persons whose very mode of appointment was undetermined by it. This objection might be waived by the proprietors, but it was not waived; and being insisted on, the colonial secretary said he was obliged to admit that it was conclusive, and he was bound further to say that it was, in his opinion, an objection founded, not on any technical rule of law, but on a sound and indisputable principle of justice,—the principle, namely, that a person who has voluntarily submitted his case to the decision of one man, cannot, therefore, be compelled, without his consent, to transfer it to the decision of another.

For these reasons, the colonial minister did not advise Her Majesty to sanction the two acts which had been forwarded, and which were, of course, intended to render the award obligatory on all who had consented to the reference. The report of the commissioners was therefore regarded by the home government simply as an expression of opinion which was not binding, and which ought not to be allowed to stand in the way of any other proposal which promised an amicable settlement of the question.

CHAPTER IX.

Bill to make the Legislative Council elective—Change of Government—Address to the Queen, craving to give effect to the Commissioners' Award—A Review of recent

Proceedings in regard to the Land Question—The Assembly willing to meet the views of Proprietors in regard to the appointment of Commissioners—The Assembly and the Commissioners right, and the Colonial Secretary wrong—The Reason-why given—The rejection of the Award unreasonable—Delegates sent to England on the Land Question—The Result.

The house of assembly met on the second of December, 1862, for the purpose of considering the present position of the land question, with a view to a speedy solution. In his opening speech, the lieutenant-governor stated that he had received a despatch from the colonial secretary, informing him that the royal assent had been given to an act (which had been introduced by the Honorable Mr. Haviland) to change the constitution of the legislative council, by rendering the same elective. This made it necessary to dissolve the house before it could enter on the special business for the transaction of which it had been convened. The new election would afford an opportunity to the people to express a decided opinion as to the award; and the issue was looked forward to with deep interest. The election resulted in a large majority approving of that document. The new house met early in March. The opening paragraph of the governor's speech referred to the marriage of His Royal Highness the Prince of Wales to the Princess Alexandra, of Denmark, which had been recently consummated. Reference was also made in the speech to the decision of the colonial secretary, that the commissioners on the land question had exceeded their powers in their report; but His Excellency expressed his conviction that the house would exert itself to find a satisfactory solution of the difficulties which had so long retarded the prosperity of the island.

On the governor's speech being read, Colonel Gray said that the members of the government having tendered their resignations, he had been commanded by His Excellency to form a new administration, and he accordingly announced the following names as comprising His Excellency's responsible advisers: John Hamilton Gray, president of the council; Edward Palmer, attorney general; James Yeo, John Longworth, James C. Pope, David Kaye, James McLean, Daniel Davies, and William Henry Pope, colonial secretary. Amongst the first business submitted to the house was an address to the Queen, in which the whole history of the appointment and proceedings of the commission was detailed, and praying that Her Majesty would cause it to be notified to the proprietors affected by the award that unless cause to the contrary should be shown before a judicial tribunal, to be appointed by Her Majesty, her sanction would be given to the bills passed to give effect to the award. That address was duly forwarded by the governor to the colonial secretary, and His Grace's decision in regard to its contents was given fully in a despatch, dated the eleventh of July, 1863. The duke observed that, as he was not aware of any method by which the question could be submitted to any court of justice, and as the council and assembly had not suggested any such method, he considered that the course most satisfactory to them would be that of ascertaining from the law officers of the Crown, first, whether the so-called award was, in itself, liable to any objection founded upon any principle of law or equity; and next, whether it was possible, by any proceeding in law or equity, to give effect to the wish of the Prince Edward Island legislature, by enabling the proprietors or tenants to show cause why Her Majesty's assent should or should not be given to the proposed bill for giving effect to the award of the commissioners. In their replies to the questions put, the law officers of the Crown, Sir William Atherton and Sir Roundell Palmer, said that they did not consider the term "award" applicable with any propriety to the report of the commissioners of inquiry. There was no reference or submission, properly so-called. The gentlemen who signed the letter to the duke, dated the thirteenth of February, 1860, were incompetent to bind the general body of proprietors of land in Prince Edward Island, and had not attempted or professed to do so. *And on the other hand, it was clear that they did not propose or intend by that letter to bind themselves individually, unless the general body of proprietors would be also bound.* The writer has put some of the words of the law officers of the Crown in italics, in order that the reader may specially mark them as bearing upon subsequent remarks which he intends to offer. The law officers were further of opinion, upon the substance of the case, that the commissioners had not executed the authority which alone was proposed to be conferred upon them on the part of the landowners who signed the letter of the thirteenth February, 1860; and that a recommendation that the price to be paid by a tenant for the purchase of his land should be settled, in each particular instance in which the landlord and tenant might differ about the same, by arbitration, was not, either literally or substantially, within the scope of that authority. The law officers of the Crown thus fortified the position taken by the Duke of Newcastle and the proprietors, in reference to the award of the commissioners.

In coming to a just decision respecting the conflicting opinions which we have endeavored to present with precision and clearness, it is necessary to review the whole proceedings.

In the year 1858, Sir Edward Bulwer Lytton, secretary of state for the colonies, intimated to the lieutenant-governor of Prince Edward Island that the whole question of the land tenures was engaging his anxious attention, and that it would give him unfeigned pleasure to receive such suggestions for their amicable settlement as could be accepted by Her Majesty's government. In consequence of the expression of this wish, the house of assembly adopted certain resolutions praying for the appointment of a commission as offering in their judgment the best means for the satisfactory adjustment of existing disputes, intimating at the same time that, in the opinion of the house, the basis of such adjustment would be found in a large remission of arrears of rent, and in giving every tenant, holding under a long lease, the power to purchase his farm at a certain fixed rate. In the mean time a change took place in the imperial government, and the Duke of Newcastle became colonial secretary, who wrote in a despatch dated the sixth September, 1869, "that any prospect of a beneficial result from the labors of the commission would be nullified if its action were fettered by conditions such as the assembly proposed. I cannot," said his grace, "advise Her Majesty to entertain the question, unless it is fully understood that the commissioners are at liberty to propose *any measure* which they themselves may deem desirable." A copy of the memorial of the house was sent by order of the Duke to Sir Samuel Cunard, requesting him to call a meeting of landlords, for the purpose of ascertaining whether there were any concessions which they were willing to make, with a view to bring the questions in dispute to an amicable issue. To the letter of his grace, Sir Samuel and other proprietors replied, that they would readily acquiesce in any arrangement that might be practicable for the purpose of settling the various questions alluded to in the memorial of the house of assembly, but that they did not think the appointment of commissioners, in the manner proposed, would be the most desirable mode of procedure, as the labors of such commissioners would only terminate in a report which would not be binding on any of the parties interested, and they—the proprietors—proposed that three commissioners or referees should be appointed,—one to be named by Her Majesty, one by the house of assembly, and one by the proprietors,—and that they should have power to enter on all the inquiries that might be necessary, and to decide on the different questions that might be brought before them, giving, of course, to the parties interested, an opportunity of being heard.

The house of assembly, instead of throwing any obstacle in the way of the proposed arrangement, at once agreed to the suggestions of the colonial secretary and the proprietors, and to abide by the decision of the commissioners, or the majority of them, and pledged themselves to concur in whatever measures might be required to give validity to the decision,—naming the Honorable Joseph Howe as commissioner in behalf of the tenantry of the island.

The duke, as previously stated, expressed his satisfaction at the promptitude of the concurrence of the assembly in the suggestions offered, and the home government and the proprietors having named the other two commissioners, a commission was drawn up, dated the twenty-fifth day of June, 1860. The commissioners executed the task committed to them, and on the eighteenth of July, 1861, transmitted their report and award to the Duke of Newcastle, who complimented the commissioners on their ability and impartiality, but at the same time objected to some of the cardinal points of their award.

Whilst the proprietors objected to the award, and regarded it as not binding upon them, the house of assembly honorably adopted it in all its provisions. Then followed the opinion of the law officers of the Crown, which was emphatically favorable to the views of the colonial secretary and the proprietors.

It is, we think, impossible to review these proceedings carefully and impartially without coming to the conclusion that the colonial secretary, the proprietors, and the Crown lawyers were wrong, and the government and the legislature of Prince Edward Island right, in the view which they took of the powers and functions with which the commissioners were invested. There is a very strong presumption, it may be remarked, that the commissioners—three gentlemen of acknowledged ability and experience— could not have mistaken, so completely as the rejection of their award assumed, the nature of their duties; and during the course of the investigation there is not the shadow of a doubt that the almost universal opinion in the island was, that the coming award of the commissioners was to be held as a final settlement of the questions at issue, so far as the parties who deliberately appointed them were concerned. That such was the opinion of the proprietors, is proved by the most important and significant fact that, in the communication they addressed to the Duke of Newcastle on the thirteenth of February, 1860, they took exception to the appointment of a commissioner or commissioners in the manner proposed by the legislature, on the specific ground that the resulting decision "would not be binding on any of the parties interested"; and, in order to make the anticipated award positively binding, they proposed an alteration in the constitution of the proposed commission, which was unhesitatingly adopted. How, in the face of this fact, Sir William Atherton and Sir Roundell Palmer could come to the conclusion that the consenting proprietors did not intend, by the letter to which we have alluded, "to bind themselves, individually, unless the general body of proprietors would also be bound," seems incomprehensible. The proprietors who subscribed the letter were perfectly aware that unanimity amongst the proprietors could not at present be obtained. They did not complain of the absence of such unanimity, nor did they even insinuate that it would by them be regarded as a necessary condition of adherence to the anticipated decision of the commissioners. It is impossible that clear-headed men, sensitively alive to their own interests, could have a mental reservation to that effect, without giving it form and substance in so important a communication; nor can the monstrous notion, that whilst they insisted on the legislature being bound, they did not regard themselves as equally bound, be for a moment entertained. Is it credible that the esteemed gentleman, J. W. Ritchie (now Judge Ritchie), whom they entrusted in the reference as their representative, could have been left in ignorance on so important a point? But the words of the Duke of Newcastle are decisive on this point. In his despatch of the second January, 1861, to the lieutenant-governor, he says: "I trust you will impress upon the commissioners, if requisite, the necessity of avoiding, as far as possible, any steps calculated to excite unreasonable expectations, or to stimulate agitation; on the other hand, while assuring the proprietors that the award of the commissioners will not be enforced by Her Majesty's government *against any persons who have not, either personally or by their representatives, consented to refer their claims to arbitration,* I should wish you also to observe to them, that their refusal to concur frankly in a measure which was intended to compose existing differences, and which, so far as it has yet proceeded, has been assented to by a large portion of their body, may materially influence the conduct of Her Majesty's government if called upon to support them in any future disputes with their tenants." If his grace regarded the proprietors who had not concurred in the reference as not bound to abide by it, it surely must be conceded to be good logic that he must have believed the concurring proprietors as firmly bound, both in point of fact and law. But it remained for the learned law officers of the Crown to put a climax to their decision by broadly asserting "that there was no reference or submission, properly so called." Now, the most effectual answer that can be given to this statement is the very words of the royal commission, "Now, know ye, that we, taking the premises into our royal consideration, are graciously pleased to nominate and appoint, and do by these presents nominate and appoint our trusty and well-beloved John Hamilton Gray, Esquire, Joseph Howe, Esquire, and John William Ritchie, Esquire, to be our commissioners *for inquiring into the said differences, and for adjusting the same on fair and equitable principles.*" If that was not, in every legitimate sense, a reference and submission, the commission was a transparent farce, and the English language has ceased to convey definite ideas. How did the commissioners regard the matter? "Perhaps," said they in their report, "no three men in British America were ever called to arbitrate upon interests of the same magnitude, or questions of greater delicacy affecting the welfare of large numbers of people. If a judge or a juror, about to decide the title to a single estate, feels the responsibility of his position, the undersigned may be pardoned for admitting that, with hundreds of estates, and the interests of many thousands of persons dependent upon their adjudication, they have only been sustained by a very sincere desire to restore peace to a disturbed province." And what did all the legal gentlemen who, as counsel, represented before the commissioners the various interests involved, think of the powers with which they—the commissioners—were invested? Why, all their speeches assumed that they were addressing themselves to adjudicators who had ample authority to solve the questions in dispute. This was admitted by Sir Samuel Cunard, as representing his co-proprietors, *after* the award of the commissioners was given; for in writing the Duke of Newcastle, the law officers of the Crown represent him as saying "that the landlords were ready to be bound by the decision of the three commissioners, but that they were not prepared to hand over their interests to the proposed arbitrators, and to embark in the expense and dispute consequent on a multitude of petty arbitrations,"—referring to the arbitrators proposed by the commissioners to determine the value of every individual property, with a view to purchase by the tenant. Yet, in the face of such overwhelming evidence, the colonial secretary had the coolness to parade the opinion of the law officers of the Crown before the government, legislature, and people of Prince Edward Island, that there was no reference or award, properly so called, very prudently abstaining from any expression of *his own* opinion on the point.

The principle on which the Duke of Newcastle rejected the award was, that a man who agrees to refer his case to one tribunal cannot, therefore, be forced to submit it to another. The equity of that principle cannot be denied. What are the facts? The commissioners, unable to conduct an examination into all the cases, recommended that arbitrators, mutually chosen, should undertake the work. They laid down general principles, and left the details to be executed by others. According to his grace's determination, as expressed in his own words, "It was very desirable that the commissioners should go into the inquiry unfettered by any conditions such as the assembly wished to impose." The commissioners were enjoined by his grace "to devote their efforts to framing such *recommendations* as should be demanded by the equity of the case," and their conclusions "would possess double weight if, happily, they should be unanimous." Their recommendations and conclusions were adopted unanimously; yet, in the estimation of his grace they, after all, amounted to nothing more than an expression of opinion; for, said his grace, addressing the lieutenant-governor, "I must instruct you, therefore, however unwillingly, to treat the commissioners' award only as an expression of opinion, which, however valuable as such, cannot be made legally binding on the parties concerned." If it was simply the opinion of the able men appointed as commissioners that was required, it could have been probably obtained without the formalities of a royal commission, and unaccompanied by some of the solemnities of a judicial tribunal; and if these gentlemen had been aware that their investigations and decisions were to be so easily "put out of the way," it is certain they would never have condescended to undertake the work; nor would the government or the legislature of the island have gone through business which they thought possible to come, through no fault of theirs, to so comical a termination.

But, assuming that the commissioners had mistaken the nature of their functions in one or two particulars, on what ground could all their decisions be rejected? Because an error in judgment was committed in certain cases, was that any good reason for superciliously brushing aside the whole report, and divesting it of all binding authority? We must leave the reader to answer the question according to his judgment. Practically, the colonial secretary said to the commissioners, on the conclusion of their labors: You have conducted the investigation with ability and impartiality; you have presented a report which has exhausted all the facts necessary to a just decision; but you, at the same time, have completely mistaken the nature of your duties, and your award, if such it can be designated, is without any binding value, and must, therefore, be treated as simply your opinion, and nothing more.

On the case being submitted to Sir Hugh Cairns, for his opinion as to its legal aspects, he stated that the commissioners were invested with authority to inquire into all differences existing between landlords and their tenants, and to propose, as a remedy for the settlement of such differences, any measure which they might think desirable,—that in consequence of the unconstitutional course adopted by the colonial office in reference to the commission, there was no legal validity in any of the proceedings which had taken place. But he expressed, at the same time, the opinion that the proprietors who proposed the commission were not morally justified in repudiating the finding of the commission merely because there were certain other proprietors who did not become parties to the proceeding. Sir Hugh Cairns might have added, that the home government were, in honor, bound to sustain the award of the commissioners, and to give validity to the acts of the assembly.

Impressed with the conviction that the home government, notwithstanding its treatment of the commissioners' award, would be disposed to give effect to principles of settlement akin to those recommended by the commissioners, the island government resolved to send Messrs. Edward Palmer and W. H. Pope as delegates to England to submit fresh conditions, which might prove acceptable. In October, 1863, these gentlemen had an interview with the colonial secretary (the Duke of Newcastle), when the land question was discussed. The proposals of the delegates were subsequently embodied in a communication addressed to the colonial secretary, and dated the thirteenth of October. A copy of that communication was sent from the colonial office to Sir Samuel Cunard, with the view of having its contents submitted to the proprietors by that gentleman. On the fourteenth of November, the baronet sent to the Duke of Newcastle a reply, in which he presented, at considerable length, his own views of the points at issue. He contended at the outset that the granting of the land originally in large blocks was "an act of necessity,—that the grantees had all lost very heavily by accepting the grants, and that no individual at present on the island had been injured by that proceeding, but, on the contrary, the grants had been a fruitful source of profit to the present generation." This novel and intensely absurd proposition Sir Samuel proceeded to establish by reference to the taxation to which the proprietors were subjected, and the various measures which had been passed by the local legislature, and confirmed by the home government. Early in December following, Sir Samuel addressed another letter to the Duke of Newcastle, enclosing a bill which, he said, would be acceptable to the proprietors if adopted in its integrity. To the baronet's letters and bill, Mr. Pope replied, in an able and exhaustive communication, dated the eighteenth of December, which concluded in the following words: "I regret to say, that I cannot construe Sir Samuel Cunard's communication, on the subject of the proposals for the settlement of the land question, in any other sense than as indicative of unwillingness, on his part at least, to make any such reasonable concessions to the tenantry as would afford that relief which is essential, in order to secure the colony generally from those much-to-be-dreaded evils which necessarily result from wide-spread agrarian agitation."

The delegates returned to Prince Edward Island, and presented an elaborate report of their proceedings. No further attempt was made to settle the land question till, at the suggestion—as we are given to understand—of the proprietors, an act was introduced, in 1864, for settling the differences between landlord and tenant, and to enable tenants on certain townships to purchase the fee-simple of their farms at fifteen years' rent. This act passed, and was supplemented in the following year by another act to facilitate the working of the previous one,—authorising the government to provide a sum not exceeding fifty thousand pounds, in order to enable tenants to purchase their lands,—no leaseholder or tenant being entitled to aid beyond one half the purchase-money of his farm.

Here we must refer to an important mission on which the Honorable Joseph Hensley was sent by the island government to England, in the year 1867. He was authorized to raise a loan of money for the public services of the island; to apply to the various proprietors of township lands in Great Britain and Ireland, and ascertain the terms upon which they would be willing to sell their lands to the government; and also to submit the views of the executive council to the imperial government in relation to a demand for the payment of nearly five thousand pounds, sterling, made for the transport and maintenance of troops. This force had been demanded to suppress disturbances which occurred on the island in 1865, and which were the very natural result of that vicious system of land tenure, for the origin and continuance of which the imperial government was responsible. Mr. Hensley poured into the ear of the colonial secretary (the Duke of Buckingham) wholesome truths concerning the constant source of trouble, expense, and discontent the system had proved, and the extent to which the prosperity of the colony had been thereby retarded. The demand of the imperial government was consequently modified. With respect to the loan of fifty thousand pounds, sterling, which Mr. Hensley was empowered to arrange, he wisely deferred, for solid financial reasons, placing the application before the public, and otherwise executed his commission with discretion, diligence, and ability.

The confederation of the island with the Dominion having been effected, in a manner hereafter to be described, and according to stipulation under the terms of union,—eight hundred thousand dollars having been placed at the disposal of the island government for the settlement of a question which, through the disgraceful supineness of successive imperial governments, had been a perpetual source of strife and bitter contention for a nearly century,—the government of the island, as a forlorn hope, resolved to take further action in order to ensure a settlement of the question, by introducing the land purchase act of 1875, *which received the formal sanction* of the governor-general of the Dominion. This act provided that commissioners should be appointed to determine the value of the various estates whose sale, under the provisions of the act, was to be rendered compulsory. The lieutenant-governor of the island was to appoint one commissioner; the governor-general of the Dominion another; and a third was to be appointed by each of the proprietors whose land was to be valued. As we write, the commissioners are sitting, and the value of the lands is being irrevocably determined. The measure, though one of absolute necessity,—so far as the local government and the interest of the tenants are concerned,—must be regarded as the most unconstitutional act that ever received imperial sanction. It may be safely affirmed, that its parallel is not to be found in the British Statute Book. In its principle, it is antagonistic to the fundamental rights of property, as universally recognized in civilized states. The act, as a precedent, will, doubtless, be cast in the teeth of the owners of British property by our modern communists, the tendency of whose views finds the solemn sanction of law in this measure. It is unjust to the landlord, inasmuch as it compels him to sell his land even when he deems it his interest to retain it; and it is unjust to the tenant, as it necessitates his paying, if he be desirous of securing the fee-simple of the land, a comparatively high price. But it is an act of governmental necessity, as further delay would greatly enhance the value of landed property, and thus render the prospects of the tenant still more unsatisfactory. Far better, however, that millions of pounds sterling were devoted by Great Britain to the compensation of the landlords and tenants of Prince Edward Island, than that so pernicious an act should disgrace the British Colonial Statute Book.

CHAPTER X.

Mr. James C. Pope and the Railway—Assimilation of the Currency—Confederation—Conference in Charlottetown—Sketch of Edward Whelan and T. H. Haviland—Opposition to Confederation—Resolutions in the Assembly—Offer of Terms to J. C. Pope—Further Proceedings—The Question of Confederation Resumed—Delegations to Ottawa—Messrs. Haythorne and Laird—Messrs. Pope, Haviland, and Howlan—Final Settlement of the Question.

To the Honorable James C. Pope belongs the honor of being the first to take legislative action of a commendably energetic character, in order to secure to the island admirable facilities for intercommunication by means of a railway. On the third of April, in the session of 1871, that gentleman submitted a resolution to the house of assembly, which was seconded by the attorney-general, Hon. Mr. Brecken, to the effect that the trade and exports of the island having much increased during the past few years, it was found impossible, in the absence of stone or gravel, to keep the roads in an efficient state of repair. It was contended that the construction and efficient maintenance of a line of railway through the island would greatly facilitate its trade, develop its resources, enlarge its revenue, and open more frequent and easy communication with the neighboring provinces and the United States. It was, therefore, proposed to introduce a bill authorizing the government to undertake the construction of a railway, to extend from Cascumpec to Georgetown, touching at Summerside and Charlottetown, and also branches to Souris and Tignish, at a cost not exceeding five thousand pounds, currency, the mile, including all the necessary appliances suitable for a good railroad, provided that the contractors would accept in payment the debentures of Prince Edward Island. The Honorable Mr. Sinclair proposed an amendment condemnatory of this resolution, on the ground that a general election for both branches of the legislature had recently taken place; that the question of constructing a railway was not then properly before the country; and that two petitions were before the house against the proposed undertaking, and none in its favor. On a division, Mr. Pope's resolution was carried by seventeen to eleven votes. A committee, consisting of the Honorable Mr. Pope, the Honorable Mr. Howlan, the Honorable the Attorney General, the Honorable Mr. Perry, and Mr. Richards, was then appointed to prepare and bring in a bill in accordance with the resolution passed by the assembly. The bill was immediately presented, read a first time, and ordered to be read a second time on the following day. The bill was accordingly read a second time, and committed to a committee of the whole house,—Mr. Beer being chairman. On the main question being put, the measure was approved by eighteen to eleven votes. The report of the committee was then received, and the bill engrossed under the title of "An act to authorize the construction of a railway through Prince Edward Island." Thus, in two days from the time of its introduction, the bill received the sanction of the assembly; and it may be safely affirmed that few measures have ever been passed by the representatives of the people of greater importance, as bearing on the material interests of the island. It is only fair to state that it was mainly through the tact, energy, and determination of Mr. James C. Pope that the scheme was carried to successful completion.

During this session an act was also passed for assimilating the currency of the island to that of the Dominion of Canada, by the introduction of a decimal system of keeping the public accounts. The act did not disturb the existing value of the current coins, but simply declared what their value should be in relation to the new system.

The question of a union of the North American Provinces was not prominently before the people of Prince Edward Island until 1864. Ten years previously, the subject had been discussed in the parliament of Nova Scotia by the parties of which Howe and Johnston were the leaders, when the latter gentleman moved a resolution favorable to union. In 1857, two members of the government of Nova Scotia had an interview with Mr. Labouchere, the colonial secretary, on the subject, when he intimated that, in the event of concurrence on the part of all the provinces, the home government would be prepared to consider any measure, with a view to the consummation of union, which might be agreed upon. Mr. Galt, in 1858, when a member of the Canadian administration, was an advocate for the consideration of the question; and, subsequently, a correspondence with the home government on the subject was opened by the Canadian government. But the official action which resulted in the consummation of union was taken in the assembly of Nova Scotia in 1861, when the provincial secretary moved that the lieutenant-governor of the province should be respectfully requested to put himself in communication with the colonial secretary, the governor-general, and the lieutenant-governors of the other North American Provinces, in order to ascertain the policy of Her Majesty's government, and the sentiments of the other colonies, with a view to the consideration of the question. This resolution was unanimously adopted by the assembly, sent to the colonial office, and subsequently transmitted by the Duke of Newcastle to the governor-general, and to the lieutenant-governors of the several provinces. On the proceedings of the assembly, his grace remarked that if a union, either partial or complete, should hereafter be proposed, with the concurrence of all the provinces to be united, he was sure that the matter would be weighed in England by the public, by parliament, and by Her Majesty's government with no other feeling than an anxiety to discern and to promote any course which might be most conducive to the prosperity, the strength, and the harmony of all the British communities in North America.

The desire of the home government to see a union of the North American Provinces consummated, having been thus indicated, a discussion of the question took place in the legislature of Nova Scotia, New Brunswick, and Prince Edward Island, in the sessions of 1864, which resulted in the appointment, by these provinces, of delegates, to meet in Charlottetown. In the assembly of Prince Edward Island there was considerable opposition to the idea of a legislative union, but the following resolution was passed by a majority: "That His Excellency the Lieutenant Governor be authorised to appoint delegates—not to exceed five—to confer with delegates who may be appointed by the government of Nova Scotia and New Brunswick, for the purpose of discussing the expediency of a union of the three Provinces of Nova Scotia, New Brunswick, and Prince Edward Island under one government and legislature, the report of the said delegates to be laid before the legislature of the colony before any action shall be taken in regard to the proposed question."

In the year 1863 the two parties in the Canadian parliament were so equally balanced, that it was found impossible to conduct the business of the country with any degree of efficiency. The leading men of both parties accordingly agreed on a reconstruction, resolving with the concurrence of their supporters to unite, for the purpose of securing a confederation of all the British North American Provinces. The governor-general addressed a despatch to the lieutenant-governor of the maritime provinces, asking whether, at the coming conference at Charlottetown, a deputation from the Canadian Government would be received, in order to give the members of it an opportunity of expressing their views regarding the proposed union. An answer favorable to the proposal was returned. A deputation accordingly proceeded to Charlottetown. The whole of the delegates met on the first of September. Prince Edward Island being represented by the Honorables Colonel Gray, premier; Edward Palmer, attorney general; W. H. Pope, colonial secretary; George Coles, M. P. P., and A. A. Macdonald, M. L. C. The proceedings of the conference were not reported, but the late Mr. Whelan, in his published account of the proceedings, says "it was well understood that the proposal to unite the maritime provinces under one government and one legislature was deemed impracticable; but the opinion of the delegates was unanimous that a union upon a larger basis might be effected; and with the view of considering the feasibility of such a union in all its details, it was proposed by the Canadian ministers to hold a further conference at Quebec, with the consent of the governments of the lower provinces, and at such time as might be named by the governor-general. This arrangement was agreed to, and the conference suspended its deliberations."

Before leaving Charlottetown, the delegates were entertained at a sumptuous banquet, by the executive council and some of the prominent citizens of Charlottetown. The entertainment was given in the Provincial Building, on the evening of the eighth of September. Speeches were delivered by a number of gentlemen, among whom were Lieutenant-governor Dundas, Hon. John Longworth, Hon. T. H. Haviland, and Frederick de St. Croix Brecken, Esq.

From Charlottetown the delegates proceeded to Halifax, where they were similarly entertained. Fredericton was next visited, and in Saint John the festivities of Charlottetown and Halifax were repeated. On the tenth of October the conference at Quebec was opened. Prince Edward Island being represented by the Honorables Colonel Gray, Edward Palmer, W. H. Pope, George Coles, T. H. Haviland, Edward Whelan, and A. A. Macdonald, which terminated on the twenty-seventh of October. From Quebec the delegates proceeded to Montreal, where they were hospitably entertained. At a public banquet given at Montreal, the Honorable Colonel Gray introduced the Honorable Edward Whelan, requesting him to respond in behalf of Prince Edward Island, when he delivered a telling and eloquent speech. We can only spare space for the concluding sentences: "It will be the duty," said the speaker, "of the public men in each and every province, whose representatives are now in Canada, to educate the public mind up to their views. The task may be a tedious, difficult, and protracted one, but no great measure was ever accomplished, or worth much, unless surrounded with difficulties. Deferring reverently to the public opinion of his own province, he would cheerfully go amongst his people, and explaining it as well as he could, he would ask them to support a measure which he believed would enhance their prosperity. Few, and comparatively poor, as the people of Prince Edward Island may be now, its fertile fields and valleys are capable of supporting a population at least three times greater than it is at present. It was once designated the garden of the Saint Lawrence; and it was a valuable fishing station for Canada during the occupation of the French, under Montcalm. It still possesses all the qualities of a garden, and its rivers and bays still abound with fish. He desired that those great resources should become as well known now, and in the future, as they were in by-gone days; and regarding the advantages which modern improvements and institutions offered as auxiliaries to the natural resources of the colony, he was satisfied that she could not fail to become very prosperous and happy under the proposed confederation."

The Honorable T. H. Haviland—who now holds the office of colonial secretary—replied to the toast of our sister colonies. "He desired to draw attention to some peculiar facts connected with the present movement. They might recollect that this was not the first time that states had met together to organize a constitution; for in times gone by the states of Holland had met to resist the tyranny of the Spanish Government; and the old thirteen states of America had also assembled under the cannon's mouth, and the roar of artillery; but the peculiarity of this meeting was, that it was held in a time of peace, with the approbation, and he believed, with the sanction of Her Majesty; that the colonies might throw aside their swaddling clothes, to put on themselves the garb of manhood, and hand down to posterity the glorious privileges for which their ancestors contended from age to age in the old country, and which had been brought into these new countries under the protecting shadow of the flag that had braved a thousand years the battle and the breeze. Although Prince Edward Island had only eighty thousand inhabitants, principally engaged in agriculture, yet, small as it was, it did not come as a beggar to the conference doors. Its revenue was not certainly very great, but there was yet a surplus of about four thousand pounds sterling to the credit of the province, over and above the thirty-six thousand pounds it spent for the government last year. Thus it had not come as a pauper, but was honestly prepared to do something—all in its power—to organize, here in America, a constitutional monarchy, which should be able to spread those institutions in which there was the soul of liberty."

The delegates proceeded afterwards to Ottawa and Toronto, where similar festive gatherings took place. But business was not neglected, as appears from the report subsequently published, which embodied the conclusions at which the delegates had arrived as the basis of the proposed confederation.

The report sets out with the declaration that the best interests and present and future prosperity of British North America would be promoted by a federal union, under the Crown of Great Britain, provided such union could be effected on principles just to the several provinces. In the federation of the British North American provinces, the system of government best adapted under existing circumstances to protect the diversified interests of the several provinces, and secure efficiency, harmony, and permanency in the working of the union, would be a general government charged with matters of common interest to the whole country, and local governments for each of the Canadas, and for the provinces of Nova Scotia, New Brunswick, and Prince Edward Island, charged with the control of local matters in their respective sections,—provision being made for the admission into the union, on equitable terms, of Newfoundland, the North West Territory, British Columbia, and Vancouver. In framing a constitution for the general government, the conference, with a view to the perpetuation of the connection with the mother country, and to the promotion of the best interests of the people of these provinces, desired to follow the model of the British constitution, so far as circumstances would permit.

The proceedings of the conference were authenticated by the signatures of the delegates, and submitted by each delegation to its own government, and the chairman was authorised to submit a copy to the governor-general, for transmission to the secretary of state for the colonies. The governor-general (Lord Monck) lost no time in transmitting the resolutions adopted at Quebec to the imperial government, which were hailed with satisfaction by the government and press of Great Britain.

The Canadian legislature met in February, 1865, when the report of the convention was discussed in both branches of the legislature, and a resolution submitted to them, respectively, to the effect that an address should be presented to Her Majesty, praying that she might be pleased to cause a measure to be submitted to the imperial parliament for the purpose of uniting the colonies of Canada, Nova Scotia, New Brunswick, Newfoundland, and Prince Edward Island in one government, with provisions based on the resolutions passed at Quebec. After protracted discussion, the resolutions were passed by large majorities. The scheme did not meet with the same degree of favor in New Brunswick; for an election having taken place before the question was discussed in the house, a large majority was returned opposed to confederation.

In Prince Edward Island the scheme of confederation was not received with any degree of favor by the people generally. Indeed, popular hostility to union found expression not unfrequently at public meetings. Early in February, 1865, a large meeting was held in Temperance Hall, at which the Honorable W. H. Pope, the colonial secretary,—who was always a decided unionist,—spoke effectively for an hour in its favor; but he was energetically opposed by Mr. David Laird and the Honorable Mr. Coles, who were regarded as two of the most able and prominent opponents of confederation. On the tenth of February, two large meetings were convened simultaneously. At one of these the Honorable Thomas H. Haviland delivered a carefully prepared opening address of some hours' duration, in which he earnestly advocated union, of which he had always been a consistent supporter. He was followed by the Honorable Mr. Coles, Mr. Archibald McNeill, the Honorable George Beer, the Honorable D. Davies, and the Honorable Frederick Brecken,—the speeches of the two latter gentlemen being specially directed to an exposition of the deficiencies of the Quebec scheme as bearing on the interests of the island. [H] The other meeting was, at the outset, addressed by the Honorable Edward Palmer, who, according to the opinion of the anti-confederates, proved conclusively that confederation could not result in permanent benefit to Prince Edward Island. He was followed in stirring addresses by the Honorable Kenneth Henderson, the Honorable Joseph Hensley, and the Honorable J. Longworth. At this meeting the following resolution was proposed by Mr. Charles Palmer, and unanimously adopted: "That in the opinion of this meeting, the terms of union contained in the report of the Quebec conference—especially those laid down in the clauses relating to representation and finance—are not such as would be either liberal or just to Prince Edward Island, and that it is highly inexpedient that said report be adopted by our legislature."

The assembly was convened on the twenty-eighth of February, 1865, and on the twenty-fourth of March the colonial secretary (the Honorable W. H. Pope) moved a series of resolutions approving of the terms proposed at the conference held at Quebec. An amendment in opposition to their adoption was submitted by the Honorable James C. Pope, and on a vote being taken, only five members voted for confederation, while twenty-three were antagonistic to its consummation.

During the session of the following year (1866) the question was again introduced to the house by a message of His Excellency the Lieutenant-Governor, transmitting a despatch from Mr. Cardwell, the imperial colonial secretary, on the subject of a federation of the British North American Provinces, when a resolution, more hostile to union than the amendment already specified, was, on the motion of the Honorable J. C.

81

Pope, submitted to the house. It was moved, "That, even if a union of the continental provinces of British North America should have the effect of strengthening and binding more closely together those provinces, or advancing their material interests, this house cannot admit that a federal union of the North American Provinces and colonies, which would include Prince Edward Island, could ever be accomplished on terms that would prove advantageous to the interests and well-being of the people of this island, separated as it is, and must ever remain, from the neighboring provinces, by an immovable barrier of ice, for many months in the year; and this house deems it to be its sacred and imperative duty to declare and record its conviction, as it now does, that any federal union of the North American colonies that would embrace this island would be as hostile to the feelings and wishes, as it would be opposed to the best and most vital interests of its people." The Honorable James Duncan seconded this resolution. An amendment was proposed by the Honorable Edward Whelan, seconded by the solicitor general (the Honorable T. H. Haviland, now a senator of the Dominion), to the effect that there should be no vote passed by the legislature as to the confederation of the provinces until the people should be first afforded an opportunity of pronouncing their judgment on the question at a general election. Mr. Pope's motion was carried by twenty-one votes to seven for the amendment. An address to Her Majesty the Queen, based on the action of the assembly, was subsequently adopted by the assembly and forwarded for presentation at the foot of the throne.

In the autumn of 1866, Mr. J. C. Pope went to England, and an informal offer was made through him by the delegates from the other provinces, then in London settling the terms of confederation, to grant the island eight hundred thousand dollars, as indemnity for the loss of territorial revenue, and for the purchase of the proprietors' estates, on condition of the island entering the confederation. But the people were not at this time in a temper to entertain the proposition for a moment.

In the autumn of 1869, the island was visited by Sir John Young, the governor-general of British North America. He was accompanied by several of his ministers, who discussed informally, with members of the government, the subject of a union of the island with the Dominion of Canada. On the eighteenth of December, 1869, the governor-general transmitted to Sir Robert Hodgson, the administrator of the government of Prince Edward Island, a minute of the privy council of Canada, relating to the question of a political union of the island with the Dominion. That minute was based on a memorandum dated the eleventh of December, 1869, from Sir George Cartier and Messrs. Tilley and Kenny, who took part in the informal discussion just alluded to, and who now submitted, for the approval of their colleagues in the Dominion ministry, the conditions on which they thought the island should be admitted to the union. These conditions received the formal sanction of the Dominion government, and were duly forwarded to Sir Robert Hodgson, who submitted them to a committee of the executive council, who, on the seventh of January, 1870, adopted the following minute: "The committee having under consideration the report of a committee of the privy council of Canada, wherein certain proposals for a union of Prince Edward Island with the Dominion are set forth, resolve, that inasmuch as said terms do not comprise a full and immediate settlement of the land tenures and indemnity from the imperial government for loss of territorial revenues, the committee cannot recommend said terms to the consideration of their constituents and the public." This minute was signed by the Honorable R. P. Haythorne, the leader of the government (now a senator of the Dominion), and his colleagues. The government subsequently presented a more detailed statement of their objections to the basis of union. These documents were forwarded to Earl Granville, the colonial secretary; and, on the seventh of March, 1870, addressing his honor the administrator, he said: "It appears to me that the government of Prince Edward

Island will not act wisely if they allow themselves to be diverted from the practical consideration of their own real interests, for the sake of keeping alive a claim against the imperial government which, it is quite certain, will never be acknowledged."

The subject of union came again prominently before the assembly in the session of 1870, on taking into consideration the messages of his honor the administrator of the government, transmitting various despatches and papers. The Honorable Mr. Kelly reported that the committee recommended that the house should adopt a resolution to the effect that the people's representatives felt it to be their duty to oppose a union with the Dominion of Canada, and to express their opinion that the people of the island, while loyal in their attachment to the Crown and government of Great Britain, were, nevertheless, almost unanimously opposed to any change in the constitution of the colony,—which resolution was carried by nineteen to four votes.

The next movement of importance in reference to the question of union was taken by the government, of which the Honorable Mr. Haythorne was the leader, on the second of January, 1873, when the executive council adopted an important minute containing new propositions, with a view to the union of the island with the Dominion of Canada. It was stated in the minute, that if Canada would accord liberal terms of union, the government of Prince Edward Island would be prepared to advise an immediate dissolution of the house, in order to give the people an opportunity of deciding whether they would go into confederation, or submit to the taxation required for railway purposes. The document was forwarded to the governor-general and submitted to the privy council of the Dominion, who suggested that a deputation should be sent to Ottawa by the government of the island, for the purpose of holding a conference on the subject of the proposed union. The Honorable Mr. Haythorne and the Honorable David Laird were accordingly appointed as delegates, representing the interests of the island; but they were not authorised to pledge either the government or the colony to any proposition that might be made by the Dominion of Canada. The delegation had several interviews with a sub-committee of the council, when the various questions connected with the important subject were fully discussed; and a minute of the terms and conditions mutually agreed to was finally drawn up. On the twelfth of March the governor-general sent a telegraphic despatch, evidently for the purpose of confirming the report of Messrs. Haythorne and Laird, intimating his ministers' opinion,—in which he expressed his own concurrence,—that "no additional concession would have any chance of being accepted by the parliament of Canada."

On the seventh of March the lieutenant-governor dissolved the house of assembly; and on the twenty-seventh of April the new house met, when the lieutenant-governor, in his opening speech, said that papers relative to the proposed union of the island with the Dominion of Canada would be laid before the house. Having dissolved the house in order that this important question might be submitted to the people at the polls, he now invited the representatives of the people to bestow on the question their careful consideration, expressing the earnest hope of the imperial government, that the island would not lose this opportunity of union with her sister provinces.

On the twenty-eighth of April the question was vigorously discussed by Mr. J. C. Pope and Mr. Laird; and on the second day of May, Mr. A. C. McDonald reported, that the committee had come to a resolution to the effect that the terms and conditions proposed did not secure to the island a sum sufficient to defray the indispensable requirements of its local government; that the strong objections hitherto entertained by the people of the island to confederation having been much modified, and the present house of assembly, feeling anxious to meet the desire of the imperial government to unite under one government all the British possessions in America, was willing to merge the interests of the island with those of the Dominion on terms just and reasonable,—such as would not involve the people in direct local taxation for objects for which the ordinary revenue had hitherto enabled them to provide. The resolution further proposed to authorise the lieutenant-governor to appoint delegates to proceed to Ottawa to confer with the government of the Dominion on the subject.

To this resolution, the Honorable David Laird moved an amendment, which was seconded by the Honorable B. Davies, to the effect that the house should appoint a committee of seven to prepare an address to the Queen, praying Her Majesty in council to pass an order in council, in conformity with the one hundred and forty-sixth section of the British North America Act, uniting Prince Edward Island with the Dominion of Canada, on the terms and conditions approved of in the minute of the privy council of Canada, on the tenth of March, 1873. The question having been put, the original resolution was carried by sixteen to ten votes.

Messrs. James C. Pope, T. H. Haviland, and George W. Howlan having been appointed delegates by the lieutenant-governor, proceeded to Ottawa for the purpose of conferring with the Dominion government on the subject of the proposed union. On the seventh of May they had an interview with the governor-general on the subject of their mission, and immediately afterwards they attended a formal meeting of the privy council. A committee of the council, consisting of Sir John A. McDonald, the Honorables Messieurs Tilley, Tupper, and Langevin were then appointed to confer with the delegates, who had drawn up a memorandum which they submitted to the committee. In that memorandum the delegates proposed to accept, as the basis of union, the offer made in 1869 by the Dominion government, namely, two hundred and forty-one thousand dollars a year for revenue, provided the Dominion government would assume the cost of the railway, as well as that of the proposed branch to Port Hill. These terms were not acceptable to the committee of the privy council. A compromise was, however, ultimately effected, and on the fifteenth of May a memorandum, embodying terms mutually approved, was signed by the committee and the delegates.

The delegates returned immediately to Charlottetown, and the terms and conditions of the proposed union, which were substantially those procured by Messrs. Haythorne and Laird, as agreed to at Ottawa, were submitted to the house of assembly, then in session. The principal terms and conditions were the following: that the island should, on entering the union, be entitled to incur a debt equal to fifty dollars a head of its population, as shown by the census returns of 1871; that is to say, four millions seven hundred and one thousand and fifty dollars; that the island, not having incurred debts equal to the sum just mentioned, should be entitled to receive, by half-yearly payments in advance, from the general government, interest at the rate of five per cent. per annum on the difference, from time to time, between the actual amount of its indebtedness and the amount of indebtedness authorised; that, as the government of Prince Edward Island held no lands from the Crown, and consequently enjoyed no revenue from that source for the construction and maintenance of public works, the Dominion government should pay, by half-yearly instalments, in advance, to the government of Prince Edward Island, forty-five thousand dollars yearly, less five per cent. upon any sum not exceeding eight hundred thousand dollars, which the Dominion government might advance to the Prince Edward Island government for the purchase of land now held by the large proprietors; that, in consideration of the transfer to the parliament of Canada of the powers of taxation, the following sums should be paid yearly by Canada to Prince Edward Island, for the support of the government and legislature: that is to say, thirty thousand dollars, and an annual grant equal to eighty cents per head of its population, as shown by the census returns of 1871,—namely, ninety-four thousand and twenty-one,—both by half-yearly payments in advance,—such grant of eighty cents per head to be augmented in proportion to such increase of population of the island as might be shown by each decennial census, until the population amounted to four hundred thousand, at which rate such grant should thereafter remain,—it being understood that the next census should be taken in the year 1881. The Dominion likewise assumed all the charges for the following services: the salary of the lieutenant-governor, the salaries of the judges of the superior courts and of the district or county courts, the charges in respect to the department of customs, the postal department, the protection of the fisheries, the provision for the militia, the lighthouses, shipwrecked crews, quarantine, and marine Hospitals, the geological survey, and the penitentiary. The Dominion government also assumed the railway, which was then under contract. The main resolutions, on the motion of Mr. J. C. Pope, seconded by Mr. David Laird, were carried by twenty-seven votes to two. The house of assembly then unanimously agreed to an address to Her Majesty the Queen, praying that Her Majesty would be graciously pleased to unite Prince Edward Island with the Dominion of Canada on the terms and conditions contained in the said address. The legislative action necessary to consummate the union of Prince Edward Island with the Dominion of Canada being thus completed, its political destiny was united to that of the already confederated provinces on the first of July, 1873.

It may seem strange, to one unacquainted with the facts, that so great a change in public sentiment in regard to union should have been effected in so brief a period. The solution of the problem is to be found mainly in the circumstance, that the mercantile community was afraid of a monetary crisis, consequent on the liabilities of the island in connection with the railway, and that the only satisfactory way of getting out of the difficulty appeared to be the union of the island, on liberal terms, with the Dominion of Canada. Fidelity to historical accuracy constrains us to say that the final settlement of the terms was in no small measure attributable to the able manner in which Messrs. Haythorne and Laird acquitted themselves when delegates at Ottawa; and it must further be stated, to the credit of these gentlemen, that they rose, when occasion required, above party prejudice, and communicated their desire to the Dominion government that further concessions should, if possible, be granted to the new delegates, so that the union might be effected without delay. But it must not, at the same time, be forgotten that the government of which Mr. J. C. Pope was the leader obtained better terms than those conceded to the previous delegation, and that to them belongs the merit, in a great measure, of bringing the question to a final solution.

CHAPTER XI.

Biographical Sketches:—Bishop McEachern—Rev. Donald McDonald—Rev. Dr. Kier—Hon. T. H. Haviland—Hon. E. Whelan—Hon. James Yeo—Hon. George Coles—James D. Haszard.

Among the early settlers of the island, prominent alike because of his aptitude for his position and the dignity with which he filled it, is the venerable figure of Bishop McEachern. While yet in early boyhood, about the year 1775, he was sent by the Scottish Bishop, John McDonald, to the Scotch Ecclesiastical College at Valladolid, in Spain. Having finished his studies there, he was ordained priest, and returned to Scotland, where he worked as a missionary for five years, under the Right Reverend Bishop Alexander McDonald. He arrived on the island either in August or September of 1790, and took up his residence at Savage Harbor. The church at Scotchfort was then the only catholic church on the island, and missionary duties were discharged at the residences of individuals in different parts of the colony. He acted as road commissioner, and laid out all the roads in the eastern portion of King's County. His assistant in this duty was a Presbyterian clergyman,—the Reverend William Douglas. He was a man of such a stamp as sometimes we find, under severe difficulties, executing work so arduous that it seems only the language of truth to call his deeds heroic. He was, in his day, the only catholic priest on the island. His flock was widely scattered. Roads were few, and travelling, always difficult, was often attended with danger. But neither difficulty nor danger could daunt the zeal of the missionary. Now in his wagon, now in his boat or sleigh, he visited the remotest settlements. Everywhere he was welcomed, both by catholic and protestant. There are yet living protestants who received the waters of baptism from the hands of the good bishop. Among his catholic flock he was at once pastor and judge. He decided differences, he settled disputes, and his verdict was, in almost every case, gracefully acquiesced in. The kindness of his nature and his shrewd forethought fitted him admirably for the duties of a missionary among early settlers, struggling with the countless difficulties of a rigid climate and a new country. One little trait recorded of him gives us a glimpse of the thoughtful beneficence of his character. He was in the habit of hanging up buckets near the springs by the roadside, in order to enable travellers to water their horses on their journeys. The same benevolence permeated all his actions, and his hospitality was unbounded. In every settlement he had a fixed place, where he resided until he had performed his priestly duties among his flock. These duties must at one time have been very onerous, for he was bishop not only of Prince Edward Island, but also of New Brunswick. He was the second English-speaking catholic priest who came to the island.

Few names call up warmer feelings of respect than that of Bishop McEachern. Full of years and wearied out with labor, he died at his residence, near Saint Andrews. He was laid in the old chapel; but, a few years ago, the remains were removed to the new church, where they rest within the sanctuary.

The Reverend Donald McDonald died in 1867. He was born in Perthshire, Scotland, on the first of January, 1783; was educated at the University of Saint Andrews; and was ordained a minister of the Church of Scotland in 1816. He labored as a missionary in the Highlands until 1824, when he emigrated to Cape Breton. Here he preached two years. In 1826 he came to the island, and commenced his labors in the spirit of the true evangelist. To him, the toil of travelling over the country and ministering to the destitute was the highest pleasure. Multitudes flocked to hear him preach. In barns, dwelling-houses, schoolhouses, and in the open air he proclaimed his commission to eager hundreds. Here and there he organized his bands of workers and ordained elders. As years rolled on, his interest in his great work increased, and great success crowned his efforts. Spacious and elegant churches began to take the place of rude shanties. His people grew in numbers, in wealth, in respectability, and in love for their minister. To have him as a guest, or to drive him from one of his stations to another, was the highest honor.

His eloquence was of a high order. Before commencing his sermon he generally gave an introductory address, in which he would refer to the national, political, and religious questions of the day, and comment freely on them. His sermons were masterpieces of logical eloquence. He would begin in a rather low conversational tone; but, as he proceeded, his voice would become stronger. Then the whole man would preach,—tongue, countenance, eyes, feet, hands, body,—all would grow eloquent! The audience would unconsciously become magnetized, convicted, and swayed at the speaker's will. Some would cry aloud, some would fall prostrate in terror, while others would clap their hands, or drop down as if dead. Seldom has such pulpit power been witnessed since the preaching of Wesley, Whitfield, and Edward Irving.

But it must not be supposed that the abundance of Mr. McDonald's labors as a preacher prevented him from giving attention to study. Far from it. His intellect was too strong and too vigorous to rest. His pen was ever busy. He was profoundly read in philosophy. He was deeply versed in ancient and ecclesiastical history. He excelled in Biblical exegesis.

No superficial thinker was he. The pen of no one but a master could produce his treatises on "The Millennium," "Baptism," and "The Plan of Salvation." He greatly admired the Hebrew and Greek languages. The Psalms of David, Isaiah's Prophecies, and Solomon's Songs were his delight. He was a graceful writer of English verse, an excellent singer, and played well on the flute. He published several collections of his poems and hymns. In the later years of his life one of his hymns was always sung at every service, set to some wild strain of his native Scotland, such as "The Campbells are coming," or "The Banks and Braes o' Bonny Doon."

To say that Mr. McDonald was faultless, would be to say that he was more than human. To say that, as a great moral reformer, he had no enemies, would be to say that he was a toady and a time-server. He was a brave man. He had strong self-reliance, and still stronger faith in God. He attacked vices with giant blows. Woe to the opponent who crossed his pathway! He had rare conversational powers. His spirits were always good. He knew the circumstances of every family in his widely-scattered flock, and remembered the names of all the children. He had no certain dwelling-place, no certain stipend, and bestowed all he got on works of charity. He was rather below medium height, stout, and powerfully built. He was hale and vigorous-looking to the last. His dress, appearance, and manners always bespoke the cultured Christian gentleman. He was never married.

In 1861 his health began to fail rapidly. It was thought he would not recover. He wrote epistles to his congregations commending them to God. But he rallied, and was able, with varying strength, to labor six years longer. More than ever did his ministrations breathe the spirit of the Great Teacher. He was again brought low. He was at the house of Mr. McLeod, of Southport. He felt that his end was near,—that his life-work was over; and a great work it was. He had built fourteen churches; he had registered the baptism of two thousand two hundred children, and had baptized perhaps as many more not registered; he had married more people than any living clergyman; he had prayed beside thousands of deathbeds; he had a parish extending from Bedeque to Murray Harbor, and from Rustico to Belle Creek; and he had five thousand followers, more attached to their great spiritual leader than ever were Highland clansmen to their chief. But he was as humble as a child. To God he gave the glory for all. He retained his faculties, and was glad to see his old friends at his bedside. Many came from far and near to take their last farewell and receive the dying blessing of the venerable patriarch. He sank gradually, suffering no pain, and on Friday, the twenty-second of February, in the eighty-fifth year of his age and the fifty-first of his ministry, he breathed his last.

The place of interment was the Uigg Murray Harbor Road churchyard, eighteen miles distant from Charlottetown. The funeral was the largest ever witnessed in the colony. All classes united in paying the last tribute of respect to the honored dead. The cortege numbered over three hundred and fifty sleighs. As the great procession moved down through the country, at the roadsides and at the doors and windows of the houses might be seen old men weeping, and women and children sobbing as if they had lost a father; and in the presence of a vast assemblage, near the church where his eloquent voice had so often melted listening thousands, and where he had so often celebrated, at the yearly sacrament, the Saviour's death, the remains of the Reverend Donald McDonald were laid to rest. A costly monument marks the spot. [1]

Amongst the first-class representative ministers of the Presbyterian body in Prince Edward Island, we may safely place the Reverend Dr. Kier, who was born in the village of Bucklyvie, in the parish of Kippen, Scotland, in the year 1779. He was educated at Glasgow College, studied theology under Professor Bruce, of Whitburn, and was licensed by the associate or antiburgher Presbytery of Glasgow about the beginning of the year 1808, and, in the autumn of that year, arrived as a missionary on the island, under the auspices of the General Associate Synod in Scotland. In 1810, Dr. Kier settled in Princetown, having been ordained in June of that year. This was the first organized Presbyterian congregation on the island. The call to Dr. Kier was subscribed by sixty-four persons, embracing nearly all the heads of families and male adults of the Presbyterian population in Princetown Royalty, New London, Bedeque, and the west side of Richmond Bay; and when the jubilee of the venerable doctor was held, in 1858, only fourteen of the number who signed the call were living. There is not one of the old Presbyterian congregations on the island, whether then in connection with the Scottish Establishment, the Free Church, or the Presbyterian Church of Nova Scotia, which did not, to some extent, enjoy his missionary labors, or experience his fostering care in its infancy. In most of them, Dr. McGregor planted; but he watered, while others have reaped.

Dr. McCulloch having died in the year 1843, Dr. Kier was, at the meeting of Synod held in the following summer, chosen his successor as theological tutor. "We have sat under men of greater originality of thought," writes one who knew him well,—"men who impressed us more deeply with a sense of their intellectual power,—but we never sat under one who produced deeper impressions of moral goodness, nor one who, in the handling of the great themes of Christian doctrine, presented them more as great practical realities."

When the jubilee, to which we have already referred, took place, the whole country round poured forth a stream of carriages and horsemen. Tables for tea had been spread for four hundred and fifty guests, and these were filled four times, and part of them five times. It may be stated, as indicative of the estimation in which Dr. Kier was held, that it was calculated that three thousand persons were then present to do him well-earned honor. The address delivered by Dr. Kier on that occasion was as chaste and modest in expression as it was deeply interesting in matter, and his hearers little imagined that the venerable speaker, who then appeared in good health, was destined, in two months and two days, to rest from his labors. The memory of the just is blessed.

The Honorable Thomas Heath Haviland, Senior, was born at Cirencester, in the County of Gloucester, England, on the thirtieth of April, 1796. More than fifty years previous to his death, Mr. Haviland came to Charlottetown, and entered upon the duties of an office to which he had been appointed by the Prince Regent. In the year 1823—the last year of the administration of lieutenant-governor Smith—he was appointed a member of His Majesty's executive council. The soundness of his judgment, his prudence, moderation, and courtly manners at once gave him influence at the council board; and for upwards of a quarter of a century—from the days of Colonel Sir John Ready until the stormy times of Sir Henry Vere Huntley, which immediately preceded the introduction into the colony of responsible government—his influence was paramount. In 1824 he was appointed assistant judge of the supreme court. From 1830 until 1839 he held the office of treasurer, which, in this year, he resigned for the office of colonial secretary. In 1839 the legislative council was separated from the executive council, and, by the Queen, Mr. Haviland was appointed its first president. On the introduction of responsible government, in 1851, he retired from office, and shortly after, with his family, visited England. His attachment to the island induced him to return to it, after a comparatively short absence. At the time of his death he was Mayor of Charlottetown,—having been annually elected to that office from 1857. He was also president of the Bank of Prince Edward Island. During his long official career he discharged his public duties with ability and dignity.

In private life he was remarkable for his generous hospitality and urbanity, for his kindly disposition and the constancy of his friendship. He was ever ready to listen to all who sought his counsel or assistance, and very many were the recipients of both. Time appeared to have laid its hand gently upon him. He was never known to the world as an ailing man. His erect figure, firm step, and good spirits gave promise of a long continuance of life, when a sudden attack, indicating severe organic derangement, confined him to his room. After a few months of suffering, which he bore with decorous fortitude, and during which he exhibited the most thoughtful concern for those who were in immediate attendance upon him, as well as for the more intimate of his friends who were absent, he passed away on the morning of Tuesday, the eighteenth of June, 1867, at the age of seventy-two years and two months. "The fine old English gentleman," said the *Islander*, "the fond father, the wise and prudent counsellor, the useful and honored citizen has been laid in the grave, leaving a memory which will long be cherished and revered in *this* the land of his adoption."

At this time the Honorable Edward Whelan was the correspondent, in Charlottetown, of the *Montreal Gazette*. Though politically opposed to Mr. Haviland, he alluded, in a letter to the *Gazette*,—which was published on the fifth of July, 1867,—to the deceased gentleman in the following touching terms: "The vacancy in the mayoralty is caused by the demise of the Honorable T. H. Haviland. He was *the* representative man of the old conservative party. Without brilliant talents, his judgment was of the highest order; he filled every situation in the colony to which a colonist could aspire, short of the gubernatorial chair; his manners to friend and opponent were always the essence of dignity, urbanity, and courtesy; and, passing through much of the contention of political life, leaving his impress on our small society, by his many useful labors, he was singularly fortunate, by his kindly nature, in disarming all opponents of the shadow of rancorous hostility."

The Honorable Edward Whelan died at his residence, in Charlottetown, on the tenth of December, 1867, at the comparatively early age of forty-three. He was born in County Mayo, Ireland, in 1824, and received the rudiments of education in his native town. At an early age he emigrated to Halifax, Nova Scotia, where, shortly after his arrival, he entered the printing-office of the Honorable Joseph Howe, then a newspaper publisher in that city. Here he gave such proofs of that great facility for newspaper writing which distinguished him in after life that he was occasionally employed to write editorial articles for Mr. Howe's newspaper during the absence or illness of the latter. At the age of eighteen he came to Prince Edward Island, which was then ruled by parties who could scarcely be said to be amenable to public opinion. Mr. Whelan, ranging himself on the side of the people, threw the weight of his influence as a journalist into the struggle for popular rights.

In 1851, Mr. Whelan married Miss Mary Major Hughes, daughter of Mr. George A. Hughes, of Her Majesty's Commissariat Department at Halifax, by whom he had two daughters—who died some time previous to his own decease—and one son,—an excellent youth, who perished by a boat accident in Charlottetown harbor, on Dominion Day, in the current year.

Apart from Mr. Whelan's oratorical power,—in which he excelled,—the great lever of public opinion, so powerful throughout the British dominions, obeyed his masterly hand as often as any fair occasion arose to resort to its agency. His political opponents will acknowledge that he never abused the power of the press, and that he knew how to combine a singularly consistent political career with conciliatory manners. Edward Whelan's nature revolted from any mean or vindictive action. He neither bullied his opponents nor begged favors; he relied upon the strong innate love of justice of every intelligent mind; and, although he died comparatively young, he lived long enough to see, to a large extent, the results of his labors in the extension of civil liberty.

Mr. Whelan was a Roman catholic. The writer of a sketch of his life, which appeared in the *Examiner*, says that "his words and thoughts, in the hour of death, were those of a Christian gentleman." The author of this work had the pleasure, in the autumn of 1867, of having an interview of several hours' duration with the deceased gentleman, during which topics connected with general literature were freely discussed, and he parted with him retaining a high opinion of his literary ability, as well as of the extent of his knowledge.

At Port Hill, on the twenty-fifth of August, 1868, died the Honorable James Yeo, in the eightieth year of his age. The deceased gentleman was a native of Devonshire, England, and was born in the year 1788. He emigrated to Prince Edward Island about fifty years previous to his death. He, consequently, was then about thirty years of age. On his arrival, he obtained a situation in connection with the firm of Chanter & Company, who were doing business in shipbuilding at Port Hill. Being a young man of good habits and business talent, he secured the confidence of his employers. He had charge of the company's books, and astonished everybody by his remarkable powers in mental arithmetic. The Messrs. Chanter having resolved to remove to England, assigned their outstanding debts to Mr. Yeo, as remuneration for what they owed him. With the small capital thus placed at his command, as the fruit of honest industry, he commenced trading and shipbuilding, which he prosecuted with remarkable success. Firmness, punctuality, and honesty were the characteristics of his business life.

Mr. Yeo entered public life in the year 1839, and from that period till his death lost but one election. He was no orator, but stated his views on the questions before the house of assembly in a few terse Saxon terms,—always strictly to the point. As a legislator, he was worth a dozen frothy orators. He died deeply regretted by a wide circle friends.

For the following brief sketch of the Honorable George Coles, we are indebted to an admirable biography of the deceased gentleman from the pen of Mr. Henry Lawson, and regret that the space at our disposal does not admit of the insertion of the entire production, which is highly creditable to the literary ability of the writer: The Honorable George Coles was born in Prince Edward Island on the twentieth of September, 1810. He was the eldest son of James and Sarah Coles. In his boyhood, Mr. Coles profited by such educational advantages as the place of his birth afforded. In 1829, when he was just entering manhood, he went to England, where he remained four years. During his stay there, he married Miss Mercy Haine, on the fourteenth of August, 1833, at East Penard Church, Somerset. Shortly after his marriage, Mr. Coles returned to the island, and commenced the business of brewer and distiller. A man of his active mind and wide sympathies could not remain long in the obscurity of private life. His influence soon began to be felt and his ability recognized. In the summer of 1842, he was elected a representative of the first district of Queen's County in the house of assembly. Seldom has any man entered public life under greater disadvantages. He was comparatively a poor man; his education was limited; and, at a time when family influence appeared to be absolutely necessary to advancement in public life, he had no powerful connections. So prominent, however, and so powerful did he become, that it was deemed expedient to appoint him a member of the government. He soon resigned his seat at the council board, and we find him, in 1848, on the opposition benches, a strenuous advocate for the introduction of responsible government.

In 1848 Mr. Coles paid a visit to the United States. When there, he became convinced of the great importance of reciprocity to the people of the island. In Boston and other cities of the great republic he met many island men who were struggling with the difficulties incident to the want of education, and it is said that he then and there determined to free his countrymen from the disability of ignorance, by establishing a system of free schools on the island. He marked the working of the machinery of popular education in the States, and, as soon as he returned home, set about framing the island education law.

In those movements which were necessary to secure responsible government, Mr. Coles was the leading spirit. His opponents were men of position, of talent, and of education, who had been until then all-powerful in the colony. He had to contend with strong social prejudices, which were even more difficult to overcome than his political adversaries; and he was under the necessity of organizing a party out of materials by no means the most promising. Without detracting from the merit of his coadjutors, he, to a greater degree than any of them, possessed the rare combination of qualities necessary to rouse a submissive people to resistance, and to infuse spirit and confidence into men who had been discouraged by a long series of defeats. When in power he introduced the franchise law, the land purchase act, and other beneficial measures with which his name is destined to continue identified.

In 1867, a melancholy change was observed in the veteran statesman. His vigorous mind, it was but too apparent, was giving way. In 1866 there had been a great fire in Charlottetown, and owners of property were kept in a state of anxiety by the suspicion that a band of incendiaries were at work in the city. The exertions made by Mr. Coles to save the property of his fellow-citizens, and the state of alarm in which he was kept, did irreparable injury to a constitution already undermined by arduous mental labor. His mental condition necessitated his retirement from public life in August, 1868. He died on the morning of the twenty-first of August, 1875. His funeral was attended by the Lieutenant-governor, Sir Robert Hodgson,—the pall being borne by the Honorable T. H. Haviland, the Honorable J. C. Pope, William Cundall, Esquire, the Honorable R. P. Haythorne, the Honorable Judge Young, and the Honorable Benjamin Davies. His body lies in the graveyard of Saint Peter's Church.

James Douglas Haszard was born in Charlottetown in the year 1797. He was one of the descendants of a spirited loyalist, who proved his attachment to the monarchical form of government by refusing to take his property, which had been confiscated, on the condition that he should become an American. In the year 1823 Mr. Haszard began business by publishing the *Register*, and successively the *Royal Gazette*, and *Haszard's Gazette*, until the year 1858. Previous to the publication of the *Register*, a total issue of fifty papers sufficed for the colony. Mr. Haszard was ever ready to do good work in connection with industrial and benevolent societies. He was the first to start a cloth-dressing mill in the colony; and, as secretary and treasurer of the Royal Agricultural Society, he introduced improvements in farming implements and machinery. During the famine of 1837 he relieved many destitute families. He died in August, 1875, highly esteemed and deeply regretted.

CHAPTER XII.

Commercial Statistics—Imports—Exports—Revenue—Government Policy—Fisheries—Education—Manufactures—Charlottetown—Census of 1798.

We shall now present a few facts respecting the commerce and other prominent interests of the island. Through the courtesy of the efficient collector of customs,—Mr. Donald Currie,—a gentleman whose polite attention and hospitality to strangers visiting the island deserve a permanent record,—we have been favored with important returns. As an illustration of the wonderful progress made in the development of the agricultural resources of the island, we may state that while the quantity of oats exported in 1862 was only 943,109 bushels, it amounted, in 1872, to 1,558,322 bushels!

The following is the value in dollars of the imports and exports of the island from 1870 to 1874, inclusive. The returns represent a rate of progress to which, perhaps, no parallel can be produced in the British Empire: [J]

YEAR.	IMPORTS.	EXPORTS.
1870	$1,928,662	$2,154,003
1871	2,336,800	1,625,635
1872	2,569,878	1,894,173
1873-4	1,908,522	1,908,461
1874-5	1,960,997	1,940,901

The island revenue was formerly derived from *ad valorem* and specific import duties, land assessments, sales of public and Crown lands. Since confederation it comes from compensatory subsidies, and the two last named sources. The revenue of 1860, in sterling currency, was £28,742, and the expenditure £41,196; in 1865 the revenue was £45,360, and the expenditure £48,350; in 1870 the revenue was £62,230, and the expenditure £70,662,—thus the revenue has been increasing from 1860 to 1870 at the average rate of £3,400. The receipts for the year 1874 were $403,013, and the expenditure for the same year was $435,207. The reason why in this latter year the expenditure exceeds the revenue is to be found in the fact of the large amount paid as compensation for land appropriated for railway purposes. It is right, also, the statement should go forth that the expenditure, which was so much in excess of the revenue in previous years, has been owing to the judicious purchase, by successive governments of the island, of freehold estates. Indeed, from 1854 to 1870 the government bought 445,131 acres of land, at a cost, in sterling money, of £98,435, of which 345,475 acres have been resold up to the year 1870. The money thus expended in the purchase of land is now in process of indirectly yielding a profitable return to the island; so that for contracting temporary debt, successive governments deserve credit instead of condemnation. They have made bold and successful efforts to shield the people from the misery and ruin entailed by the reckless disposal of the land by the Crown, and from the gross injustice of successive home governments in not making full and honorable compensation for the evil consequences of their action.

Mr. John Ings has placed at the temporary disposal of the writer a most interesting little manuscript book containing extracts from the survey of Captain Holland, in 1765, and exhibiting penmanship and neatness of arrangement of the first order. At this period the number of acres cleared in the three counties was 11,235; houses, 391; churches, 2; mills, 11.

The number of acres of arable land held by all families in 1861 was 368,127. The number held in 1871 was 445,103,—the increase in ten years being 76,976 acres!

Prince Edward Island is the best fishing-station within the Gulf of Saint Lawrence. But this important department of industry has not been cultivated to anything like the extent it ought,—being mainly carried on with United States capital. The following table from the census of 1870 shows that there had been, from 1860 until 1870, little, if any, progress:—

	1860.	1870.
Fishing Establishments,	89	176
Barrels of Mackerel cured,	7,163	16,047
Barrels of Herrings or Alewives,	22,416	16,831
Quintals of Codfish or Hake,	39,776	15,649
Gallons of Fish Oil,	17,609	11,662
Boats owned for fishing,	1,239	1,183
Men engaged in fishing,	2,318	1,646

In 1870 the total number of schools in the three counties was 372; and of scholars, 15,000. In 1874 the number of schools was 403; of scholars, 18,233. The salaries of teachers range from $113.56 to $324.44,—only about twenty teachers receiving the larger sum,—an allowance which cannot, by any possibility, command the necessary talent, and which must be increased if the educational system is to be put on a proper basis.

The manufactures of the island are such as promise further development. The importance of diminishing the import of articles which can be produced cheaply on the island as elsewhere cannot be overestimated. Merchants who send money from the island to procure manufactured goods which they can obtain to equal advantage at home are enemies to the material progress of the island. Is furniture required? Men like Messrs. John Newson, Mark Butcher, or John E. Ferguson can supply it. Are carriages or wagons needed? Visit Messrs. McKinnon & Fraser's establishment, or that of Messrs. J. & R. Scott. Are castings needed? Messrs. McKinnon & McLean, or Mr. Edward Morrisey can accommodate customers. Are window-sashes or similar woodwork in request? Lee & Gale are prepared to execute orders. Is tobacco required? Messrs. Hickey & Stewart and Charles Quirk produce a superior article. Are mowing-machines needed by our farmers? Mr. Archibald White makes them in great numbers and of excellent design and quality. Is well-made cloth required? It can be supplied in abundance by the manufacturing establishment of Mr. John D. Reid, Tryon. The men of whom these and similar firms consist are practical tradesmen, who are not ashamed to earn their bread by the sweat of their brow, and who naturally look to their fellow-islanders for that support to which their skill and enterprise entitle them.

The railway, under the management of Mr. McKechnie, prospers beyond the most sanguine expectations of its promoters. It was opened in the month of April, 1875. We give a statement of traffic earnings from the date of its opening till the close of August, 1875:—

No. Passengers.	Amount.	Freight.	Mails.	Express.	Total.
47,847	$35,655	$14,381	$1,737	$1,391	$53,164

Mr. Stronach manages the mechanical department efficiently, and the amount paid annually in wages is such as confers signal benefit on Charlottetown.

One word about Charlottetown. If the city were to represent the intelligence and enterprise of the fair and fertile isle of which it is the capital, it would be celebrated in the Dominion for the excellence of its sidewalks, its copious supply of water, its thorough system of drainage, and the delightful salubrity of its atmosphere. Since our arrival on the island, our head has been more than once in danger of coming into violent contact with the dilapidated wooden structure beneath. "I smell you in the dark," said Johnson to Boswell, as they walked on one of the then unwatered and undrained streets of Edinburgh, and certainly, the redolence of Charlottetown can hardly with truth be said to be elysian. The return of Mr. William Murphy, the representative of pure water, to a civic seat, from which he ought never to have been ejected, augurs that the legislative and municipal steps already taken to furnish a remedy for evils which can no longer exist without injury to the health of the inhabitants, will lead to a speedy consummation devoutly to be wished; and then Charlottetown will stand, in the estimation of tourists, in the position which its natural advantages warrant.

In hotel accommodation, the extensive and well-equipped Island Park Hotel of Mr. Holman, which we visited, is a credit to the island. The hotel of Mr. John Newson, at Rustico, is also well reported; and we are given to understand that Miss Rankin, determined that Charlottetown should no longer lag behind the times, is about to have a handsome house erected in a most suitable locality. A few first-class hotels will not only be mutually profitable to the owners, but also beneficial to respectable houses of all grades.

A Return of the Inhabitants on the Island of Saint John, taken in April, 1798, by order of His Excellency Governor Fanning, &c., &c., &c.: By Robert Fox, Deputy Surveyor. [K]

No. of Lots or Townships	Names of the Heads of Families	Males			Females			Total Males and Females
		Under 16 yrs	From 16 to 60	Above 60	Under 16 yrs	From 16 to 60	Above 60	
Lot No. 34.	Rev. Theo. DesBrisay	5	1		2	4		12
	Neil & Mal. Shaw		2	1	1	1		5
	John Auld	1	1			1		3
	Sandy Marshall		1		1	1		3
	Peter Leech	1	2		3	1		7

	John McGreggor	1	1		2	1		5
	Robt. Auld	1	3	1	1	4		10
	Lan. Brown	1	2		6	3		12
	John Millar		1	1		1	1	4
	Rod. Steele	1	1		1	1		4
	Corn. Higgans	3	3		1	2		9
	James Curtis		3			1		4
	Wm. Lawson	2	2	1	3	2		10
	Dun. Shaw	4	1		2	1		8
	Ronald McDonald	3	1		1	1		6
	Arch. McDonald			1			1	2
	Stephen Bovyer	2	3		3	3		11
	John McDonald	3	1		1	1		6
	John Brown		1			1		2
	Dan. Roper	2	1		2	1		6
	Col. Jo. Robinson	1	2		1	3		7
	John McCormack	3	1			1		5
	Caleb Sentner	1	1	1		2		5
	Mr. McCaustin		1			1		2
	Geo. Vickerson	2	1		4	1		8
	Old McCormick			1				1
	Peter Mattox		1					1
Lot No. 33.	Neil McPhee		2	1			1	4
	Allan	2	1		2	1		6

	McDonald							
	Angus McLeur	4	1		2	1		8
	Don. McKinnin	2	1		2	1		6
	Dun. McCullum	2	1		4	1		8
	James Griggor		1			1		2
	Peter Greggor	2	1	1	1	2	1	8
	Hugh Campbell	2	1		2	1		6
	Don. McFarlane	3	1	1	2	1		8
	Sam. Hyde			1				1
	Robt. Urquhart		1		2	1		4
	John McCullum	3	1		1	1		6
Lot No. 24.	Peter Gallong	3	1		4	1		9
	Matin Ryan	5	1			1		7
	Jos. Gallong	2	2		3	1		8
	Peter Martin	4	2		2	1		9
	Sapplion Gallong		2					2
	Widow Shasong		1				1	2
	Jo. Peters	2	1		1	1		5
	Widow Martin		1				1	2
	Cha. Martin		1		1	1		3
	Mich. Doucette	3	1		2	1		7
	James Peters	2	1		2	1		6
	Fran. Blanchard		2			1		3
	Cha. Gallong		1			1		2

Bonang Martin	1	1			1		3
John Blanchard		3		3	2		8
Widow Guthroe	4			1	1		6
Fabian Gallong	1	1		1	1		4
Fran. Brown	1	1		3	1		6
Alex. Dourong		2	1	1		1	5
Widow Mewes	4	1		4	1		10
John Ducett	2	2		4	1		9
Fran. Ducett		1			1		2
Brazil Gallong	2	1		3	2		8
Cha. Gallong	2	2		4	1		9
John Gallong	1	3		2	2		8
Leman Gallong		1		2	1		4
John Durong	4	1		1	1		7
Jos. Durong	2	1		2	1		6
Fran. Botlea	3	2		1	2		8
Peter Gooday	2	1		2	1		6
John Peter, Jr.	3	1		1	1		6
Lewi Gallong			1		2		3
Joe. Martin	1	1			1		3
Charles Golly	1	1		1	1		4
Feoman Martin	1	1		5	1		8
John Peter, Senr.		1	1		1		3
Joe. Penean	3	1		2	1		7
Peter Leclair	2	1		1	1		5

	Lewi Blakair	6	1			1		8
	Peter Peter	3	1		1	1		6
	Widow Gallong				2	1		3
	John Gootia		1			1		2
	James Adams	1	1		2	1		5
Lot No. 23.	Capt. Wm. Winter		4			3		7
	John Grant		1					1
	Jacob Buskirk	3	1		4	1		9
	John McNeal	6	1		2	1		10
	Wm. Simpson, Senr.		2	1		1	1	5
	Wm. Simpson, Jr.	1	1		3	1		6
	Wm. Clark	2	1		3	1		7
Lot No. 22.	Tho. Adams	1	2			1		4
Lot No. 21.	Robt. Anderson	3	1		2	1		7
	David Cole	2	1	1		1		5
	Alex. Anderson	3	1		2	1		7
	Widow Anderson		1				1	2
	Wm. Pickering	6	1			1		8
	John Adams, Jr.	1	1		1	1		4
	John Adams, Senr.		1	1		1	1	4
	James Murphy		1		1	1		3
	Wm. Vincent	4	1			1		6
	Saml. Barnett	5	1		2	1		9
	Richard Moorfield		1			1		2

	Richard Shepherd		1					1
	Michael Murphy			1				1
	James Campbell	1	4		4	1		10
	Barthw. Brislar	1	1		1	1		4
	James Townshend	3	2	1		2		8
Lot No. 20.	Wm. Marks	4	1			1		6
	John Barefoot		1					1
	John Crowley		1		1	1		3
	James Dunn	6	1		1	1		9
	Daniel Delaney	3	1		3	1		8
	John Cousins	3	1		2	1		7
	Robert Heathfield	1	1		3	1		6
	Ben. Warren	2	1		4	1		8
	James Brander	2	1		2	1		6
	John Poor	3	1			1		5
	Geo. Warren		1		1	1		3
	Mrs. Rieley	2			2	1		5
Lot No. 18.	Archibald McCoy	5	3		1	2		11
	John Lawler		1			1		2
	John Murchland	2	1		3	2		8
	Widow Green		1				1	2
	Peter Heron	1	5		5	1		12
	James McNutt, Esq.	2	1		4	1		8

	Dennis Rafter	2	1		2	1		6
	Patrick Sennott		1			1		2
	Ronald Morrison	2	2		4	1		9
	Peter McDougald	4	2		3	3		12
	Dougald Stewart	1	1			1		3
	Wm. Donald	1	2			1		4
	James Woodside, Jr.	1	1		1	1		4
	Arthur Owens	2	1		3	2		8
	Hugh McKendrick	1	1			1		3
	Neal Ramsay	5	2		1	1		9
	John Sinclair	1	1		3	1		6
	Donald McDougald		1		3	1		5
	Baldy Mathews	4			2	1		7
	Donald Taylor, Jr.	1	1		4	1		7
	Chas. McNeal	5	1		2	1		9
	Malcom Ramsay	2	1		4	1		8
	Alex. Boyce	3	1		3	1		8
	Alex. McCoy		2	1		1	1	5
	Angus Stewart	3	1			1		5
	Andrew Gray	1	1		1	1		4
	Angus McLelan		3			1		4
	John McLelan	7	1		1	1		10
	Angus Gillis	4	1		1	1		7

Royalty of Princetown	James Mountain	3	1			1		5
	David Palmer		1		1	1		3
	Tho. Cochran, Senr.	5	2		1	3		11
	John Whealan			1			1	2
	Tho. Sutton	3	1			2		6
	Benj. Warren, Senr.	1	2		2	2		7
	John Henry	1	1			1		3
	John Thompson	3	1		1	1		6
	Tho. Cochran, Jr.	2	1		1	1		5
	James Ferguson	3	1		4	1		9
	Jane Allen	2	1		1	2		6
	Kenith McKenzie	3	1		1	1		6
	Widow McNeal	3			2	1		6
	Geo. Thompson	1	1	1		2		5
	Widow McCoy		3		1	3		7
	Don. Taylor, Senr.	1	2	1		1		5
	John Mathews	4	1		2	1		8
	John McKenzie	2	1			3		6
	Mal. McKendrick	4	1		1	1		7
	Chas. Stewart, Esq.	4	3		3	4		14
	John McGougan	2	4			2		8

	James Woodside, Senr.	1	5	1		3		10
	Hugh Montgomery		3	1	1	2	1	8
	James Stewart	1	4		1	1		7
	Wm. Craig	2	1		1	1		5
	Danl. Montgomery, Esq	3	1		4	1		9
	Arch. Ramsay	3	1		2	1		7
	Wm. Baker	1	2			1		4
	John Ramsay	1	1		2	1		5
	Edward Ramsay	2	1		2	1		6
	Joseph McLean	1	2		1	2		6
	Tho. Simpson	2	1		1	1		5
	Mal. McNeal		1	1		1	1	4
	John McPherson		1		1	2		4
	Don. McKenzie	3	1	1	1	1	1	8
	Alex. McKenzie	2	1	1	2	1	1	8
	John McMullan	1	1		2	1		5
	John McNeal	2	1		1	1		5
	Penney McDonald				1	1		2
Lot No. 19.	Dav. Downing	2	1		1	1		5
	Dugald Steele		2					2
	Wm. Holmes		1		2	1		4
	James Nowlan	1	1			1		3
	Doodia Russel	3	1		6	1		11

	John Gallong, Senr.	1	2	1		2		6
	John Gallong, Jr.		2			1		3
	John Perrie		1		5	1		7
	Joe Gooday, Senr.	1	2	1	1	1	1	7
	Bazil Perrie	4	3		5	1		13
	Jos. Deroche	4	1			2		7
	Fearman Arsnoe	2	1		2	1		6
	Prosper Perrie	4	1		1	1	1	8
Bedeque Bay.	George Mabey	2	1		5	1		9
	John Leforgee	1	1		4	1		7
	James Warf	3	1		2	1		7
	Jonathan Palmer	3	2		2	1		8
Lot No. 17.	Lewi Arsnoe	1	2			1		4
	Cyprian Arsnoe	5	2		3	1		11
	Chas. Ducett	1	1				1	3
	Joe Gooday	2	1		1	1		5
	Yaco Shasong		1	1		1	1	4
	Peter Arsnoe	3		1	2	2		8
	Widow Gallong		1		1		1	3
	Chas. Rushaw	5	1		2	2		10
	Cyprian Gallong	6	5		1	2		14
	Minie Gallong	1	3			5		9
	Larriong Bernard	1	1		3	1		6
	Joe Bernard		2	1	2	2	1	8

	Placid Arsnoe	1	1		1	1		4
	Paul Arsnoe	2	2	1	1	1	1	8
	Alex. Arsnoe	1	1	1		1	1	5
	Joseph Rushaw	3	3		2	1		9
	Peter Perrie		1	1			1	3
	Joseph Arsnoe	1	2		3	3		9
	John Arsnoe	3	2		2	3		10
	Joe Arsnoe	2	2		2	3		9
	Fearman Gallong	2	1		1	1		5
	Widow Ducett	1			2	1		4
	John B. Gallong	2	3		4	3		12
	Stephen Arsnoe	2	1		1	1		5
	Joe Ducett		1		3	1		5
	Stephen Gooday	2	1			1		4
	Peter Bourke		1	1	2	1		5
	John Babtist St. John	2	1		1	1		5
	Benjamin Darby	4	1		3	3		11
	Daniel Green	5	2		4	1		12
Lot No. 16.	Babtist Arsnoe		1		1	1		3
	Mal. Ramsay, Esq.	3	1		4	1		9
	Fran. Gallong	3	1		1	1		6
	Owen Hickey		3					3
	John Shassong	5	1		4	1		11
	Peter Perrie	4	1		1	1		7
	Gregwar Bernard	1	1		1	1		4

	Antonie Gallong	5	1		2	1		9
	Lewi Arsnoe	4	1		3	1		9
	Peter Bernard	3	1		3	1		8
	John Arsnoe			1	1	1	1	4
	Bazile Perrie	4	1		4	1		10
	John Wedge	4	1		5	1		11
	Francis Gallong	1	1		1	1		4
	Widow Arsnoe		2		1	1		4
	Alex. Cameron	2	3		2	2		9
	Donald Campbell	2	3		3	2		10
	Hugh McCarter	2	5			2		9
	Angus McGinnis	2	1		5	1		9
	Widow McDonald		2			1	1	4
	Don. Forbes	2	1		5	1		9
	Archibald Cameron	2	2		4	1		9
	Allan McLean	2	1			1		4
	John McDonald	1	1		3	1		6
Lot No. 14.	Donald McDonald		1	1		1	1	4
	Angus McKinnion	1	2		1	1		5
	John McLelan	2	1		2	1		6
	John Gillis	3	1		1	1		6
	Laughlin McIntyre	4	1			1		6

	Alex. McCarter	3	1		1	1		6
	Murdock Campbell	1	2		4	1		8
	Donald Gillis	2	2		2	2		8
	Tho. English	1	1		1	1		4
	Patrick Rochfort	2	2			1		5
	Michael McIntosh		2	1		3		6
Lot No. 13.	George Blood	2	2		1	2		7
	Rodk. Gillis	2	2		1	1		6
	Widow Ramsay	2	4		1	2		9
	George Penman	1	3		1	2		7
	Dougald Campbell		1	1			1	3
	Donald Murphy			1			1	2
	Wm. Hunter	1		1		1		3
	John Ramsay	2	1			1		4
Lot No. 11.	George Linklater		3	1		1		5
	James Smith	4	1		3	2		10
Lot No. 6.	George Hardey	5	1		4	1		11
Lot No. 5.	John Murray	3	1		1	1		6
	John Brownyoung	3	2		3	1		9
	Jacob Vigo	3	1	1		1		6
	Hugh Ross	1	1			2		4
	Alexander McKinnion	2	1		2	1		6

	Tho. Duffee	2	1		2	1		6
	Michael McNamara		1			1		2
Lot No. 25.	Angus McDonald	1	1		2	1		5
	Ronald McDonald	1	1		3	1		6
	Samuel Rix	2	1			1		4
	William Wright	2	1	1	2	2		8
	Jessie Strang	2	1		1	1		5
	John Murray		1	1	2	3	1	8
	David Murray	3	2		2	2		9
Lot No. 26.	William Schurman	3	4		3	2		12
	Peter Schurman	1	1			2		4
	Samuel Chatterton	2	1		3	1		7
	John Baker	4	3			3		10
	Major Hooper		1		2	1		4
	Joseph Selliker	1	2			1		4
	Thomas Hooper, Esq.	1	1	1		1		4
	William Barrett		4					4
	Peter Mabee	4	3		1	2		10
	John Strickland	2	1		2	1		6
	Nathaniel Wetherall	1	1			2		4
	Widow Robins	3			3	1		7
	Benjamin Cole	1	2		4	1		8

	Richard Price	2	1		1	1		5
	Moses Hives	2	1		1	1		5
	Alexander Anderson		1		2	1		4
	Archibald McCullum	2	1		2	1		6
Lot No. 27.	Daniel Woods	2	1		2	1		6
	John McDonald		1		2	1		4
	Dennis Flyn		1					1
	John McGinnis	1	1		3	1		6
	Dougald McGinnis	1	1		2	1		5
	Donald McKenzie	2	2			2		6
Lot No. 28.	Peter Rubere	2	1		2	1		6
	William Clark	1	1	1	1	1		5
	George Molart		2			1		3
	John Gould	2	1		2	1		6
	George Stagman	2	1		4	1		8
	Tho. Gamble	4	1		2	1		8
	Dav. McWilliam	4	1		1	1		7
	Widow Pollard	4			3	1		8
	Adam Fullmon		3	1			1	5
	Widow Lard		2		2	1		5
	James Hewit	1	2	1	1	1		6
Lot No. 28.	Morris Quinlan		1		2	1		4
	John Taylor		1		1	1		3
	Joseph Woods	1	1		3	1		6

	Dav. Penman		1	1	2	1		5
	William Warren	1	1		2	2		6
	John Lord	2	2		2	4		10
	Nathaniel Wright	4	1			2		7
	John Foy, Esq.	1	1		3	1		6
	Philip Callbeck	1	1		2	1		5
	Ebenezer Ward	1	3		3	1		8
	Peter Clymer	2	1		1	2		6
	Paul Clymer		1	1			1	3
Lot No. 30.	James McDougald		1		6	1		8
	Jno. McDonald	1	1	1	1	1	1	6
Lot No. 31.	Johnson Basto	2	3		4	3		12
	Michael Seeley	1	1		4	1		7
	Wm. Wilson	1	1					2
	Benjamin Nicholson		1			2		3
	Lieut. John McDonald	2	4		2	2		10
	Thomas Hyde	3	1		1	4		9
Lot No. 32.	John Wilson	2	1		3	2		8
	Wm. Crosby	1	1	1	1	4		8
	Wm. Hyde	2	2		3	2		9
	Jno. Creamer		1		3	1		5
	Wm. Dockendorff		1		1	1		3
	Wm. Long	3	1			1		5
	Donald McNab		1		1	1		3

	Jacob Hartze		3	1	3			7
	Jer. Myers	1	1		1	1		4
	Conrod Yonker		1			1		2
	Wm. Fisher		1		1	1		3
Lot No. 65.	Rob. McConnel	2	2			1		5
	Angus McGinnis	3	1		2	1		7
	Robert Fox	1	1		2	1		5
	Peter McMahon		1					1
	Ben Wood		1					1
	John Clark	3	3		6	3		15
Lot No. 49.	John McGinnis	4	1		2	1		8
	Wm. Hassard	1	2		1	3	1	8
	Wm. Jetson	1	1		6	1		9
	Barney McCrossen	2	1			1		4
	John Burho	3	3		3	2		11
	Wm. Wood, jr.		1			1		2
	Wm. Wood, senr.	5	1		3	1		10
	Joseph Smith	2	1		3	1		7
	John Costin	2	1		2	1		6
	John Eacharn	1	1		4	1		7
	Nicks. Jenkins	6	1		3	1		11
	George Hayden	1	1			1		3
	James L. Hayden	3	1		3	1		8
Lot No. 50.	—— Rynolds		1			1		2
	Joseph Beers,	1	1		3	1		6

	Esq.								
	Frederick Praught	3	1		2	1			7
	Richard Myers	3	2		2	1			8
	Tho. Pendergast	3	1		2	1			7
	James Carver	4	1		1	1			7
	Peter Musick	3	1		2	1			7
	Spencer Crane	2	1			1			4
	Don. McPhee	2	1		3	1			7
	John Praught		1			1			2
	John McDonald	1	1		1	1			4
	Wm. Young	4	2		4	1			11
	James Lard	1	2		3	1			7
	Wm. Laws		1		1				2
	John Van Niderstine	1	2		1	1			5
	John Haley		1						1
	Geo. Coughlin	2	1			1			4
	Wm. Morris		1		2	1			4
	John Monlin		1						1
	Fred. Shultze			1			1		2
Lot No. 64.	Nickl. Hughes	1	1			1			3
	Wm. Shenshabach	3	1			1			5
	Mrs. Forster	4				1			5
Lot No. 63.	Wm. Graham	1	2			1			4
Lot No. 61.	John Griffin	3	1		1	1			6
Lot No. 59.	William Creed	4	2			2			8
	Dav. Young	1	1		4	1			7
	Jos. Clark		1	1		1			3
	Dav. Ervin,		2	1			1		4

	Esquire							
	Wm. Ervin	3	1		3	1		8
	Jno. Aitkin		1	1				2
	Wm. Keoughan		1		1	1		3
Lot No. 54.	Duncan McSwain	1	1		3	1		6
	Farquhar Campbell	3	1		2	1		7
	Angus Steele	2	2		2	2		8
	Dun. Campbell		1			1		2
	Alex. McLelan		2	1			1	4
Lot No. 55.	John McLean		4		1	2		7
	Alex. McLean	2	1		1	1		5
	John McLean		1		1	1	1	4
Lot No. 56.	Don. McCormick	4	1		1	1		7
	Angus McCormick		1		1	1		3
	Rod. McDonald	1	1		2	1	1	6
	Don. McDonald		3		1	1		5
	Angus Walker	1	1			1		3
	Hugh Morris	3	1		1	2		7
	John Carpenter	1	1				1	3
	Wm. Blackett	1	2		3	1		7
	Wm. Hayne			1				1
	Joseph Brown	1	1		3	1		6
	Wm. Dingwell	2	1			1		4
Boughton Island.	Hugh McCormick	4	1		1	1		7

	Alex. Steele	1	5		1	1		8
Lot No. 50.	Dan. Shiverie		2		2	1	1	6
	Peter Shiverie	4	1		2	1		8
Lot No. 43.	Lewi Longapee		1		2	1		4
	Lewi Longapee, senr.			1		1		2
	John Longapee		1		3	1		5
	Brazile Shasong	4	2		1	1		8
	Lemong Shasong	2	1		1	1		5
	John Shasong		1			1		2
	Paul Shasong		1	1			1	3
	Rusile Shasong			1	1	1		3
	Babtist Launderie		1			1		2
	Paul Peter	1	1		2	1		5
	Naurie Mashell			1				1
	German Shasong	5	3		2	1		11
	Joe Peters, senr.		1	1			1	3
	Joe Peters, jr.		1			1		2
	Simon Burk	2	1		1	1		5
	John Burk		1		1	1		3
	Ambrose Burk	1	1		2	1		5
	Lavia Peter	3	1		3	3		10
	Peter Shiverie		1					1
	Joseph Burk, senr.	5	2		2	1		10

	Joseph Burk, jr.	1	1		1	1		4
	Simon Burk		1			1		2
	James Aitkin	3	1		1	1		6
	Robert Dingwell				1			1
	John Hipwell				1			1
	John McPhee	1	1		2	1		5
	Dond. McPhee	1	1		2	1		5
	Neal McPhee	1	2		4	1		8
	Dond. McCormick	3	3		2	1		9
	Mary Sutherland	1				1		2
	Rod. McDonald	1	1		4	1		7
	Laughlin McDonald	5	1			1		7
	Dond. McDonald	2	2		2	2		8
	Allen McDonald			1			1	2
	Hector McDonald	3	1		2	1		7
	Rod. McDougald	1	1		3	1		6
	Rod. McIntosh	3	1		3	1		8
	Don. McDonald	2	1		4	1		8
	John McDonald	1	1		1	1		4
	Angus McDonald	1	1	1	3	2		8
	Angus	1	1		2	1		5

	McFarrish							
	Allan McDonald	1	1		3	1		6
Lot No. 40.	John McKenzie	2	1		2	1		6
	John Duke	6	1		2	1		10
	Cha. Saunders	2	1			3		6
	Wm. Webster	1	2			1		4
	Saml. Hutchinson	3	3		2	1		9
Lot No. 39.	Alex. Dingwell	2	1		3	1	1	8
	James Dingwell	1	2		2	1		6
	Arch. McKenzie	1	1	1	2	2		7
	Jacob Taylor	2	1		1	1		5
	John Dingwell			1				1
	Tho. Wright, Surv. Gen.	3	4		3	2		12
	Dond. Peyton	4	2		3	2		11
	John Moore	2	1			1		4
	Tho. Webster	3	1		1	1		6
	John McKie	3	1		1	1		6
	James McIntire	1	1		2	1		5
	Don. McIntire	1	1		2	1		5
	Dav. Anderson, senr.	1	4			2		7
	Dav. Anderson, jr.		1			1		2
	James Anderson		1			1		2
	Wm. McKie, Esquire		3		4	1		8

Robert Banks	2	1		1	1		5
Angus McIntire	1	1			1	1	4
Rond. McDonald	1	1		3	1		6
John McDonald	2	1		1	1		5
John McEachran	2	1		2	2		7
Widow Fisher	4			1	2		7
Rod. McDonald	2	1	1		1		5
Angus McFarrish	2	1		1	1		5
Hugh McFarrish	1	1		3	1		6
Joseph Dingwell		1		1	1		3
Angus McDonald	1	3	1	1	3		9
Duncan McEwin	4	4		2	2		12
Wm. Robins	1		1		1		3
Allen McDonald	2	1		2	1		6
Allen McDonald	2	2	1	2	1		8
Allen McKisick	2	1		4	1		8
Laughlin McDonald	1	1		2	1		5
Uriah Coffin	2	2	1	1	2		8
Fred Simonds	4	1		1	1		7
John Ford & Peebles		1	1				2
John Broh		1	1	1	1		4

	John Murrough	4	1			1		6
	Edwd. Allen	3	1	1	2	1		8
	John Campbell	2	1		1	1		5
	Peter Rose		1			1		2
	Angus McDonald		1		2	1		4
	Angus Campbell	5	4		1	2		12
Lot No. 42.	John McKinnion	2	1		4	1		8
	Rod. McKinnion	3	1		3	2		9
	John McDonald	1	1		3	1		6
	(Little) John McKinnion		1			1	1	3
	Hector McKinnion	2	1		2	1		6
Lot No. 41.	Angus McKisick	7	1			1		9
	Neil McCormick	3	1			1		5
	John McKinnion		1		3	1		5
	John McDonald	5	1		2	1		9
	Angus McIntire		1		1	1		3
Lot No. 38.	Don. McAdam	3	1		1	1		6
	Alex. McAdam	3	1		2	1	1	8
	Laughlin McAdam	3	1		4	1		9
	Allen McDougald	2	2		3	1		8

	John McEachran	2	1		3	1		7
	Widow McEachran		3		3	1		7
	Hugh McEachran	3	1		1	2		7
	Hugh McEachran, senr.		2	1	2		2	7
	Revd. Angus McEachran		1					1
	Angus McDonald	2	2		2	1		7
	Arch. McPhee		1		1	1		3
	John McPhee		1		1	1		3
	Rod. McDonald		2	1			1	4
	Allen McIntire		1		1	1		3
	Don. McIntire	4	2		1	2		9
	John McEachran	1	3		1	1		6
	Dun. McMullen	4	1		1	1		7
	Allen Morrison	1	1		2	1		5
	Ellisha Coffin	4	1		3	1		9
	Widow Coffin		2				1	3
	Kemble Coffin	1	1		1	2		5
	Benj. Coffin		1		2	1		4
	Dond. McMullen	1	1		3	1		6
	John McMullen	2	1		1	1		5
	Alex. McMullen	1	2		1	1		5

	Joseph Smallwood	3	1		3	1	1	9
	Neal McDonald	2	1		1	1		5
	Angus Curry	2	1		3	1		7
	Call Curry	2	1		2	1		6
	Wm. Douglas	4	3		3	2		12
	James Hewick	1	1		1	1		4
	John Anderson	3	1		1	1		6
	Angus McPhee	1	2		5	1	1	10
	Angus McPhee	2	1	1		1	1	6
	Angus McDonald	3	2			1	1	7
	John McDonald	2	2		1	2		7
Lot No. 37.	Cha. McKinnion		1		4	1		6
	John McCaskill	2	2		1	1		6
	Dond. McCaskill		1			1		2
	Duncan McGinnis			1			1	2
	Gallen McGinnis	1	1		2	1		5
	John McMullen	1	2			3		6
	Widow McGinnis	2	1		2	2		7
	John McDonald	1	1		1	1		4
	Angus	2	3		3	1		9

McCormick							
Alex. McCloud		1		1	1		3
Capt. John Stewart	1	3		2	1		7
Alex. McKinnion	1	2		2	1		6
Allen McKinnion	1		1			1	3
Rond. McDonald	2	1	1		2		6
Angus McDonald	2	1		1	1		5
Murd. McCoy		1		1	2		4
John McDonald	1	1		2	1		5
Allen McDonald	3	1			1		5
John McDonald		1	1		3	1	6
Alex. McDonald	2	2		5	1		10
Dond. McDonald	4	2		4	1		11
Archd. McDonald	4	1		3	1		9
Duncan Gillis		2			1	1	4
Alex. McDonald	1	1		3	1		6
Dond. Grant		1	1			1	3
John McKinnion		1		1	1		3
Wm. Gillis	1	1			1		3
Angus McEachran	2	1		2	1	1	7
Dond.	1	1		2	1		5

	McEachran							
	Widow McKinnion	2	2	1		2		7
	Hugh Gillis	4	1		4	1		10
	Widow Frazer	1	1		1	1		4
	Laurence Barrett	3	1		1	1		6
	James Flanigan	1	1			1		3
	John McCormick	2	1		3	3		9
	Hugh McNab	1	1		2	1	1	6
	Archd. McPhee			1			1	2
	Hugh McPhee	1	1		3	1		6
	Archd. Campbell		1		3	1		5
	Walter Walsh		1			2		3
	Wm. Campbell	2	1			1		4
	Saml. Street		3					3
	Rond. McDonald	1	2		2	3		8
Lot No. 36.	Alexr. Curry		4			3		7
	Angus McKenzie	2	1			1		4
	Colin McKenzie	2	2		2			6
	Donald McIlray		1					1
	Donald McGraw	6	2		3	1	1	13
	Angus McDonald		4	1		1		6
	Chas.	5	3		3	3		14

	McDonald							
	Widow McDonald		1			1	1	3
	John McIlray		3	1			1	5
	Martin McIlray	2	1		5	2		10
	Dond. Gillis	1	2	1	1	2		7
	Dun. Gillis	1	1		2	1		5
	James McDonald	3	1			1		5
	John McDonald	3	1			1		5
	John Stewart	3	1		5	1		10
	Dond. Morrison	2	1		2	1		6
	Hugh Walker	2	1		2	1		6
	Rond. McLean	2	1			1		4
	John McKenzie	1	1		2	1		5
	Widow McDonald	1	1			1	1	4
	Capt. John McDonald	2		1	1	2		6
	John McPhee	4	1		1	1		7
	Alex. McIntosh	2		1	1	1		5
Lot No. 35.	John McIntyre		1		3	1		5
	John Pringle		2				1	3
	James Chaytor	2	1		1	1		5
	Dond. McIntosh	2		1		1		4
	Moses Keho		1		2	1		4
	Rod. McIsaac	2	1			3		6
	John		2			2		4

	McIntosh							
	Edward Elvert	1	1		2	1		5
	Edwd. McAdam	4	1	1		1		7
	Dond. McIlray	1	1		5	1		8
	Patk. Curry	2	1		2	1		6
	John McIntire	1	1		3	1		6
	Dond. McKisick	1	1		3	1		6
	Dond. McDonald	1	1		4			6
	Angus McIlray	3	1		2	1		7
	Don. McEachran	3	2		1	1	1	8
	Don. McDonald	1	3			1		5
	Don. McDonald		4		2	2		8
	John McDonald	1	1		1	1		4
	James Lawson		1		3	1		5
	Rond. McDonald	1	1		2	1		5
	Don. Campbell	3	1		1	1		6
	John Campbell	1	1		1	1		4
	Hugh Campbell		2	1			1	4
Lot No. 48.	Alex. McDonald	1	1	1		1		4
	Neal McDonald	2	1		2	1		6
	Murd. McCloud	5	1		1	1		8
	Wm. Ferguson	2	1		2	1		6

	Dond. Curry		1		1	1		3
	Alex. Mutch	2	1		3	1		7
	John Bovyer		2					2
	Chief-justice Stewart		4	1	1	3		9
	Angus Curry	1	1		2	1		5
	Angus McDonald	1	2			2		5
	Rodk. McDonald		1		2	1		4
	Benj. Crossman		1		1	1		3
Royalty of Ch'town.	Patk. Oneal	1	1		3	1		6
	J. Gellespie	3			2	1		6
	Ben. Grosvenor		2		1	1		4
	Rond. McDonald	1	1		3	1		6
	John Carrol	2	2		2	1		7
	Mrs. Hillman	2			1	2		5
	Dav. Ross		1		3	1		5
	Mrs. Cambridge	2	2		2	2		8
	John Brecken	3	3		2	3		11
	Colo. Lyons	1	3		4	4	1	13
	Widow Smith		1				1	2
	Benj. Chappell	1	2		1	1		5
	David Laughry		1	1		1		3
	Henry W. Perry	2	2		1	2		7
	Rob. Hodgson, Esqr.	3	1			2		6
	Serjt. Deering	3	1		2	1		7

	John J. Potcher		1		1	1		3
	John Hall		2		1	1		4
	Rob. Callehan		1				1	2
	John Webster, senr.			1	1		1	3
	John Coxen		1			1		2
	Wm. Townshend. Esqr.	3	2		1	2		8
	John Revel	1	1			1		3
	Robert Jeffrys			1				1
	Doctor Patton			1				1
	Tho. Alexander	2	1		2	1		6
	Peter Connoly	3	1		3	1		8
	John Condon		1			1		2
	Alex. Rea	4	2			2		8
	Saml. Bagnal	2	3		1	2		8
	Alex. A. Rind	1	1		3	1		6
	John McKinnion	2	1		2	2		7
	Dond. McPhee		2			2		4
	Joseph Robinson	2	2		2	1		7
	Alex. Richardson		3		2	2		7
	Widow Clark				2	1		3
	Ser. McCloud	3	1		2	1		7
	—— Ross, Esq			1				1
	John Hawkins	2	1		4	1		8
	His Ex. Gov. Fanning	4	4		6	4		18

	Robert Lee	2	2		1	1		6
	Thos. R. Hassard	1	3		1	1		6
	John Webster, jr.	3	1		1	1		6
	Peter McGowan		3		1	2	1	7
	Doctor Nicholson		3		1	1		5
	James Douglas, Esquire	2	2		4	1		9
	John Jones	1	1		2	1		5
	John Wright		1			1		2
	Angus McEachran	3	1		1	1		6
	John Lewis	4	1			2		7
	Lieut. A. Smyth		1	1		1		3
	Angus McPhee	3	1		1	1		6
	Tho. Geary	1	2			1		4
	Andrew Ladner	1	1		2	1		5
	Geo. Hopps	1	1		1	1		4
	Nath McDonnell	1	2		1	1		5
	Dond. McDonald	1	1		2	1		5
	Lieut. Cha. Stewart	5	2		3	2		12
	Nichs. Counahan	1	1		1	1		4
	Jos. Aplin, Esqr.	2	2			1		5
	Fran.	1	1		1	1		4

Longworth							
Robt. Kiley	3	1			1		5
Saml. Braddock	1	2		2	1		6
John Gardner	3	1		1	1		6
Doctor Gordon	3	2		1	2		8
Colo. Desbrisay		2			1		3
Colo. Gray		4		1	3		8
Wm. Burk	3	2	.	4	1		10
Dond. Kennedy	2	1		1	1		4
Rob. Emmerson	1	1		2	1		5
John Jerome		1			1		2
Willm. Amos		1		2	1		4
Martin Dwyre	2	1			1		4
Peter Stafford		1			1		2
James Connoly	3	1		2	1		7
Thos. Murray		1					1
James Ferguson		1					1
Saml. Byers	1	1		1	1		4

Total Number of Inhabitants:—

Males under 16 years	1217
do. from 16 to 60 years	1014
do. Above 60 do.	104
	2335
Females under 16	109

years	2	
do. from 16 to 60 years	867	
do. Above 60 do.	78	
		203 7
	Tot al	437 2

Footnotes

[A] The Rev. Mr. Sutherland, in his Geography, estimates the population at about four thousand, which corresponds with the estimate of the writer. See History of Nova Scotia, page 143.

[B] The writer has obtained his information from manuscript copies of the original minutes of the Commissioners of Trade and Plantations.

[C] The method of granting the lots was the following:—The Board of Trade ordered all petitioners for grants to appear before them personally or by deputy on the 17th and 24th June, and 1st July, 1767, in support of their respective claims. During these days, after hearing parties, they selected those whose claims seemed preferable, and on the 8th of July the list was completed, and finally adopted. The balloting took place on the 23rd of July, 1707, in presence of the Board. The name of each applicant was written on a slip of paper or ticket, and put in the balloting box,—the lots being granted in running numbers as they were drawn.

[D] See manuscript minute of meeting of Commissioners of Trade and Plantations, dated eighth July, 1767.

[E] This gentleman was not John Stewart, of Mount Stewart. The latter was only twenty-three years of age when John Stuart was appointed by the assembly their agent in London, and he had been only three years on the island at the time of the appointment. His Honor Sir Robert Hodgson, the Lieutenant Governor, has taken the trouble to peruse the correspondence which passed between Governor Patterson and John Stuart, and in a note addressed to the writer, says: "I feel convinced that John Stuart was the person whose name appears on the Island Statute of 30 George III, cap. 5, of the year 1790, as the owner of ten thousand acres of land; and who, I have always understood, was a personal friend of Governor Patterson, and if not an original grantee, must have acquired his land by the instrumentality of his friend the governor, under the sale of the lands for the non-payment of quitrents, so frequently alluded to in the correspondence." The writer has carefully gone over the list of original grantees, in which there is one named John Stewart, but not one who spelt his name Stuart.

The following is a copy of the despatch addressed to Fanning:—

"Whitehall, 5th April, 1787.

"Sir,—Your despatch, number one, of the fourteenth of October last, in answer to my letter of the thirtieth of June last, was duly received, and I have since been favored with your letters, numbered two, three, and four, giving an account of your arrival in the Island of Saint John, and of certain proceedings which have taken place subsequent to that time.

"His Majesty, from the very extraordinary conduct of Lieutenant-Governor Patterson, has thought it advisable to dismiss him at once from office, and has been graciously pleased to fix you in the government of that island, persuaded, from the proofs you have given of your zeal for his service, as well as of your prudence and discretion, that you will make a suitable return for the confidence which has been placed in you by a faithful and diligent discharge of your duty.

"I am, sir, your obedient servant,

"Sydney.

"To lieutenant-governor Fanning."

The following is the letter of Lord Sydney, formally intimating to Patterson his dismissal, as well as the reply to the communication of Patterson to his lordship, already given:—

"Whitehall, 5th April, 1787.

"Sir,—I have received your letter, number thirty-one, of the fifth November last, in answer to one from me of the thirtieth of June preceding, wherein you have stated certain reasons which have induced you to delay the carrying into execution His Majesty's commands, which were sent to you by me, for delivering over the charge of the Island of Saint John to Colonel Fanning, and for your returning to England to answer certain complaints which have been exhibited against you.

"Without, however, entering into the grounds upon which you have proceeded to justify disobedience of His Majesty's orders, I must acquaint you that I have received his royal commands to inform you that His Majesty has no further occasion for your services as Lieutenant-Governor of Saint John.

"Colonel Fanning, who has been appointed your successor, will receive from you all the public documents in your custody, and such orders and instructions as have been transmitted to you which have not been fully executed.

"I am, sir, your obedient, humble servant,

"Sydney.

"Lieutenant-Governor Patterson."

In Dr. Patterson's memoir of the late Rev. Dr. James Macgregor, there is an interesting reference to an interview which the latter eminent missionary had with Mr. DesBrisay. "I afterwards," wrote Dr. Macgregor, "became acquainted with him, and was always welcome to preach in his church, which I uniformly did when I could make it convenient. His kindness ended not but with his life." Dr. Macgregor states incidentally that at this period Charlottetown was a wicked place. We may safely affirm that it was not more wicked than any other seaport of its population.

[H] The Honorable Mr. Brecken and the Honorable Mr. Davies were favorable to union, on what they conceived equitable principles, but opposed to what was termed the Quebec Scheme.

[I] The author is indebted for this graphic sketch to the kindness of Mr. John T. Mellish, M. A., who was personally acquainted with Mr. McDonald.

[J] The island having entered the confederation with the Dominion on the first July, 1873, Canadian manufactured goods since then have not come under the head of "imports," which explains the apparent decrease. The same remark applies to exports, because all island products sent to Nova Scotia, New Brunswick, Magdalen Islands, and Canada, which were formerly "exports," are not so reckoned now. In the value of exports is included the price of the tonnage sold or transferred to other parts.

[K] The orthography of this list is strictly according to the original document.

CPSIA information can be obtained
at www.ICGtesting.com
Printed in the USA
LVHW011010111020
668495LV00012B/2461